LOST *in* THE ARK

a novel

VAL AGNEW

Lost in The Ark
Published by Angel Hill Press
San Diego, CA

Names: Agnew, Val, author.
Title: Lost in the ark / Val Agnew. Description: San Diego, CA: Angel Hill
Publishing, 2022.
Identifiers: ISBN: 979-8-9850024-0-9 Subjects: LCSH Cults--Fiction. |
Girls and women--Fiction. | Family--Fiction. | Bildungsroman. | BISAC
FICTION / Coming of Age Classification: LCC PS3601.G58 L67 2022 |
DDC 813.6--dc23

Cover by Shira Lee Designs, and interior design by Victoria Wolf,
copyright owned by Val Agnew

ANGEL HILL
PRESS

This book is dedicated to family, friends, and forgiveness. I need you all.

CHAPTER 1

"DO NOT DOUBT. Stand firm in your faith. Trust God to smash the obstacles in your path." Pastor Steve's voice boomed out of the car speaker.

I pictured the veins bulging in his neck, his hand pounding the pulpit. I slapped the steering wheel and shouted back, "I do trust God. It doesn't matter what Ma says. I will go to The Ark. I'm eighteen and she can't stop me."

His sermon ended as I pulled into the driveway. My headlights shined on Gram's Buick parked in Dad's spot.

Although it was a warm June night, a shiver ran down my spine. Gram didn't drive at night. That's when her lover, Smirnoff, visited. Light blared from every window on the first floor and flooded out the open front door. My heart hammered as I hurried up the steps.

Quiet roared inside the house. I rushed down the hallway toward the den and stopped. The furniture was cockeyed like we'd been robbed. *Please God, let everyone be safe.*

I backed toward the front door and called out, "Anyone here?"

"Kate, I'm in the kitchen." It was Gram's hoarse voice.

She sat at the table caressing the familiar glass of vodka. Her heavy rose perfume competed with the stink of a full ashtray.

"What happened?" I said, afraid to touch anything.

Gram turned to me with watery eyes. Her gnarled hand clutched an empty package of Camels. "She told BB her head hurt. She fell to the floor." Each word sounded heavy in her mouth. I willed myself to stay calm.

"Gram, what are you talking about?"

"For Chrissakes, Kate. Your mother."

"Where is she?" I grabbed the edge of the table. "And where's everyone else?"

The pain etched in her blotchy face stabbed my gut. "She's at the hospital. Your father's with her."

"We've got to go too," I said.

Gram's arm shot out. Her icy hand caught my wrist. "No. He wants you all to stay here."

"Okay." I nodded until she let go. "I'm going upstairs."

At the second-floor landing, Pam stood waiting for me with her arms crossed. She glared at me as if she were the older sister. "Were you at one of those Bible studies again?"

"I was at work. Why didn't anyone call me?" I jingled the keys in my hand. "What hospital is she at?"

"Dad said to stay home."

"What's wrong with you? We have to go."

"Don't do it." Pam wagged her finger at me just like Ma would.

I left her and went into BB's bedroom. She sat on the floor hugging Precious, her purple stuffed cat. BB looked more like a scared little kid than a twelve-year-old, and I knew she wouldn't be going to the hospital with me either.

The lamp on her nightstand cast a long shadow across the floor. I sat cross-legged opposite her and our knees touched. "You all right? What happened?" A storm churned in my stomach.

"We were watching TV." BB laid the cat on her lap and stroked its back. "Ma said her head hurt and told me to get her some Tylenol. When I got back, she was on the floor. I shook her, but she didn't say anything."

I put my fingers to my mouth and breathed fast through my nose. BB tried to be brave, but the way her lip quivered, it crumpled my heart.

"Ma wouldn't wake up. I must've screamed because Pam and Dad came running. Pam called 9-1-1. Dad rolled Ma onto her side. Checked her mouth to see if she was choking. When the ambulance got here, he told us to call Gram and wait in our rooms."

"When did all this happen?" I said.

Pam stood at the threshold. "About three hours ago."

For three hours they sat and waited. I couldn't believe it, but held my tongue since BB kept talking.

"Red lights were flashing. I looked out my window. They'd strapped Ma to a stretcher. She didn't move." BB rocked back and forth. "She's not going to die, is she?" Tears pooled in her eyes. "Sometimes I wished she was dead. But I didn't really mean it. You know about God. He wouldn't do that, right?"

I tried not to gasp. Pastor Steve's words echoed in my head. *Trust God to smash obstacles.* This was BB's first question about God, and I was afraid to answer her.

"Dad will be back soon. He'll tell us everything is going to be all right." I reached out to pat her knee. It was as close as I could get to her.

Pam came in and sat beside us. No one moved. No one spoke. I silently pleaded with God for Ma's recovery. *She's not an obstacle.* Minutes later, tires crunched on the gravel driveway. We went to the window and saw Dad's SUV. I raced down the stairs with my sisters following close behind me.

"Come in the kitchen and wait with me." Gram's words slurred from the alcohol.

Like robots, Pam, BB, and I took our regular places around the table. Gram stayed in Ma's spot and stirred the ice in her drink with her finger. Pam shredded a napkin while BB rolled and unrolled the hem of her T-shirt. I tried to pray, but the words wouldn't come.

The second hand clicked twice around the clock before Dad thumped up the back stairs and opened the door. He came into the kitchen stooped over like an old man. More than anything else, it was his red-rimmed eyes that made my hands tremble. I swallowed hard.

"The doctors said it was a stroke." Dad's voice sounded hollow. "A blood clot burst in her brain. They've put her in a coma...she's on life support." He paused and whispered, "There's no brain activity."

I could barely listen to his words and jumped up. "Ma. You're talking about Ma." No one met my eyes. "Listen, please. God will heal Ma if we all pray for her. I'll call everyone at Bible study—"

"Kate, didn't you hear your father?" Gram shook her head. "Praying won't fix her. Your mother's brain dead."

Her voice struck me like a slap. I couldn't breathe.

Ma's last words crashed over me: *"You'll go to that cult over my dead body."*

CHAPTER 2

A WEEK LATER, we buried Ma. The relatives stopped visiting and Dad went back to work. Pam, BB, and I bumped into each other and mumbled apologies. The house seemed twice as big without Ma there.

BB started having bad dreams and ended up in my room in the middle of the night. I left an extra comforter for her on the floor. Pam showed us her dark side. She'd turn on Ma's favorite TV shows full blast and then leave the room.

Several times a day my mind played tricks on me. I'd hear a teakettle whistling and run into the kitchen thinking Ma was making tea. Finally, I hid the kettle in the cabinet under the sink.

Ma wasn't the only one missing. Dad seemed a million miles away. Before Ma died, he was never a big talker, but now when we tried to start conversations with him, he answered in one-word sentences.

We'd learned three things from Ma: how to cook, how to clean a house her way, and most importantly, how to leave her the hell alone. After all the donated meals were eaten, I tried to get things back to normal, but Pam and BB checked out of making dinners and doing their chores. Dad hated all the bickering between my sisters and me and ended up stocking the freezer with frozen meals. Family dinners ceased, and we ate whenever we wanted.

At first, I stopped cleaning the house. When the mold in our bathroom sprouted a mushroom, I had a fit. Pam laughed and BB said, "I'm not touching that." I couldn't believe they weren't grossed out.

I think my sisters knew that if they did nothing, I'd take over. So, in addition to my job at the mall, I cleaned the house and did my dad's laundry. All of it made me tired and snippy.

One hot night, Pam came into the basement where I was pulling towels out of the dryer. "Really, Kate. What's wrong with you? Ma's not ordering us around anymore. We can finally do whatever we want and you choose to do chores."

I wiped sweat off my forehead and finished folding a towel in thirds the way Ma liked it. "It's what she would've wanted us to do."

Pam groaned. "Don't act like Ma was some kind of saint."

"What's that supposed to mean?"

"It means…" She twisted a hunk of her hair. "Just stop trying to be our mother."

"Well, I don't like living like a pig, and no one else seems to be doing anything around here."

Pam barked out a laugh. "You know, there's nothing you can do *now* to fix anything."

I whipped around. She flashed me her mean victory smile. It took all my will and a prayer not to swear at her.

"I heard Dad talking to Aunt Linda on the phone last night." Pam put her hands on her hips. "He said if you didn't have that big fight with Ma, we wouldn't be in this mess."

Her words cut sharp as knives. "That's not true. Dad would never say that."

"Go find out for yourself. He's upstairs watching the news." She kicked a pile of clothes and left.

"Fine. I will." I hid my fists behind the laundry basket. Even though Ma and I fought over The Ark, what happened to her wasn't my fault. We'd all taken turns pestering her to take her blood pressure pills.

I stood outside my parents' bedroom gathering the right words to say. The closing music of the late night news trickled into the hallway. Dad couldn't see me, but I saw his bare feet on the bed. Ma's bureau was crowded with velvet jewelry boxes, perfume bottles, and Hummel figurines. A Danielle Steel paperback still lay on her bedside table. Dad hadn't touched a thing of hers. My heart hurt because I'd never thought about him missing Ma.

One of the last times I'd been in their room was to help my aunts pick Ma's outfit for the funeral. We squeezed into her closet, but I had to get out. The scent of her leather shoes and handbags overwhelmed me. And all of the sleeves of Ma's blouses brushing against my body felt like a hundred of her arms trying to touch me.

When my sisters and I stood at her casket, we stared at the blue satin dress she'd only worn at Dad's work parties. None of us said a word or shed a tear. I wondered if Pam and BB also thought Ma might spring up at any moment and yell at us.

The sudden silence in the hallway meant Dad had clicked off the TV. I stepped closer to the door and knocked twice.

"Come in," he said.

My breath caught. Ma's side of the mattress still had the indentation of her body. I had to steady myself against the footboard.

"Do you want something?" Dad picked up the newspaper lying beside him.

I waited a few moments while he scanned the front page. "I was wondering. All Ma's stuff, do you want help with it? We can donate her clothes to Goodwill or someplace like that."

He sighed. "Just leave everything alone."

"I'm only trying to help."

Dad spoke in a voice I didn't recognize. "I think you've done enough already."

The house swayed. My face burned. Pam wasn't lying—Dad blamed me. I stumbled out to the hallway, my arms grasping for something solid: a wall, a railing, a door. I reached my room and crumpled to the floor. Grabbing a pillow, I hugged it tight and let the tears I held back at Ma's funeral burst out. Crying and rocking. Crying and shaking.

Close to exhaustion, a calming thought found me. There was a place where everyone loved me. Now was the time to go.

CHAPTER 3

BY THE END OF AUGUST, I'd worked enough hours at my mall job to cover my first semester tuition at The Ark. Saying goodbye to the ladies I'd worked with for the past two years was harder than I expected. A couple of the older ones fussed extra over me after Ma died. Some brought me homemade cookies and others called me "poor thing."

On my last day, our supervisor called us into the stockroom for cake. I didn't understand why it was decorated with scissors and combs made out of frosting.

"Kate, you've gone through a lot these past weeks." She put her hand on my shoulder. "A new career choice is just what you need. If going to barber school doesn't work out, you're always welcome back here."

How Bible school morphed into barber school, I had no idea and I didn't have the heart or energy to correct her.

The next Saturday morning, I was packed and ready to leave home. I put my suitcase and a plastic garbage bag full of bedding near the front door. Dad dozed in his recliner while a golf tour-nament droned in the background. I let him be. When we had the talk about my going to The Ark, all he said was, "Do whatever you want. It doesn't matter anymore."

I heard Pam in the kitchen. She stood at the counter pouring juice in a glass.

"Just want to say I'm leaving now."

She came toward me. "Want some OJ or do you prefer Kool-Aid?"

"You're hilarious." I tilted my head in the direction of the den. "Hope you and BB will be okay with him."

"We'll be fine. You're the one joining a cult."

"Hey, don't you be Ma now." For the first time in weeks, Pam laughed with me. It was more than I'd hoped for.

BB waited for me on the staircase. "Can I help?"

"I'd love your help."

She raced down the last steps, wrapped her arms around the puffy plastic bag, and headed out ahead of me. I took one last look around the house. Too many bad memories lived here. At The Ark, I'd make new ones, good ones. I grabbed my shoulder bag and suitcase and wondered when I'd return, and if Dad would want me back.

One good thing happened. Dad didn't try to take my old Subaru away from me even though he'd paid for it. He hadn't done anything with Ma's car either. It sat parked in the driveway under layers of dust and leaves. I shuddered thinking that's how Ma was too.

BB and I heaved the suitcase and plastic bag into the trunk. After slamming it shut, I said, "I'm going to miss you."

She squirmed away when I tried to hug her. "I wish I could leave too. It sucks here."

"It'll get better. It's just going to take a while for Dad to get over Ma." I opened the car door and got in. "I'll give you my dorm phone number when I get to campus…if you ever want to call."

"Really? I can call you there?" She ended each question on an upbeat.

"Yes, on this." I handed her my cell phone. "They aren't allowed on campus."

"Wow." BB held it like a precious jewel. "Ma said I couldn't have one until high school. Thanks."

"I cleared all my stuff off it, but if you get any calls you don't recognize, just ignore them."

A shadow crossed BB's face. "What if you break down or have an emergency?"

"Don't worry. The Ark is a very safe place, and I won't be going too far off campus. Oh, one more thing. I don't know how Dad will feel about me coming home for the holidays. Be my spy and find out for me."

BB leaned in the car window and rested her elbows on the frame. She gave me a goodbye gift, her crooked smile.

My eyes filled with tears. "Don't forget, I love you, little sis."

She didn't know how to say it back so she turned and walked away. A few tears trickled down my cheeks. Nothing was easy in this house. It was an endless Tilt-a-Whirl ride, and I had finally gotten off.

CHAPTER 4

MY NEW BIBLE SAT on the seat next to me. I traced the gold lettering. Lifting the cover, I read again what was written on the first page.

The Gift of Life and Truth
Presented to:
Kate Bennett

Pastor Wayne gave it to me. I remembered the first time I met him. About a year ago, during my junior year at Salem High School, Julia sat down at my lunch table.

"Hi, Kate," she said. "Is it okay if I join you and your friends?"

I nodded, a bit confused because even though we were in home-room together, she'd never spoken to me. With her shiny blonde hair and perfect makeup, I thought she hung with the popular girls.

The two other girls at my table pretended not to listen. We ate at the designated quiet table where students could do homework and act like that was much more interesting than having a best friend or being asked to a dance.

"Thanks for letting me interrupt your lunch," Julia said. "My youth group is looking for new members." She pulled some colorful papers out of her shoulder bag and passed them to us. "I think you'd all like it. The details are in this flyer. The best part is our next meeting is tomorrow morning. And don't worry about breakfast because we have free donuts. Do you think you'd like to come?"

When none of us replied, Julia smiled and stood. "Bye for now."

I watched her work her way into the food line and then spoke to the other girls. "Do either of you know what she's talking about?"

One said she thought they were religious. The other said she wouldn't get up an hour early for any school group. I stuffed the flyer in my binder to read later.

Before I went to bed that night, I remembered Julia's invitation. The flyer listed the meeting times in the cafeteria and that everyone was welcome. But what caught my eye were the words, *If you don't fit into the mold of aimless, superficial youth, Break the Mold. Don't be a leaf blowing in the wind. Be a tree that stands firm in a storm. Be Someone who is Going Somewhere.*

My goal in high school was to get through it with minimal attention. I figured if I didn't go to the meeting at least once, Julia would see me in homeroom every day and I'd feel bad. What did I have to lose? If I hated it, I wouldn't go back.

The next morning about a dozen boys and girls had already assembled at the cafeteria door. They seemed too cheerful for so early in the morning.

Julia spotted me and rushed over. "I'm so glad you came. Pastor Wayne will be here soon."

I stepped back when she said Pastor Wayne.

"Oh, it's not like church." She pushed her bangs out of her eyes and led me to a table where we put down our books. "First, he leads us in song. After that we talk about what's going on in our lives. You'll love it."

A moment later, a youngish man wearing jeans and a sports jacket headed toward us. He carried a Bible and had a guitar slung over his shoulder. Behind him, a girl carried a pink box from Dunkin' Donuts. Other students jostled each other trying to catch up to the man who had to be Pastor Wayne.

I stood at Julia's side as she introduced me to the others. I'd never seen so many happy faces in high school before. No one played football or was a cheerleader, but no one seemed too weird either, except for a boy with pink ears and blotches on his face. I relaxed and waited for the last person in line.

"Pastor Wayne." Julia bounced from foot to foot. "This is my new friend, Kate."

He looked at me with kind gray eyes and shook my hand. "Welcome, Kate. We are blessed to have you join us today."

Pastor Wayne had no airs about him. His warm handshake and gentle voice made me think of the word *genuine*. He asked us to take a seat, and we spread out over one long table. Julia made sure I sat right next to her.

I glanced at the others who seemed to adore Pastor Wayne, all waiting for his next move. He tuned his guitar for a minute and played a song I'd never heard. It had a good beat and everyone sang along with him about rejoicing in the Lord.

Who'd believe a bunch of high school kids got up early to sing about God in the school cafeteria and apparently liked it? But there was something real about it and that made me like it too. Pastor Wayne put his guitar away and nodded to each of us. I paid more attention.

"Last week, we talked about the pressure to fit into the different groups like popular, smart, druggies, and jocks. And in order to fit in, there are the smaller challenges of what clothes you wear and the words you speak. Then there are bigger temptations like choosing whether to smoke on the bus or drink that beer behind the bleachers." Several of the boys laughed and Pastor Wayne joined them. "Hey, it wasn't so long ago that I was in high school."

He opened his Bible. "Today's verse is from John 3:16. It is the most important verse in the New Testament. 'For God so loved the world that he gave his one and only Son, that whoever believes in him shall not perish but have eternal life.'"

On our few visits to church on Christmas Eve, I'd never heard this verse before. We sang carols and admired the pretty decorations. I'd never thought too much about death or what happens afterward.

"God loves all of us the same. Not just those who believe, but everyone. That is very important to remember as Christians. If we don't remember it, we will judge others. Never think you're better than anyone else. God's grace is a gift. We did nothing to earn it. Our job is to show others what his grace is all about."

I didn't know what grace was either. Pastor Wayne asked what we could do in school to be a witness for God.

I heard, "Stop a bully." Another said, "Help someone who is struggling in class." As the others shared, I tried not to flinch whenever someone said *Jesus*. It was a major word in Ma's swear arsenal.

After a quick prayer, we grabbed donuts and left for our classrooms. Julia and I walked to homeroom together.

Before we went in, she said, "I hope you liked it today and that you'll have lunch with us too. We meet at the same table as this morning."

As the weeks flew by, Julia and I became close friends. We passed notes between our classes and went to all the school meetings together. Her friendship and learning about God stirred something inside me. I liked it so much that on the nights I didn't work, I went to Bible studies in people's homes. *Hey world, Kate Bennett actually has a social life.*

At home, I tried to talk to Pam and BB about God. Pam said, "Could you be even more boring than you already are?" BB didn't insult me, but she didn't want to hear about "that religion stuff" either.

Ma didn't pay any attention to my comings and goings as long as I made dinner on my nights and did all my chores on the weekend. Dad said, "Better God than drugs," and pretended to listen to me, but I knew he was reading the newspaper and just nodding.

As much as I admired Pastor Wayne, there was another pastor I'd heard a lot about. His name was Pastor Steve. Whenever anyone talked about him, awe filled their voice. I pulled Julia aside one night after a Bible study.

"It seems like everyone here knows who Pastor Steve is except me."

"I forget how new you are to all this." Julia suppressed a laugh. "Pastor Steve is the founder of The Ark. That's where Pastor Wayne comes from. And guess what?" Her eyes turned dreamy. "I go there every Sunday to hear his sermons. Want to come see for yourself? Lincoln's only a two hour drive from here, and it's so beautiful up there in New Hampshire. You can even see the White Mountains from the campus."

The smile on Julia's face was hard to resist.

"Tell me when we leave."

CHAPTER 5

THE FOLLOWING SUNDAY I met Julia at her house. We always met there. She'd never been to my house—I'd made up enough excuses that she didn't press it. I couldn't bear what embarrassing thing Ma might say in front of her.

It was early, but Julia's parents and little brother were up eating homemade granola and drinking fresh-squeezed orange juice. Her parents reminded me of hippies who outlived the 1960s. They all had long hair (even her little brother) and the house smelled like incense. Musical instruments were strewn everywhere. She told me her parents were in the music production business, but I didn't really understand what they did.

"Enjoy God's love today," her mom said. She hugged Julia goodbye. And when it was my turn, everyone in her family laughed.

"You need more practice, Kate. One day you won't wince when you're hugged," her dad said.

Ma and Dad never touched us in a loving way. I imagine they must've when I was a baby because when BB came around, Ma showed me how to comfort her.

On the drive to New Hampshire, I probably asked Julia a hundred questions about Pastor Steve and The Ark. She teased me, saying she didn't want to ruin the surprise. But I did figure out that there was more to it than a Bible school. There was also a high school on the campus. Both attracted lots of students and trained them to be missionaries. In fact, it had doubled in size every year over the past three years.

Julia pulled off the highway and we passed a sign for the town of Lincoln. "We are getting close," she said. "Ten minutes to arrival."

I could barely sit still. When I saw the campus, I shouted out in a preachy voice, "Welcome to The Ark World Outreach Headquarters."

Julia bent over the steering wheel in silent laughter.

The campus was a collection of white rectangular buildings, split rail fences, and parking lots. Julia pulled into a spot in front of a newer structure that reminded me of a gymnasium except that it had beautiful octagonal windows. Each one had a perfectly proportioned wooden cross embedded in the glass.

"This is the chapel," Julia said. Her face beamed.

The air buzzed as we joined the folks scurrying toward the entrance. My body absorbed the energy around me, sending a shiver of anticipation down my spine.

"Is anybody else from our youth group here today?" I searched the crowd for familiar faces.

"Not that I know of. So when we go inside, stay with me." Julia took me by the arm. "Pastor Wayne saved us seats up front.

They're usually reserved for pastors and teachers."

"Awesome." If I had both hands free, I would've clapped.

Several folks waved to Julia as we entered the chapel. The foyer opened into a large auditorium full of people. Indoor/outdoor carpeting covered the floor and rows of metal folding chairs flanked the aisle.

"Wow. How many people can this place hold?" I said.

"About three hundred," Julia said.

I looked for statues of saints and Jesus on the cross but found neither. Instead, colorful banners decorated with Bible symbols hung on the white walls. On the stage were a pulpit, some fancy velvet chairs, a set of drums, and two tall speakers. Soft light streamed in from the high windows and the murmur of voices filled the air.

Pastor Wayne's face lit up when Julia and I reached him. He looked the same as when we saw him at school, but today he was freshly shaved and wore dress slacks instead of jeans. "It's so wonderful to see you both here this morning." Our eyes met. "Kate, most folks never forget the first time they hear Pastor Steve preach. Right, Julia?"

Julia squeezed my arm. "One hundred percent right."

The band members took the stage, which appeared to be the signal to quiet down and be seated. After entertaining us with some worship songs, the lead singer, a cherub-faced young woman, asked us to stand and sing "Amazing Grace." Hundreds of voices, some low and some high, blended together with hers. I mouthed the parts I knew and let the beauty of the words wash over me.

Then some folks started talking in a language that sounded like it came from aliens. Others moaned while rocking back and forth. I gasped, crouched, and tried to pull Julia down with me. "What's happening?"

Julia's mouth opened, but she didn't answer me. I looked at Pastor Wayne for help, but his eyes were closed and his face serene. We had to get out of this weird place.

"Tongues," Julia finally blurted out. "It's okay. They're speaking in tongues." She pulled me up trying not to laugh. "Oh, Kate, it's a spiritual gift."

Without glancing behind me, I smoothed out imaginary wrinkles on my skirt.

The band stopped and an older man wearing an ill-fitted suit jacket came to the pulpit. He pulled out his handkerchief to dab his sweaty brow. After adjusting the mic, he smiled down at us. "Please be seated."

"Is that him?" I whispered to Julia. "Is that Pastor Steve?"

She held a finger to her lips and shook her head. Some part of me was relieved; in my mind I'd imagined Pastor Steve as a younger man and more polished.

"Let us bow our heads in prayer. Lord, help us to hear the living word of God. Amen."

The prayer guy sat down and a tall man in a sharp navy suit with a red tie climbed up a set of side stairs to the stage. He walked like a movie star. Now, this had to be Pastor Steve. I knocked Julia's knee with mine. She gave me thumbs up and slid her Bible between us so I could follow along. Pastor Steve had a Bible too, but he didn't open it. He quoted a verse out of II Corinthians.

"'For God, who commanded the light to shine out of darkness, hath shined in our hearts, to give the light of the knowledge of the glory of God in the face of Jesus Christ.'" He paused and said, "We have a choice. We can let the light of God shine in our hearts or we can let darkness abide."

He spoke for several minutes in a soothing tone. I glanced at Julia who seemed hypnotized and noticed Pastor Wayne jotting notes in the margins of his Bible. I crossed and uncrossed my ankles. My stomach growled.

"Can you hear God?"

Pastor Steve's commanding voice startled me. I swallowed hard and when I met his eyes, he seemed to be focused only on me.

"Have you ever felt like you were drowning? Did you reach up to take God's hand?"

Pinned against my seat, the memory of BB and the pond overtook me.

An eight-year-old never forgets a promise. So on a cold February morning, I kept my promise and took BB ice skating. We walked to the pond with our skates slung over our shoulders. BB chatted nonstop about her favorite princess.

The morning sun shimmered over the ice, creating a light mist on the deserted pond. We found a dry sandy area to lace up our skates.

Pretending to be Frankenstein, I lurched on the ice toward BB. She shrieked and giggled. The wind lifted our hair as we glided across the smooth surface.

BB raised her arms in the air. "Someday I'm going to twirl like they do at the Olympics."

"Do you know how much they practice to get that good?"

"How much?"

"They're at the rink every day at 5:00 in the morning with their coaches, and *then* they go to school."

BB shrugged. "I could do it. And I can also beat you to the other side."

The sound of our blades scraping the ice filled the air. I'd forgotten how exhilarating speed felt. BB headed toward some reeds, and that's when I noticed that the clear blue ice we'd been skating on now looked flaky.

A hot wave shot through me. "BB, don't move."

"Ha, ha. I won." She swirled and bowed.

"I mean it. The ice isn't the right color here." Her smile vanished at the pitch of my voice. "Slowly skate back toward me."

BB pressed in one blade. Then, gently, she pressed in the other. I willed her toward me, afraid if I moved a muscle I might change the weight on the ice.

I heard the sickening sound before I saw it. A second later, BB disappeared. *No! This can't be happening.*

A scream tore from my throat, and then BB's hand burst out of the water. A moment later, her head broke the surface.

I dashed toward her, ice shards flying in my wake. I slowed as I got closer, unsure where the thinner ice began. BB sputtered and gasped for air. "Kaaaaate!" Her tiny voice disappeared as she sank. My heart broke into pieces.

Dropping to my knees, I crawled to her. *Please God, don't let this ice crack underneath me.* She surfaced again.

The world slowed to this single moment, our two hands reaching out to touch each other.

"I got you, BB." She locked on, but the weight of her body on my hand was too much. I started sliding toward her. *She's going to pull me in with her.* My soul cried as I broke free of her icy grip. Her face crumpled in disbelief.

She went under again and bobbed up. "BB, it's going to be all right." I kept the terror out of my voice. "Can you climb out?"

"I can't." She thrashed in the water. "I can't feel the bottom." Her lips had turned blue. She sank again.

Please God, I begged, *don't let her die. I swear I'll do anything for you.*

I didn't have a second to waste and dug the toes of my blades into the ice to anchor myself. BB's hair floated to the top. I reached into the icy water to grab it and missed. "Shit!" *She's going to freeze to death.*

Inching even closer, I plunged both my hands into the water and got a handful of hair. I tugged hard and BB's head rose. The emptiness in her eyes made me scream, "Lift your arms out now!"

One soaking arm reached up. "That's it, BB." Digging my skates in deeper, I pulled her soaking wet body with strength I didn't know I had. My arms ached but I didn't stop until she lay beside me. I panted into the ice to catch my breath, and then wrapped my arms tight around her. The wisp of a moan escaped and she coughed.

With heavy breaths, I dragged her to the sandy area and sat her up. I whispered in her ear, "BB, we made it."

Her body trembled as I peeled off her wet jacket, replacing it with my warm one. Just then, a ray of sun poked through the clouds. We turned to it like baby birds. BB looked at me with clear loving eyes, and I knew we were going to be okay. *Thank you, God.*

The sound of the band playing "How Great Thou Art" brought me back to the chapel.

Pastor Steve scanned the crowd. "God's been waiting for you. Let him show you his love and compassion. Do you want everlasting life? Come to the front of the stage and accept the Lord into your heart."

A warm tingle started in my chest and spread to my fingertips, making me weak and strong at the same time. I couldn't deny it. God wanted me and I owed him. Tears of gratitude pooled in my eyes. I rose to join the others in the aisle.

"Lord, thank you for these souls," Pastor Steve said.

He walked down the side stairs and met us. Pastor Wayne and some other men joined him. They formed an outer circle around us, each with a hand resting on our backs. The kindness of that gesture broke me and I couldn't stop the tears from falling.

After Pastor Steve finished praying for us, we took our seats. The glorious expression on Julia's face made me cry even more. She reached for my hand and lifted it in the air with hers. I wasn't used to praising God like this, but my heart burst with love because now I knew what being saved felt like.

CHAPTER 6

I'D DONE IT. I'd been accepted as a student at The Ark and soon my training to be a missionary would begin. As I drove, I thought about why being a missionary appealed to me. I'd have to live in another country, deal with unknown hardships, and talk to strangers about God. But I'd be with other young people like me, and together we'd enjoy fellowshipping and the rewards of making a difference.

A crushing doubt fell over me. How could I be a missionary in the world when not one person in my family would listen to me about God? I prayed again for Ma's soul. When I couldn't pray a second longer, Pam, BB and Dad invaded my thoughts.

To stop all the noise in my head, I listened to one of Pastor Steve's sermons. He read from Philippians and his words rang true. "'We must forsake all for Christ. A true believer will lose all to gain salvation.'"

When I finally arrived at The Ark, I parked in front of Carlson Hall, the administration building bearing Pastor Steve's last name, and blew out a huge sigh. The campus was quiet since school didn't officially start for another week. I lowered the windows and shut off the engine. It was the still time of day when the birds and insects napped. Pine trees scented the air and covered the nearby mountains in a green blanket.

God was here. I'd made the right decision. Pumped, I climbed the steps up the building and pulled open the glass door. The jingle of bells and a strong gush of air conditioning greeted me.

"Hello…I'm down the hall," a woman's voice said.

And smack, the first day of school jitters punched the confidence right out of me. If only Julia wasn't taking a year off to learn Spanish before she came to The Ark. Having a friend here would've been so much better.

I laughed at myself. This wasn't high school where I had to worry about fitting in. Students came to The Ark for the same reason: They loved God. Closed doors with nameplates that read WORLD OUTREACH, TREASURER, and YOUTH MINISTRIES lined the hallway. I reached an open door. A slim young woman waved me in. She'd put her dark brown hair in a tight bun. I'd seen her before but couldn't remember where.

She extended her hand. "Hi, I'm Elizabeth Carlson."

Oh, God. *She's Pastor Steve's wife. Should I bow? No. Act normal. Shake her hand and introduce yourself.* "I'm Kate Bennett."

"Nice to meet you, Kate. Pastor Wayne told us you'd be arriving a few days early. I'm very sorry about the passing of your mother."

My breath caught, and I looked away. "Thank you."

"Please, have a seat." Elizabeth opened a desk drawer and took out a set of keys. "Your student ID and dorm key are in the treasurer's office. Make yourself comfortable. I'll be right back."

Her flats tapped down the hallway. If she knew about Ma, I wondered who else Pastor Wayne told. I distracted myself by checking out Elizabeth's office. She had her own printer and copier and a pair of filing cabinets took up an entire wall. A glass vase full of wildflowers adorned the corner of her desk. A ladybug crawled out of a daisy and landed on the back of a silver frame. I turned it around and saw her wedding photo.

Pastor Steve gazed at Elizabeth with such devotion it made me wonder if there'd ever be a man who'd love me that much. Footsteps in the hall warned me to put the frame back. I did it with a few seconds to spare and sat with my hands on my lap.

Elizabeth's light blue jersey dress floated as she walked—more like glided—back into the room. On the wall behind her desk, a poster of Degas' ballerinas caught my eye. Elizabeth could have fallen right out of it.

She motioned toward the poster. "Are you a fan of the artist or ballet?"

"Both I guess. And you, you move just like a ballerina."

Her laugh floated like a musical note. "A long time ago, I was a dancer. But I had an accident that ended my career." She paused and bowed her head. "Those were dark days for me."

"I'm sorry."

Elizabeth met my eyes. "Thank you."

"How did you meet Pastor Steve?" I hoped it didn't sound like I was prying.

She smiled and tilted her head. "It was an older friend of mine. She said that my pity party needed to end. And it was time to lift myself up. I asked her how she expected me to do that. She told me that I needed to hear this amazing preacher. To make her happy, I went to church with her. That's when I heard Steve Carlson speak." Her eyes shone. "And I guess you know how that story ended."

Something warm trickled into my heart. "That's a great story," I said.

"You know, Kate. You're a good listener. What a wonderful gift. It is one of the finest attributes a woman in God's service can have."

Pastor Steve's wife said I had a gift. I couldn't believe it. I'd heard about spiritual gifts and thought God had passed me over.

"Well, that's enough about me," Elizabeth said. She opened a file on her desk I hadn't noticed. She studied it for a moment. "We like to ask all our new students a few questions. What inspired you to come to The Ark?"

I fiddled with my watch strap. "I want to be a missionary."

"Well, you've come to the right place. You'll love our mission-ary training program."

"Is it okay that I'm not fluent in any language other than English?"

"Oh, don't worry about that. You'll get paired with someone in the field who is fluent. I've heard you learn real fast when you have to."

Elizabeth smiled and went on to explain my class schedule and gave me a campus map, a dorm key, and my student ID card. My head swirled with all the information. I jotted down as many notes as I could.

"To limit student distraction, there's a no cell phone policy on campus, but there are pay phones in every building. And last, but not least..." Elizabeth patted her flat stomach. "Food. Our cafeteria doesn't open until classes start, but the snack bar is open and there's a Price Chopper not too far if you want to buy some groceries."

She started to stand and I did as well. "Thank you for doing my orientation early, Mrs. Carlson."

"Please call me Elizabeth. And don't be a stranger." She came close and hugged me. "I'll look for you at chapel tomorrow and save you a seat up front."

A good shiver traveled down my back. It was like the feeling I'd get when my sisters and I pretended to crack eggs on each other's head. I bounced down the stairs and back to my car. My first day and already I'd met Pastor Steve's wife. I couldn't wait to meet my roommates and start school.

The campus map showed me the way to the girls' dorm, a long two-story building in need of a paint job. I parked in the empty lot. Leaving my stuff behind, I walked up the two steps to the entrance and unlocked the front door. Hot stuffy air engulfed me in the small lobby. Someone must have thought pink was a good idea for wall color, but it looked like they'd been painted in Pepto-Bismol. An ancient pay phone with a small shelf under it occupied one wall and a huge cork bulletin board hung on another. The faded pieces of colored paper covering it reminded me of a patchwork quilt.

I read the notices: *Will fix your car if you do my laundry. Almost new winter coat—going to Costa Rica—will trade. Subway is hiring. Wedding dress for sale—only worn 3 times.* That one made me smile. Julia told me that by the end of the first year, half of the students were either engaged or married. I couldn't imagine being married, but having a boyfriend at The Ark sure would be nice.

Beyond the lobby was a staircase with long corridors on both sides. My room was on the first floor down a dim hallway. The reek of Lysol warned me I'd come close to the bathroom area. I peeked in and saw toilet stalls with curtains for doors. Yuck.

Two doors down, I found my room. With the shades drawn, all I could make out were the shapes of three sets of metal bunk beds. If things went well, one of my roommates would be a new friend.

I flicked on the wall switch for the overhead light just as something gray with a long tail scurried under a bunk in back of the room. My loud "eek" bounced off the walls as I bolted into the hallway and crashed into someone. I screamed again.

The person thumped against the wall. My heart banged as my hands braced to prevent a full body slam. Our noses grazed. I pushed myself away. Thank God, it was a girl like me. I hadn't killed her.

My sentences came out in spurts. "You scared me... I'm so sorry... Are you hurt?" I backed up a few more steps and saw a pale girl with inky hair that matched her black turtleneck sweater and long skirt. It made me sweat just to look at her.

"Did you see a spirit in there?" she said, her eyes wide.

I tried to speak in a calmer voice. "Ah, no. I think I saw a mouse or something."

"Not many people know." The girl's eyes darted around the hallway as she spoke. "A long time ago, a boy died in one of these rooms. His spirit is stuck here. God wants me to find him."

With no idea of how to reply to this odd girl, I offered her my hand. "I'm a new student. My name's Kate."

She took it and traced some lines on my palm. "Yes, you are a Kate. I'm Daisy."

For the first time since she died, I could hear Ma's voice. *"Hey Miss High and Mighty, you picked this over college? Friggin' brilliant."*

CHAPTER 7

I WOKE UP DISORIENTED the next morning. Soft light peeked under the yellowed window shades. While my eyes adjusted to the room, I made out the shape of Daisy lying asleep on a bottom bunk in the middle of the room. She didn't use sheets, just a toss pillow and a worn blanket. The top bunk I picked was furthest from where I saw the rodent run and hide.

An unexpected happiness rolled over me. My first day of freedom. No more cleaning, cooking, or taking care of anyone. If Daisy wasn't sleeping, I might've done a touchdown dance.

Even though the dorm seemed a bit lonely now, I imagined it full of more girls like me, eager to do God's work. Most important of all, today was Sunday and Pastor Steve preached twice. It was called a double blessing day. When school started, our first class every morning would be with him. I could hardly wait.

A thud in the room caught my attention. Thank goodness it wasn't Daisy falling out of bed. My shoulder bag had slid off the dresser to the floor. Without a sound, I kicked off my sheet, jumped down to pick it up, and dumped out the contents on my bed. The foil on my Hershey's chocolate bar had been scratched, *with teeth marks*. Silent screams of rabies and black plague ricocheted in my head. I slammed the candy bar into the trashcan. Grabbing my robe and towel, I raced down the hall to the bathroom.

Under scalding water, I showered with a sliver of old soap until it disappeared. I wrapped a towel around my head and pressed my forehead against the sink mirror. *God, are you testing me? My first roommate talks to ghosts and a rodent lives in my dorm room. This is not the mansion I thought you prepared for me.*

My breath steamed the mirror. Morning service started in a few minutes so I'd have to rush to sit with Elizabeth. Someone left a hair dryer in a basket under the sink, and thankfully it still worked. After a quick drying, I rushed back to my room.

The bright overhead light was on, but Daisy's bed was empty. A scrawny older guy in a green uniform appeared from the far end of the room. I held in my shriek and backed toward the hall.

"Hey, Missy. Didn't you hear me yell out that there was a man in the dorm?"

I wrapped my robe tighter.

"Just got a few more traps to set." He hobbled around until he placed a trap under every bunk bed. When he finished, he picked up the trashcan and pointed to the candy bar in it. His breath reeked. "You tell the other girls that Charlie said no food in the dorm rooms. Jeez, we'll never get rid of the rats in this place."

I locked the door, dressed, and raced to the chapel, but the service had already begun. Crushed, I took the first seat I found in the back. Elizabeth probably forgot all about me. Today's crowd was mostly people my age along with a few senior ladies and some families with older children.

As the service started, a young teen girl took the empty seat beside me. During the sermon, she fidgeted with her purse like it was a Mary Poppins bag. She dug out gum, lip-gloss, Kleenex, sunglasses, and gel pens. When she shook out some Tic Tacs, I bit my lip to keep from groaning. My only consolation for missing most of the sermon was that I could hear it again tonight. Nothing would stop me from being early and sitting in the front row.

One of the elders closed us in prayer and announced that the cafeteria would be open for fellowship and brunch. I followed the crowd to the back of the admin building and stood in line at the long food counter. The smell of maple syrup reminded me of my Sunday tradition with BB. She'd beg me to make her pancakes even though she knew how to do it herself. I sighed thinking BB might be the only one who missed me.

I kept our tradition alive and chose a short stack of pancakes and a glass of orange juice. As I glanced around, voices buzzed and silverware clanked, but I didn't recognize a soul. I carried my tray to a table with some empty seats. Just as I lifted my first forkful, a pair of lanky boys—who seemed all arms and legs—asked if they could sit with me.

"Sure." I couldn't believe how much food they had on their trays.

"Hi," the taller one said. "I'm DJ and this is my little brother, Rich." DJ shoved him in the shoulder.

"Hi, I'm Kate. I'm new at The Ark. What about you guys?"

"We go to the high school." DJ stared at my plate. "Did you just get pancakes?"

"Yes. That's all I wanted."

"Listen, lady. Let's make a deal. We can only go through the line once, so if you get everything and can't eat it, slide it on over," DJ said.

Lady? I wasn't old enough to be called lady.

The cafeteria hushed. Pastor Steve had walked in. He'd loosened his tie and seemed to be headed straight toward our table.

"Hey, boys," Pastor Steve said. "Are we going to have a winning basketball team again this year?" He smiled and put his hands on a chair. "May I join you?"

Rich and DJ nodded and kept on eating like Pastor Steve joined them for every meal. If I was a teakettle, I would've sputtered out hot water. I didn't know what to do or where to look.

"Can I get you something to eat?" I cringed at how dumb that sounded.

Pastor Steve stifled a laugh. "No, thank you. Boys, I haven't met your friend yet."

"Oh, sorry. This is Kate." Rich wiped at his mouth with the back of his hand. "She's new here."

"Welcome to The Ark." Pastor Steve held out his hand and we shook. "Nice to meet you."

"You eating here today?" Rich said.

"Actually, I've got a craving for bacon. Elizabeth's a health nut and won't make it for me." He patted his flat stomach. "Without her, I'd pack on the pounds."

I never imagined Pastor Steve talking about normal things like bacon and getting fat.

"Be right back." He hung his suit jacket on the chair opposite me. I watched him greet people as he walked across the room.

When he got into the food line, no one would go before him, which was exactly what I would've done. He finally gave up and went to the front.

"Rich, hurry up. We've got to get to practice. You know how Coach Luke is about being on time." DJ pushed back his chair from the table.

I grabbed the edge of his plastic tray. "Don't go yet." They couldn't leave me alone with Pastor Steve. The room heated up and the back of my neck started to sweat.

DJ's wide grin showed a mouth full of crooked teeth. "Hey, you're not afraid to sit with him, are you?"

"What do I say?" Panic churned the pancakes in my stomach.

"You're worried about what to say. That's funny," Rich said. "He's a preacher. You'll be lucky if you get a word in edgewise."

That's what Ma used to say when Pam, BB, and I were little kids. We'd come home from school and burst through the back door all yammering at the same time. Ma would yell, *"Enough already. A person can't get a damn word in edgewise."* My job was to shush my sisters with a snack, make Ma a cup of tea, and bring it to her in the den where she watched her TV shows.

The hungry boys left. I couldn't just bolt. I searched for someone, even Daisy, to come sit at my table. A minute later, Pastor Steve returned with a tower of bacon and three fried eggs. He sat and bowed his head in prayer—something I always forgot to do. I silently said another prayer, "God, please, don't let me do anything stupid."

Pastor Steve said something I couldn't understand.

"I'm sorry, I didn't get that."

"No, I shouldn't talk with food in my mouth. Bad habit. I was just asking why you chose to come to The Ark."

Thankfully, a question with an easy answer. "To train to be a missionary."

He scooped a forkful of eggs in his mouth and a drop of yolk hit his tie. I tried not to stare at it.

"Now I recognize you. Kate from Wayne's ministry, right? I remember when you came forward to accept Jesus."

I couldn't believe it. How could Pastor Steve remember that?

"Wayne told me about the loss of your mother." His eyes filled with compassion. "You have my deepest sympathy."

"Thank you."

Pastor Steve paused. "I sense something else troubling you. Did your family oppose your decision to come to The Ark?"

My hands trembled in my lap, but the tone of his voice pushed away my shame. "Yes," I said in a whisper.

He lowered his voice. "Kate, God's love is abundant. You have spiritual brothers and sisters here who will encourage and help you through all your difficult times."

I nodded, afraid my voice might crack.

He ate, and I sipped my orange juice. Close up, I noticed his clean, manicured nails and deep laugh lines around his mouth. Some gray touched his eyebrows and sideburns. He could've been any ordinary guy, but he changed so many lives. A new lightness touched my soul, and I thanked God for putting me here at this perfect time.

"If you're not busy tomorrow morning, would you like to drop by the studio and hear me do my radio show?"

No way. I couldn't believe Pastor Steve asked me to a live show. I'd heard *God's Disciples* on the radio plenty of times. Pastor Steve started each show with a specific topic, and then he opened the line to callers. It amazed me how fast he got to the root of each person's problem. He knew what God wanted to tell them. If I ever called, I'd ask him about Ma's soul and if she went to Heaven.

"Really? I mean, yes. I'd love to." My smile felt too big for my face.

"Great. The conference room we use for the radio show is at the end of the hallway in the admin building. Try to be there a few minutes early. We shut the door at 9:50 sharp." His eyes met mine. "Tomorrow, I'll be taking calls from those dealing with the burden of guilt."

Pastor Steve's words tunneled deep. I covered my mouth with my napkin. He kept speaking but I couldn't hear him. Pam's words haunted me: *"Dad said if you didn't have that big fight with Ma, we wouldn't be in this situation."*

I snapped back to the present.

"...there are two kinds of guilt. One is Godly sorrow. It leads a person to repentance. The other kind of guilt comes from the devil. It condemns and accuses."

CHAPTER 8

MONDAY MORNING ARRIVED and I felt jumpy, like my skin was too tight. What if Pastor Steve forgot he'd invited me to his radio talk show? I'd spent part of the night wrestling with why Dad blamed me for Ma's death. An argument didn't kill a person. He knew I tried harder than anyone to get her to take her medicine.

I swayed from foot to foot in front of the admin building. Tamping down my nerves, I climbed the steps and went in. A phone rang and I heard Elizabeth's voice answer it. She gave me a quick wave as I walked by.

Further down the hall was a door with red and white lights above it. The white one was on, and I peeked into a small office arranged with a long table and mismatched chairs. A pair of microphones, a water pitcher and glass, and a large black box sat on the table. Wires snaked around the room and ran up the wall to the ceiling.

I picked a folding chair in one of the corners and waited. Fifteen minutes until showtime. Ma used to joke that I'd be early to my own funeral, but she was the one who made me that way. She'd put me in charge of getting my sisters ready for school so she could sleep in. I had to make their breakfasts, check that they wore the right clothes, and then rush them out the door on time.

A younger, taller version of Pastor Steve came into the room. He didn't notice me as he went straight to the microphones and fussed with the cables. I tried not to stare, but he had the muscular build of an athlete. His sandy blond hair curled where it touched the collar of his polo shirt. The seconds ticked by so I coughed. When he saw me, his face lit up.

Butterflies danced in my chest. His piercing green eyes made me forget how to breathe.

"Oh, hey there. Sorry I didn't see you." He came toward me and shook my hand. "I'm Luke Carlson."

"Hi, I'm Kate Bennett. Your dad invited me today…to sit in… I got to The Ark a little early." Oh God, I didn't need to give him my life story. "I mean, nice to meet you."

"Same here. Oh, and he's not my dad. He's my uncle." Luke glanced at the wall clock. "Okay, so for the next few minutes it's going to be a little crazy in here."

"Am I in the way?"

"Not at all." He scanned the room. "I could use your help though. Would you mind grabbing that pitcher and filling it? There's a water cooler down the hall."

"No problem." My hand shook as I picked up the pitcher, but Luke didn't seem to notice. His name sounded familiar, and I wondered if he was the same Luke the hungry boys mentioned.

He sure had the height to coach a basketball team. I filled the pitcher and returned to the room.

"Thanks," Luke said. "Once we close that door, the audience—looks like just you today—will need to be silent. Nothing personal."

I pretended to zip my lip closed. *Good grief, way to make an impression if you're ten years old.* I went back to my seat and fanned my hot neck with my hand.

Pastor Steve and Elizabeth burst into the room. He sat behind a mic and looked over the pages she'd given him. Turning to her, he said, "Great job, dear. I don't know how you read my scribbles."

Elizabeth did a curtsy that made us laugh. "I don't want to be trapped in here for an hour, so have a great show." She shut the door behind her. Out in the hall, I imagined her switching the white light to red.

Pastor Steve smiled at me. "Kate, so glad you could make it. Welcome to the show." He checked his watch with the wall clock. "Luke, count us down."

Silence overtook the studio except for the countdown, which reminded me of a NASA rocket launch I'd seen on TV. At five seconds, Luke took the seat beside Pastor Steve.

"Welcome to *God's Disciples*. This is Pastor Steve Carlson of The Ark Outreach Ministries. For the next hour, you will be able to call in with your questions, comments, and prayer requests. Before we open the lines, let's ask God to bless our time together."

After praying, Pastor Steve rested his hands near the base of the mic. He quoted some verses from Hebrews, and said, "Listeners, if guilt is the obstacle that has kept you from growing in your spiritual life, won't you lay that burden at the cross? Accept God's forgiveness."

I didn't have time to let his words sink in because he took a call.

"Tina, it is my privilege to hear your burden today."

Her voice was soft. "Is Hell a real place?"

A conversation I'd had with Ma sped back to me. It was soon after I started going to youth meetings with Julia. I found Ma kneeling on a beach towel clipping away at some roses in the garden.

She saw my shadow but didn't turn around. "Did you come to help me or do you want something?"

Sitting beside her, I inhaled the heavy fragrance of red velvet roses. "I have a question. What religion are we?"

"I guess this is because you've been going to all those Bible studies." The sun lit the gray in her dark hair.

"What about you? Do you believe in God?" Hope filled my heart.

"I'll tell you a story about what Jesus did for me." Ma sat next to me and took off her gardening gloves. A sparrow sang from a nearby tree. "When I was twelve, Gram took me on a trip."

Stories about Gram usually had bad endings. We called Ma a mean witch behind her back because she yelled and swore at us all the time. But Gram, she was a monster. She'd get drunk and beat her kids.

"What kind of trip? A vacation?" I said.

Ma held up her hand. "Let me tell the story." After a deep breath and exhale, she continued, "It was after my pop died. She got meaner."

The thorns on the roses seemed sharper. The sun burned hot on my shoulders.

"We were all afraid. My brothers lied about their ages and

enlisted in the army. I was left alone with her. One day she told me to pack a suitcase for a long trip. It was the first day of summer, and I thought we were going to visit one of my aunts." Ma reached for a cigarette but didn't light it. "She drove a couple hours to a place I'd never seen before. Left me with an old couple and said they'd be taking care of me for a while."

Ma's voice changed and sounded tighter. She had a faraway look on her face.

"Gram left you with strangers?" I cringed as I said the words.

"After she left, I learned the truth. I was taking care of *them*. I was so scared and lonely. I missed my brothers, Pop..."

I sat in silence and imagined wrapping my arms around her. *Please God, just let this one story have a good ending.*

"During the day, while I did my chores, I sang the hymns Pop taught me. At night, I prayed on my knees. Prayed to Jesus that my mother would come back and take me home."

I let out the breath I'd held. It was such a sad story, but God helped her and now we could share more stories like this together. "So, you do believe?"

Ma's dry laugh made the hair on my arms stand up. "Jesus didn't hear me. I lived there for two friggin' years. No school, no friends. When she finally came back for me, I was too embarrassed to go to high school."

My mouth dropped open. I couldn't move.

"So now you know, I never graduated. And to answer your question, it doesn't matter how many Bible studies you go to, there's no one up there." She glanced at the sky and back at me with frightening intensity. "And don't be scared by that Hell bullshit either. Hell can be right here on earth."

The sound of a woman crying brought me back to the present. She sniffled and said, "Then if a child dies, do they automatically go to Heaven? Even if they've never been to church?"

Whew, it sounded like the same caller. I sat up straighter to listen.

"I feel your loss, Tina. I'm so sorry. Please know that children are not held responsible for their sins until they reach the age of accountability. By the grace and mercy of God, children are granted entrance into Heaven."

"My child was sixteen. He overdosed."

I slapped my hand over my mouth and stared at Pastor Steve, and then at Luke, who avoided my eyes.

Pastor Steve didn't flinch. "Tina, only God knows a person's heart. We don't know what happened during the final seconds of your son's life. Trust God and let go of this tremendous burden you're carrying."

A flicker of hope touched my soul. *Dear Lord, I hope Ma made her peace with you before she died.*

Pastor Steve prayed for Tina and took another caller. Frank spoke about the guilt he had over impure thoughts. "Frank, you bring up a good point for all of us. We all have choices. This is because God doesn't control us, God gives us freedom. Think of it this way. Our spirit is God-conscious, our soul is self-conscious, and the body is world-conscious." His voice rose and filled the studio. "Listeners, where do you choose to live? Frank, we are all joining hands in the studio to pray for you."

Luke and Pastor Steve motioned for me to join them.

God, please forgive me for my wandering thoughts. Don't let me be the weak link in this prayer circle.

I walked to the table and took their hands. God's presence surrounded me. Everything I'd gone through at home was worth it for this healing moment.

CHAPTER 9

THE BROADCAST ENDED and I walked back to the dorm realizing my efforts to stay God-conscious were doomed. My mind wandered to what was going on at home. With sharp detail, I could see BB flopped on the couch eating a bag of chips. Pam would be rifling through my closet to find something to wear. But not Dad, his face faded into shadows.

Dwelling on my family wouldn't help me with my immediate goal of finding a job. Fortunately, Lincoln was a good-size town by New Hampshire standards, with chain restaurants and stores. Each day I tried a new place and struck out.

My diligence finally paid off at the Price Chopper supermarket. I met Wanda, the night shift manager, who said the magic words, "Yes, we're hiring."

Wanda reminded me of someone Dad would call a tough cookie, someone you don't mess with or point out that she needs her roots done. She took me to the employee lounge to fill out an application. Overhead, the fluorescent lights flickered and ticked.

"I'll be back in fifteen minutes," she said.

When Wanda returned, she sat beside me and tapped the table with her acrylic fingernails. "Good, you've used a cash register. Available nights and weekends. And you're from The Ark."

"Yes, I'm a new student." *Please God, let her like The Ark.*

"I sure don't get all the fuss about that preacher, Carlson. But, I got to say, you've all been honest workers."

"I promise I won't let you down," I said, almost squirming in my seat.

Wanda laughed big enough to show a missing tooth in the back of her mouth. "Oh, aren't you're a cute one. You're hired. You'll start off as a bagger. Oh, don't give me that sad face. We all started as baggers."

On the way out, Wanda gave me my work schedule for the first week: three weeknights and Saturday afternoon. I thanked her and shook her hand goodbye.

"Well, they sure do teach you good manners at that school. See you on training day."

Good manners came way before The Ark. Ma told us many times, *"You don't have to be royalty to have good manners."* She had us saying please and thank you as soon as we could talk. I even said "no, thank you" to the bad guys who chased me in my dreams.

I hummed a few praise songs on the drive back to The Ark. In the dorm hallway, a patch of light shone from my room. My happy mood disappeared. Either Crazy Daisy was there or the janitor was back to check the rat traps.

It turned out to be neither of them. A girl with bouncy copper curls was making up the bunk below mine.

"Hi, there. I'm Kate. Top bunk."

"I'm Sheila." A dusting of freckles covered her smiling face. "Nice to meet you."

I offered her my hand, but she wrapped her arms around me. "I'm a hugger. Handshakes are for strangers." Sheila let me go and stepped back. "You okay that I picked the bunk under you? I did a little decorating."

Paper flowers wove through the metal bars of our bunk bed and posters with scripture verses decorated our bleak walls. Her best idea of all: gauzy fabric tacked to the ceiling for a privacy curtain between our bunk and the rest of the room. I brought it to my face and breathed in lavender.

"How'd you know to do all this?" I said.

"I remembered these rooms can be a little gloomy."

I loved Sheila already. "Then you must be a second year?"

"Yes. And I'm your room captain and your newest friend."

"I'm so happy you're here." My voice cracked.

"What's the matter? Oh, dear." Sheila pulled me into another hug and patted my back. "Long journey to get here?"

I nodded on her shoulder.

"Let me pray for you."

We sat on her bed. Sheila closed her eyes and I bowed my head. "Dear Lord, my new friend is troubled. You have given us many things. One of these gifts is strength. Shine your light into Kate's heart. Fill her with courage and bless her decision to be here. May she find joy as she casts all her cares upon you. Amen."

I silently thanked God for my new friend. We'd go to chapel together in the morning and at night, we'd whisper about what happened during our day.

"Praise the Lord! There's that smile again. Have you had lunch yet?"

We walked to the cafeteria arm in arm. Sheila also wanted to be a missionary. She filled me in on more of The Ark's history. "So this campus used to be a prep academy for boys. They closed it about five years ago. Something about one of the students dying from harsh discipline. Guess it made the papers. All the parents pulled their sons out."

I shivered. "I met someone named Daisy. She said a boy died in our room."

"God bless our Daisy. She's still trying to find that boy's spirit."

Before I could react to the idea that Daisy might be a second year student as well, Sheila pointed out a grouping of small single-story houses. "There's where our anointed ladies live. They're some of the original members of Pastor Steve's church from Rhode Island. When his ministry outgrew their building, this property came up for sale. He prayed for God to touch the hearts of those who could give. Four ladies stood up and offered to sell their homes to help finance the purchase of The Ark. They will now live here for the rest of their blessed years."

I whistled softly. "That's dedication."

We reached the cafeteria and the hungry boys waved at me from a table, mouthing *get everything*. I laughed and made an okay sign.

"I see you've made some friends already," Sheila said.

"And I got a job, too. At the Price Chopper," I said. "What about you? Have you started looking?"

"Oh, I'll go back to the job I had last year. I work at a group home for mentally challenged children."

My breath caught. "What's that like?"

"When everyone's calm, I play the piano and sing to them. The joy on their faces..." Sheila looked toward Heaven and smiled. "It's such a blessing."

"And when they're not calm?" I clasped my hands together.

"On those days, there's spitting, kicking. They soil themselves. We have a special safe room for them to quiet down." I winced at the image hoping Sheila didn't notice. "It's demanding, but God chose me to work with those children. He rewards those who serve him diligently and love unconditionally."

Sheila showed more kindness to those kids than Ma ever showed us. When we aggravated her, we had five seconds to get out of her sight. We'd bolt to our rooms with her words chasing us, *"If I ever lay a hand on you friggin' kids, I'll kill you."*

This is why I'm here, God. Teach me to be more like Sheila and not anything like Ma.

CHAPTER 10

I SURVIVED MY FIRST FEW SHIFTS at Price Chopper with an aching back and scratched wrists from stuffing groceries into paper bags. Halfway through the week, Wanda and I nearly collided in the breakroom.

"Oops, sorry about that," I said.

"You sure have lots of enthusiasm." Wanda glanced at her watch. "And you're early again." She clutched a clipboard to her chest and sighed.

"Everything okay?" I said.

"One of the new cashiers. Damn, if she didn't give her boyfriend free groceries. Now I'm down a cashier."

She arched her drawn-on eyebrows. I could almost hear her brain whirling.

"Can I help?" I flashed my most honest face. The one I used when something broke in the house and Ma tried to figure out who was guilty.

"Well, I normally don't promote baggers this soon, but let's give it a try."

The promotion came with a small raise, so I stood a little taller. Wanda paired me with a bagger named Nick, a student at the local junior college. His dark hair and eyes gave him a tough guy look, one I wasn't sure I could trust.

On our first night alone, Nick said, "Hey Kate, I like the way you handle those bananas."

At first I didn't get it and ignored him. Then he said, "Does that cucumber remind you of something?"

I glared at him. He grinned and continued his produce commentary. The more flustered Nick made me, the faster I slid the canned food toward his hands, trying to bash his fingers.

When we got a break between customers, I faced him. "What if a customer hears what you're saying?"

Nick shrugged. "Better go round up some carts."

To calm myself down, I imagined putting on God's armor. For the rest of the night, I ignored him and it worked. He teased the cranky kids that came through our line instead of bugging me.

By the time I returned to campus, two more dorm mates had showed up. Sisters named Hannah and Alice shared the bunk against the far wall. They told Sheila, Daisy, and me that they lived on a cattle farm. Their rough man-hands, sunburned faces, and muscular arms showed it. Hannah rolled up her pant leg and pointed to a scar on her shin where a branding iron had burned her. Daisy tried to touch it, but Hannah frowned and covered her leg again.

One bunk still lay empty on the night before school started. Sheila worried that the new girl would miss her first day. It was ten o'clock, an hour before lights out, and quiet time in our room. Daisy had already fallen asleep. Hannah and Alice sat cross legged on one bed playing something like "guess which book of the Bible I'm reading from." I talked to Sheila with my head and arms hanging down over my bunk.

The door banged open and everyone but Daisy jumped. Bright light from the hallway illuminated a girl from behind. She carried in the smells of spice and night air. Her dark hair flashed gold highlights, and her white blouse and black jeans fit her like a fashion model. No one at The Ark ever looked this glamorous. I couldn't wait to hear her story.

Sheila sat up, hitting her head on the bunk rail. *Ouch.*

"Suite 108?" the girl said. A look of confusion crossed her blemish-free face.

I held in a laugh as she scanned the room. She had no idea it looked worse in daylight when the water marks on the ceiling and the rust stains on the floor showed up bright and clear.

"Yes, right place," Sheila said. "Welcome. Let me get you checked in." She rubbed her head and rummaged through our nightstand.

"I'm Bobbi Young." She gave us a beauty queen wave, flashing her bright red nails. "Well, this is going to be cozy. What are you all in for?" Only Bobbi laughed at her joke. "Geez, anyone have a sense of humor around here?"

Sheila found her clipboard. She loved rules, order, and Jesus, which kept our room tidy and our sleep time peaceful. I appreciated her because I didn't have to be the mom for a change. *Oh, shoot.* In all the excitement of school starting, I hadn't called BB yet. By now she must've thought I'd forgotten all about her. I had to remember to get some quarters for the pay phone and laundry next time I was at work.

"Okay. Let's see…" Sheila flipped through some paperwork. "I'm Sheila and I'm your dorm room captain. You've arrived during quiet time. But of course, you don't know the rules yet… Roberta Young."

"Oh, God. Don't call me Roberta." She tossed her silky hair. "It's Bobbi. Always Bobbi."

"Okay, Bobbi. Let me introduce you to your dorm sisters."

In the middle of the introductions, Bobbi pointed at Daisy. "Hey, when's the last time someone checked the pulse on that one? She hasn't moved since I got here."

Hannah, Alice, and I hid our smiles.

Sheila cleared her throat. "She sleeps a—"

Bobbi interrupted, "Hey, if anyone's modest, you might want to cover up. My driver's right behind me with my trunks."

Sheila fumbled with the belt of her white terry bathrobe and tied it tight. "You mean one of your parents?"

"Oh, no." Bobbi's smile quivered for an instant, and then she recovered. "My parents are abroad. Ricardo drove me." She rolled both of the R's.

Pink anger washed over the freckles on Sheila's face. "Men are not allowed in the girls' dorms."

"But it's move-in day. I couldn't carry them by myself." Bobbi used a fake-sweet voice that reminded me of the popular girls in high school.

I'd never seen Sheila flustered like this before. Nervous energy raced through my body. The sound of squeaky wheels made us turn toward the door. An honest-to-goodness chauffeur in a suit and driving cap appeared holding a two-wheel dolly loaded with trunks. I covered the front of my worn T-shirt with my bed pillow.

"Miss Young, is this where you want them?" He glanced around the room and back at Bobbi.

"Oh, Ricardo." Bobbi's index finger tapped her chin. "Where am I going to put all my clothes? Oh well, just leave my autumn trunk for now. You can bring the others back later in the year."

Sheila set her furious eyes on Bobbi. "He will not be allowed back. And, Mr. Ricardo, you must leave this building immediately."

"Sorry to bother you." He lifted his cap to her, pulled the top trunk off the dolly, and placed it on the floor by Bobbi. "Ladies. Ms. Young. Goodnight."

Sheila announced, "Lights out in thirty minutes."

Bobbi opened her trunk and took out some sheets. She threw them on the bed and put her hands on her waist. I bet she'd never made a bed by herself. Hannah and Alice went back to their Bible game while Sheila busied herself with her clipboard.

Nice roommates. I went over to Bobbi's bunk. "Let me give you a hand with that." Her sheets weren't scratchy like mine. They felt as smooth as satin and her pillows were full of down. I wanted to hug one of them.

"Thanks." Bobbi gave me the hint of a smile. "Kate, right?"

"Yes." I lowered my voice. "We're much more lively during the day."

Bobbi tilted her head, but said nothing.

Lights went out a few minutes later. Drifting off to sleep, I thought about how Bobbi didn't fit the profile of most students at The Ark. I imagined how great her life must be and couldn't wait to ask her why she decided to come here.

Hannah and Alice left the room at daybreak. Sheila and I were the next ones up and went to breakfast together. While we ate, she told me where all my classes were and a bit about each of the instructors. Basically, all classes at The Ark were taught by men except for one, God's Golden Woman class.

"You'll learn the seven qualities of a godly woman." Sheila raised her fingers as she listed them. "Submissive, resourceful, loyal, patient, humble, productive, and God-fearing."

"How did you remember all of those?" I tried to sound impressed but was distracted by Ma's voice in my head: *"So you went to the cult to learn how to be a dog."*

Sheila stopped talking mid-sentence. I followed her gaze and saw Bobbi entering the cafeteria. I started to raise my hand to wave her over, but Sheila pulled it down. "Be careful. She doesn't follow our dress code. Look at all that makeup she's wearing. She's already broken a bunch of rules."

The Ark's dress code for women was simple: Do not wear clothes that draw attention to your body and away from God. Even so, Sheila's harshness surprised me.

"Don't you think she just needs some time to figure things out? She just got here," I said.

"I know her type. We had one like her last year." Sheila lowered her voice. "It was all hush-hush. She left between semesters."

I didn't like this side of Sheila. "We don't know her yet. Let's give her a chance."

Sheila stood and picked up her tray. "Enough about that. Let's go so we can get good seats at chapel."

We raced to the chapel and snagged two seats in the front row. First, Pastor Steve welcomed all the new students. Then he introduced the theme for the week, "Being God's Servant." This was real. Happy bells rang in my heart. No more waiting a whole week to hear him preach.

Pastor Steve asked us to turn to John 12:26, and he read, "'If any man serve me, let him follow me; and where I am, there shall also my servant be: if any man serve me, him will my Father honor.'"

My notebook filled up with Pastor Steve's inspirational words and scripture references. The hour sped by, and he closed in prayer. "Lord, may the work we do bring new hope, life, and courage to all we come in contact with this semester. Amen."

As we filed down the aisle to the exit, I saw Luke still seated in a discussion with another guy. Right as I passed him, the heel of my shoe caught a seam on the carpeting. I stumbled forward, leaving my shoe behind. Before I hit the floor, Luke rose and caught my elbow.

Oh God, what a klutz.

"You all right?" Luke's hand felt warm and strong.

"Yeah, thanks for catching me." I couldn't look him in the eye.

"It's nice to see you again," Luke said.

"Guess I should go." I wiggled my foot back into my shoe.

Sheila and I walked out into the bright September sun. My eyes teared. "How embarrassing was that?"

"Forget about that. How do you know Luke?" Sheila said.

"I met him before school started. Pastor Steve invited me to sit in on his radio show. Luke was there too."

"You should've seen his smile. I think he likes you. He's quite the catch, *and* he'll be a pastor soon." She took my hand and swung it as we walked. "And best of all, he's Pastor Steve's nephew."

My footsteps slowed. A bird chirped a sweet song. Could it be true? Could Luke Carlson like me?

CHAPTER 11

I PULLED OUT MY CLASS SCHEDULE for the tenth time.

> 8:00 – Chapel
> Morning break
> 10:00 – Understanding the Old Testament
> Lunch
> 1:00 – Introduction to Mission Life
> 3:00 – God's Golden Woman

Sheila and I separated after chapel. As I walked across campus, I couldn't stop smiling. I'd followed my heart for the first time in my life and here I was. *Thank you, God.*

Paul Carlson, Pastor Steve's oldest son, taught my Old Testament class. He was tall like Luke, but not as athletic. About thirty well-used desks and chairs filled the room. We were divided into two separate groups: girls on one side and boys on the other.

I sat with my roommates, Hannah and Alice, and whispered to them that we'd been separated by the Red Sea. They burst into laughter and when I realized why, I joined in.

The first assignment on our syllabus was to memorize the names of all thirty-nine books. This would be right up there with trying to remember all the elements on the periodic table.

After lunch, I went to Intro to Mission Life held in a smaller classroom where the instructor let us sit wherever we wanted. He spoke to us about the countries in Central America where The Ark had active missions and encouraged us to think about where we might fit in. Julia's decision to learn Spanish before coming to The Ark would definitely give her a boost.

I couldn't wait to meet Mrs. Huffman who taught the God's Golden Woman classes. Despite Sheila's explanation of the seven qualities that matched those of a golden Lab (*thanks for that image, Ma*), Mrs. Huffman had to be someone special. She was the only woman on The Ark's teaching staff.

Bobbi was in this class too, so I motioned for her to join me up front. She shook her head and took a seat alone in the last row.

"Young ladies, I am so blessed to share with you the joys of being God's Golden Woman. The first class of each semester is very exciting," said Mrs. Huffman.

Mrs. Huffman barely reached five feet tall and ran out of breath at the end of each sentence. Well, I'd never forget her last name.

"Isn't the Lord wonderful?" She looked up to Heaven and back to us, her face beaming as if she'd seen Jesus himself. "God's goal for you in this class is to polish your spirituality. Make you shine like gold."

I tried not to laugh at her quirkiness.

"God's Golden Woman is a two-year program. In year one, we learn scriptures about appropriate behavior for a single Christian woman." She stopped for a long inhale. "Year two, you'll learn all the skills necessary to be a missionary in the field, or a pastor's wife." She clasped her petite hands together and made a cooing noise before going on. "But most importantly—what every woman dreams about—how to honor your husband and his ministry."

"Oh, brother."

I didn't have to turn to know it was Bobbi and tried to concentrate on Mrs. Huffman's words. Would I end up being a missionary or a pastor's wife? The idea of being a pastor's wife had never crossed my mind. The only one I knew was Elizabeth, Pastor Steve's wife. I couldn't even imagine how you trained for a job like that. And as soon as I thought about how to honor a husband, Ma's voice laughed in my head: *You're eighteen, don't you friggin' dream about being someone's wife.*

The squeak of Mrs. Huffman's marker on the whiteboard sounded loud as we read the syllabus. "Young ladies, you will want to memorize the Bible verses I have written down. They are from Paul to Timothy and the basis of our class. Even though they were written to the early church, at The Ark we believe the Bible is the living word of God, and it applies to us today. Take a few moments to read this to yourselves."

She wrote down the verses from 1 Timothy 2:11-15. "'Let the woman learn in silence with all subjection. But I suffer not a woman to teach, nor to usurp authority over the man, but to be in silence. For Adam was first formed, then Eve. And Adam was not deceived, but the woman being deceived was the transgression. Notwithstanding she shall be saved in childbearing, if they continue in faith and charity and holiness with sobriety.'"

All women had to pay the price for one woman's sin. Ma would've flipped if she'd heard this. It made me a bit uncomfortable.

"Oh, Mrs. Huffy. I mean, Huffman, I've got some questions."

Bobbi again. Even though it was immature to make fun of the teacher's name, I giggled inside. When I glanced in Bobbi's direction, she gave me the slightest of nods.

Mrs. Huffman moved toward her. "Young lady, no speaking out in class."

Bobbi continued in a louder voice, "So, let me put those verses into real words. Are you saying that because some ancient lady tricked her man, the rest of us have to be silent now?"

The whole class turned toward Bobbi. Her face lit up. "Then, we're not supposed to drink? And after all that, we'll be saved in childbirth?"

"Please, we have rules." Mrs. Huffman's face darkened a deep shade of pink.

"Honestly, I don't think silence and sobriety are the way most babies are made."

The other students and I gasped in unison. Mrs. Huffman looked mortified, but she spoke in a controlled voice. "Young lady, please state your name for the class."

"Bobbi Young." She gave us her princess wave.

"Thank you. Now, Miss Young has introduced us to the topic of classroom etiquette. This is a lecture classroom and questions should be held until the end of each session." Mrs. Huffman paused to run her fingertips over her Bible. "When asking questions, you will speak in a demure tone as appropriate for women of God."

Bobbi rolled her eyes and shook her head.

Mrs. Huffman ignored her. "So that we all understand the passage, we will go over the meaning of each word." She started with the word *silence*. The discussion was short. Then she explained the next word.

"Subjection is not about who is the boss. God placed women in the care of men. Those of you who are single, you're in the care of your pastor. A married woman is in the care of her husband. She's sheltered by his provisions. If she truly subjects herself to her husband, she actually gains security and contentment because her husband has subjected himself to Christ. He knows his needs will be met by the Lord..."

I doodled in my notebook and wondered if I had what it took to be God's Golden Woman. Was security better than independence? Being Anne Bennett's daughter didn't give me a good role model for a submissive woman. Mrs. Huffman finally dismissed us and asked Bobbi to stay behind.

Bobbi ignored her and rushed outside. I followed her down a back route to the dorms. She went through a path of trees where bits of sunlight filtered through the cool green shade.

"Hey, wait up." She slowed. "That was pretty bold, what you said back there."

"Remember that movie *Stepford Wives*? Mrs. Huffman is the Christian version. Soon we'll all be like her." In a mechanical voice she said, "Isn't Jesus wonderful? Isn't Jesus wonderful?"

I shushed her, but she wouldn't stop.

"And how come she gasps for air? Maybe they forgot to program her to breathe like a real human."

Before I could stop them, silent laughs wracked my body. I bent over and grabbed the trunk of a pine tree. My hand stuck to the sap. *God forgive me.*

"Hey, I heard you work at Price Chopper. Can you bring back some bakery cookies one night?"

Almost composed, I said, "Yes. I will. Tonight."

Classes and work kept me busy that first week. A break to do laundry came on the weekend, and I made sure to keep some quarters to call home. Bobbi entered the room as I folded a stack of my boring underwear. She pranced around in colorful lace bras and matching undies when she got dressed. Sheila scolded her, but I secretly wished I felt that confident about my body.

Growing up, Pam, BB, and I never undressed in front of each other. Ma didn't even know when we got our periods. She gave me a booklet called something like *Your Changing Body* on my eleventh birthday and only figured out that Aunt Flo had come to visit when we started stealing her feminine products.

Bobbi eyed my neat piles of folded clothes. "Now I see what your problem is. No color. No pizazz. It makes you invisible."

She rifled through the closet that I shared with Sheila. On my side, a sea of beige tops floated over dark pants.

"Obviously, you need my help. But first, you have to make me a promise." She grabbed my hand and put it on my heart. "Promise me you'll never buy another beige thing. This looks like a moth's wardrobe."

With my hand still in hers, she led me to her side of the room. Bobbi had an entire closet to herself since Daisy kept her meager wardrobe in a box under her bed. She pulled open the door. "This is what a closet should look like."

Her clothes were put together as outfits. Bright patterned tops shared padded hangers with pants in every color. After a few moments of searching, Bobbi found a floral scarf and tied it around my neck. It smelled like cinnamon and felt like silk. Next, she opened the top drawer of her dresser jammed full of makeup, brushes, and nail polish.

"Now relax and close your eyes."

I felt Bobbi's breath on my face as she swept brushes over my cheeks and eyelids. She lined my lips and ran some lipstick over them. I worried she might overdo it, but when she told me to open my eyes, I looked in the mirror and all my features seemed to pop out.

"Wow, how'd you do that?"

"It's a natural talent." She yanked at my headband. "No more of these either. They make you look like you're twelve."

I swallowed my "yikes" and rubbed my head. The magazines said pulling your hair back made you look older, but Bobbi acted like somebody who knew what she was doing. No one had ever paid this much attention to me or cared how I looked.

Sheila's warning to keep my distance from Bobbi flashed in my head, but I pushed it aside. This moth girl found a new light. She didn't want to be Beige Kate any longer.

CHAPTER 12

ON SUNDAY AFTERNOON, I grabbed my quarters and headed to the pay phone in the lobby to call home. No one answered so I left a message that everything was fine at school. I could've called BB on the cell phone I gave her, but if she was out with Dad and Pam, I didn't want to interrupt them.

Then I thought of a great idea—BB loved getting mail. I went back to my room and wrote her a letter telling her how much I liked school and that I missed her. I tucked a stamp in so she'd write me back. It worked! I looked forward to her letters every week even though she'd forget to answer my questions about how Dad and Pam were doing. BB had a knack of sharing whatever was on her mind at that moment.

As the weeks passed, I spent more time with Bobbi and less with Sheila, who Bobbi nicknamed The Saint. Although I loved Sheila, her passion for rules made hanging out with her much less entertaining.

One night near curfew, Bobbi convinced me to sneak out with her. We dressed in T-shirts and sweatpants and raced like ghosts to the one building on campus that was always open, the chapel. It was so peaceful and beautiful there. The moonlight lit up the room like an old black and white movie.

Bobbi picked a spot up by the podium where Pastor Steve spoke. We made bets on how long it would take for Sheila to find us.

"What's the prize if I win?" Bobbi said.

"You get to wear anything in my closet," I said. We both laughed over that. There was so much about Bobbi I didn't know. Most of her stories involved fights with her mother, or the *Queen Mum*, as she called her. "Hey, I've been wondering, do you have any brothers or sisters?"

"Nope, I'm an only child. What about you?"

"I've got two younger sisters. They think I'm crazy for coming here."

The whoosh of the chapel door sliding open interrupted us.

"It's The Saint," Bobbi whispered. "Slain in the spirit."

For someone who hardly attended classes, Bobbi surprised me with her spot-on biblical references. We dropped to the floor and lay flat out on our stomachs. Bobbi's fingers crawled toward me until she hooked her pinkie with mine. We were in this together.

Sheila's shoes squeaked down the aisle toward us. My pulse beat in my ears, and I kept my eyes closed. Her feet tapped up the stairs to the podium. I squinted and saw she'd stopped inches from my face.

"Do you two realize it is past curfew?"

I pictured her face red with fury and arms crossed over her chest. My hipbones dug into the wooden floor.

"Would you like to join us in prayer?" Bobbi said, using her sweetest voice.

"Honestly. Back to the room when you're done."

Sheila huffed and puffed her way out. Bobbi elbowed me when it was safe to get up.

A few days later, Bobbi found me in between classes. She waved a green flyer in my face. "You have to do this with me."

It announced cheerleading tryouts for our basketball team, The Crusaders.

"Oh, that's not going to happen," I said. "I can't be a cheerleader. I'm not coordinated enough." Plus, the thought of people staring at me trying to do high kicks was unimaginable.

Bobbi made a pouty face.

"I'm sorry, but I promise on my nights off, I'll cheer from the stands. By the way, I kind of know one of the players."

Bobbi's eyes lit up. "Which one?"

"Luke Carlson." I couldn't hide my smile.

"Oh, him. He's all yours." She put her hand on my shoulder. "But I got dibs on the rest of the team."

My first night off from work, I kept my word and went to a game. Bobbi saw me and gave a pompom wave. She led three other girls in a pre-game cheer with her ponytail swaying in time with the chant. They wore shiny green pants and white crew neck tops. Somehow, Bobbi managed to make the leprechaun colors look good.

The lead changed several times. With ten seconds left on the clock, the score was tied. The star of our team was a student from

Quebec named Henri. He passed the basketball to Luke who lined up for the shot and then passed it behind his back to Henri. Waiting until the last second on the clock, Henri floated the ball into the hoop. The Ark's side of the gym went wild yelling so loud we drowned out the cheerleaders.

When the teams left the floor, Bobbi bounced over to see me. "You picked the best game to come to. They aren't all this exciting." She pulled the elastic off her ponytail and shook out her hair. "Let's celebrate the big win at the Pizza Palace."

"Okay. Should I wait here for you to change?"

"Yep, and by the way," she said, "we'll have company."

"What did you do?" I grabbed her arm.

"I invited Henri and Luke. Oh, come on. You don't look very excited now, but you'll thank me later."

I wiped off my frown and decided it wasn't so bad to have Bobbi with me on my first whatever this was with Luke. She'd probably do the talking for both of us. I paced the floor in front of the bleachers until my favorite rat-catching janitor, Charlie, came out with a mop and started wiping the shellacked floor. Climbing to the top of the bleachers, I checked my face in my compact mirror and waited.

His hair still wet, Luke was the first one out of the locker rooms. He looked handsome in a light blue polo shirt and jeans. When he smiled and waved, I waved back with a shaky hand.

"Can I join you up there?"

I nodded. *Be cool, Kate. Don't make a fool of yourself.*

Luke sat so close beside me, the clean scent of his soap floated between us. "So how'd you like the game?"

I could barely look at him. My stomach turned into a basket

of flutters. I just needed to talk about something safe. *Sports. I know sports.* "It was a very exciting finish."

"Henri's been a great addition to our team this year. He really knows how to work the crowd too."

"Yeah, he does. But your behind-the-back pass was awesome." Being this near to Luke sent hot waves through me. "How about we wait outside for the others?"

"Great idea." Luke offered me a hand.

I took it, but he didn't let go when I stood. My hand felt small wrapped in his large one. I'd never held a guy's hand before and hoped mine wasn't too sweaty. Shy Kate was holding hands with Pastor Steve's nephew. I didn't want to blow it. I'd just let Luke take the lead and everything would be fine.

We reached the bottom of the bleachers as the other players filed out of the locker room. Luke let go of my hand, and I understood why. Mrs. Huffman told us that holding hands was a privilege allowed to official couples. I wanted to ask her what being an official couple meant, but after she reprimanded Bobbi, I wasn't brave enough to ask.

Outside, I breathed in the cool air and pointed to where I parked. "That's my car over there." We walked over and I dug my keys out of my shoulder bag. "You want to drive?"

Luke took the keys and walked around the car to open my door for me—another first for me tonight.

When he started the ignition, the speakers blared out music from my favorite Christian station. I grabbed for the volume button to turn it down, but Luke stopped me. Together, we sang off key to a remake of "The Old Rugged Cross" until Bobbi and Henri got inside and begged us to stop.

For most of the drive, Henri and Luke went over the big plays of the game. Then, they switched to the Celtics. Bobbi commented on the three-second rule. I joined the laughter when they compared Luke's pass to the likes of Larry Bird.

Luke found a parking spot right in front of the Pizza Palace. The restaurant wasn't too busy and the lone waitress said, "Sit wherever you like."

"Let's get a booth," Bobbi said. "But I call dibs on the outside spot." She waited for Henri to get in first. Luke did the same and I sat on the edge of the bench on Luke's side. Bobbi gave me a couple of head tilts that meant move closer. I scooted in a couple of inches more and she winked.

The waitress put some waters on the table and took our order. We chatted more about the game, and when our pizzas arrived, Henri started eating his slice with a knife and fork. We all laughed at him. "What do I do that is so funny?"

Bobbi leaned in close to give Henri a detailed explanation of how Americans eat pizza. I glanced at Luke and noticed a five o'clock shadow covered his jawline. He was cute, but not exotic like Henri. Luke was more the kind of guy you wouldn't look at twice until you looked twice.

As we ate, I realized Luke was left-handed. We should've traded places because whenever he picked up a slice of pizza or went for his water glass, our arms touched. Not really our arms, more like the swirly blond hair on his tickled the hair on mine. Each time I moved an inch away from him, he moved closer. A low volt of electricity ran through me.

Back at The Ark, Bobbi and Henri went to the gym to search for some earrings Bobbi thought she'd lost. Luke and I walked side by side in the blue-black darkness toward my dorm. An owl hooted and we looked up. The moment seemed magical, and neither of us spoke. Luke reached for my hand, and I could've twirled for joy.

We reached my doorway. "Could I have my keys back?" I kept my voice light and playful.

Luke let go of my hand to dig into his pocket for them. I wasn't sure which of us was more nervous. I climbed the steps and turned toward him, our eyes at the same level.

"Thanks for escorting me back," I said.

"Sure. But don't go in yet." Luke looked down at his feet and then back up at me. A cool breeze sent goosebumps up my arms. "Before you go in, I want to ask you something. Would you like to come with me tomorrow night on the witness bus?"

I'd heard about the witness bus and avoided it. The idea of talking to strangers made me cringe, but to tell them about God scared me even more. Worse, what if I screwed up in front of Luke and the other students? The truth was I had to do it eventually, or the whole reason I came to The Ark—to train to be a missionary—was pointless.

"I'd like to, but you need to know something." I gnawed at the inside of my cheek. "I've never witnessed before."

"Oh, that's no problem." Luke clapped his hands together. "I'll help you. We'll be a team."

His earnestness made my heart lurch. "Okay."

"And we'll have a special guest leading us." Luke's smile grew. "My best buddy from seminary and someone you know well, Pastor Wayne."

Pastor Wayne never ceased to amaze me. In addition to his youth ministry at my old high school, he worked crazy hours remodeling an empty warehouse into a place of worship for his ministry in Salem. He also made it up to The Ark whenever he could. He never looked tired or complained. And to think, he and Luke were best buddies. God was generous.

"I can't wait," I said.

Luke filled me in on the details, and then we said timid good-nights to each other.

I couldn't wait to talk to Bobbi, but she was still out with Henri. Sheila liked our last hour before curfew to be quiet time anyway. I hadn't known Luke very long, but all the time we'd spent together had been wonderful. With him on my mind, I slept like a happy cat curled up in a ball.

Sheila was a regular on the witness bus, so the next morning I found her in the cafeteria and snuck up behind her in line. "Can I cut in?"

"Yikes." Sheila jumped. "You're up early. And you're glowing. What's happening?"

"Guess what? No, don't guess." I couldn't keep still. "I'm going on the witness bus tonight."

Sheila's face lit up. "Praise God. He answered my prayers." She wrapped me in her arms. I counted to five Mississippi before she let me go.

We moved a few steps closer to the front of the line. The smell of bacon and maple syrup made my stomach growl. I touched Sheila's arm. "Tell me, what's the worst thing that's ever happened to you out there?"

"It's when someone doesn't care about salvation. They look at you like you're crazy and your heart breaks because you might be the only one who'll ever talk to them about God."

We were quiet for a few moments. Once you got past her freckles, Sheila's gold-specked brown eyes became her best feature.

"Have you ever been afraid to witness to someone?" I said.

Sheila thought for a moment. "I always pray for God's protection when I go out. There are guys who try to show off. They say rude things because the devil rules them. But I've learned something." She took my hands. "If you ask them if you can pray for someone they love—like their mother or sister—it scares the devil away. And maybe you've planted a seed for the next time God touches them."

Her words rested on my heart. "That was beautiful. You're going to be the best pastor's wife someday."

"If it's in God's plan." Sheila let go of my hands and fiddled with a loose string on her shoulder bag. "Oh, and you should dress modestly. Nothing flashy. Nothing of Bobbi's. And comfortable shoes. We walk a lot."

Sometimes I pictured Bobbi on one of my shoulders dressed in a red satin dress with a pitchfork in her hand. On the other shoulder, Sheila wore white choir robes and held a harp. I admired Sheila more, but Bobbi took me on adventures.

"One last question. What's the best part about street witnessing?"

Sheila leaned against the gray wall and closed her eyes. When she opened them, they shone. "It's when you're holding a stranger's hand and they ask Jesus to come into their heart. It's better than anything you can imagine." She sighed. "It's divine. It's why we're here."

CHAPTER 13

THE SUN DROPPED BEHIND the mountains on my walk to the chapel parking lot. The yellow bus painted with the words The Ark Outreach Ministries was easy to find, but no one was there yet.

Searching for any familiar face, I spotted Bobbi heading down the path to the snack bar and called her over. She glanced at me and then at the bus. "Well, that explains your horrid outfit."

Bobbi could always make me laugh. "Luke invited me."

"Oh Lord, we've got some work to do."

She yanked my pink blouse out of my pants, took off her skinny leather belt, and cinched it around my waist. "Now, unbutton the top two buttons. You look like a nun. And, you are *not* wearing that granny sweater. If you get cold, snuggle up to your man."

I handed Bobbi my sweater while she fumbled around in her shoulder bag for her makeup. She brushed some blush on my cheeks and patted my nose with powder. Her spicy perfume tickled my nose.

"Not my best work." Bobbi pulled an elastic band from my hair. "No on the braid. You look like one of those Amish ladies. Now, bend over and shake it out."

Checking to make sure no one saw us, I did what she said.

"Wow, those waves give your hair some body. New rule: Kate wears a braid to bed every night."

"Thanks for the makeover." I ran my fingers through my hair and hoped Sheila wouldn't say anything.

"Hey, gotta go. Someone might try and guilt me into doing this with you. Good luck with Luke." As she walked away she shouted back, "Save a few souls for me."

I buttoned my shirt, still perplexed about why Bobbi came to The Ark. The first time I asked her, she said, "The same reason as everyone else." When I tried to get her to say more, she changed the subject to boys. If she were husband-hunting, The Ark would be the place to find a great guy.

Several more minutes passed before Sheila arrived. "Praise the Lord, you're here." She hugged me and pretended to push my hair away from my face, but I knew she was trying to wipe the blush off my cheeks. "Can you help me hand these out?" She gave me a stack of postcards. "Just put a dozen of these tracts on each seat."

The tracts were printed on both sides. One side explained the steps to salvation and the other listed the times of services at The Ark. The smell of diesel fuel hit me as I stepped onto the bus. Most of the vinyl seats where I placed the tracts were patched with duct tape. When I finished my job, I picked a good seat to wait for Luke and tried to calm the butterflies flitting around my rib cage.

Denise's hoarse voice caught my attention as she walked past me. The first time we met, her scarred purple lips made me feel queasy. To speak, she had to slip her finger under the scarf around her neck. Sheila told me later that when Denise was younger she tried to kill herself by drinking drain cleaner. To save her life, the doctors performed a tracheotomy, but Denise believed God gave her a second chance.

To stop my knee from bouncing, I hopped up to open the window and then again to shut it. The bus started to fill with clean-cut boys and plainly-dressed girls. Bobbi's remark about the Amish was pretty accurate.

Pastor Wayne boarded the bus and caught my eye. He nodded and I smiled back at him. When the bus driver got on a few minutes later, I panicked. Where was Luke? I couldn't do this without him. It was so dark I could only see my reflection in the window. If he didn't show up, I'd have to beg Sheila to be on her team. The bus roared to life.

"Don't leave yet," Pastor Wayne said and put up his hand. "Here comes one more."

Luke scrambled aboard, dressed like a casual businessman. He spoke to Pastor Wayne and then headed down the aisle. When he saw me, his face lit up and my heart flip-flopped.

"Your hair looks nice like that. Any room for me?"

"Sure, sure." I gathered up the tracts I'd spread across the seat and silently thanked Bobbi. The driver shifted into gear, and the bus lurched forward. On the sharp turn out of the school drive-way, I banged into Luke's strong shoulder.

"Sorry, sorry," I said, the closeness heating my face and neck.

"Are you going to say everything twice tonight?" Luke leaned closer. Distracted by the crisp smell of his aftershave, I only caught the end of his sentence. "…make witnessing difficult when we get out on the street."

I wanted to ask him more about where we were going, but Pastor Wayne started playing his guitar. After leading us in several songs, the bus drove onto the highway and he stood to speak.

"Our mission tonight is in a new area. There's a few stores, restaurants, bars, and lots of people out on a Saturday night. We've got about five more minutes on the bus, so if you haven't done so already, get into your witness teams."

I faced Luke. "What do I do? Can I watch you for the first few times? I don't know what to say." My fingers drummed the tracts on my knee.

Luke put his hand over mine to hold it still. "Of course. Don't worry. There isn't any right or wrong way." His voice was soothing but my heart kept drumming.

We parked in the lot of a closed post office. Pastor Wayne spoke again, "Tonight we are God's ambassadors. Don't be fooled into thinking someone's religion is so personal we shouldn't talk to them about it. What would have happened if no one had talked to you about Christ?" He closed with a prayer asking the Holy Spirit to anoint us.

When I opened my eyes, Luke was looking into them. "You ready?"

I nodded. *Oh dear Lord, please don't let me make a fool of myself.*

We paired off from the rest of the students and walked for a few minutes. Just as we reached a strip mall, we saw a young boy trip over a parking curb.

His father called out, "Tommy, how many times do I have to tell you, no running in parking lots?"

Luke approached Tommy and crouched beside him. "You okay?"

Tommy pointed at his scraped knee. Luke brushed some dirt off it. "Hey, that's not too bad, just a few scratches. I bet you can stand up and it won't even hurt."

Putting on a tough face, Tommy stood and tried not to wince. "Mister, you sure are tall. Are you a Celtics player?"

Luke laughed. "No, but I do play basketball."

The dad caught up to us and we introduced ourselves.

"Daddy, he plays basketball, but not for the Celtics."

The father tugged at his son's arm trying to move him along. "Thanks for helping my boy."

"Looks like it's time to go." Luke smiled at them. "Your dad really loves you, little guy."

Tommy's dad patted him on the head. "Yes, I do."

"Sir, I'd like to give you something." Luke handed him a tract. "Our heavenly Father loved his son too, and he sent him to die for our sins."

The man shook his head. "You born-agains or something?"

"We're students at The Ark, over in Lincoln."

I sensed something sad about this family and spoke before I could stop myself. "Are you raising your son alone?"

"Mommy died in a car accident. She's up in Heaven." The boy looked so brave. I wanted to hug him.

"Can we pray for you?" Luke said. Without waiting for an answer, he put his hand on the man's shoulder. I took Tommy's hand in mine. Neither of them moved away.

"Lord, this family has been through a tragic time. Please help them heal from their great loss and fill their hearts with your love. Amen."

The dad's eyes welled up. "Thank you."

"We'd like to invite you to one of our services. We have a great Sunday school too," Luke said. "The times are on this tract."

"Tommy, my mommy's in Heaven too. Maybe they're friends." I patted him on the back, afraid to do more or I'd cry. The dad and son walked away hand in hand. I heard the word *ice cream* a few times. Luke and I shared a look that filled my heart with peace.

"You had a real connection with that boy." Luke reached for my hand.

I squeezed back. "Good thing he likes basketball players too."

An elderly couple approached us. The man held his wife's purse so she could manage her cane. He spoke to us in a loud voice. "It's nice to see young people doing good things for a change. Were you praying for that man and boy?"

Luke answered him as a beater Chevy drove by, distracting me with its noisy muffler. It stopped about twenty feet away from us. A hand motioned for me to come over. Strengthened with God's love, I walked to it.

The car was full of guys like the ones Sheila warned me about. I'd made a rookie mistake and turned to catch Luke's eye, but the old couple still had his attention.

"Hey, what ya got there?" the driver said. His arm was bare and muscular. Tattoos covered most of it and he had some letters inked on his knuckles. An unlit cigarette dangled from his lips.

I looked at the tracts in my hand and tried to remember what Sheila said to do. Embarrassment clouded my mind—these guys were trouble. *Please God, protect me.* Without making eye contact, I mumbled, "Our church is spreading the good news that Jesus died for our sins."

"Did you hear the pretty lady?" He slapped the dash and turned to his friends in the car. "Any sinners in here?"

One of the guys yelled, "I'd like to sin with her." Howls filled the car.

I backed up a few steps and forced myself to sound normal. "I've got to go. My boyfriend's over there waiting for me."

"Wait up, little lady." It was one of the guys in the back seat. "Sorry 'bout my friends. They have no manners. Can I have one of those things you're handing out?"

He was older than the others, with some dark stubble on his chin. Maybe God did want me here. I handed him a tract. He took it and smiled. "You keep up the Lord's good work."

After glancing at it, he stuck his hand out to shake, and I gave him mine. He pulled it tight and wrapped his fingers around my wrist. I tried to pull back. With his other hand, he stroked the inside of my palm with his middle finger. "You like that?"

I froze. His thick pink tongue made a wet circle around his lips.

"You scumbag." I wrenched my hand away. "I hope you rot in Hell."

He banged the side of the car and hooted. The driver took that as the signal to peel out of the parking lot.

I wiped my hand on my pants until it felt raw and hot. Someone grasped my shoulder. I screamed and swung around wildly, sending my shoulder bag flying.

Luke held up his palms. "Kate, it's me. What happened?"

It took all my power not to spurt out every swear word I'd learned from Ma. "Take me back to the bus. I can't do this."

Tears threatened. I shook as I bent over to pick up my bag and the compact that had skidded out of it. A car came around the corner with blinding headlights. I put my hand over my eyes.

Luke stood guard in front of me like a gladiator. When it passed, he said, "Let me help you."

"I'm fine. I don't need any help."

He waited until I finished gathering my stuff before offering me his arm. I took it and held on tight during our silent walk to the bus. Once inside, he waited for me to sit and then he sat sideways in the row in front of me.

After a few moments, he said, "Do you want to talk about what happened out there?"

I held back hot tears. "I think I failed."

In a gentle voice, he said, "I don't believe that."

I rested the side of my head against the cool window and let out a long breath. "I was so excited about the little boy and his dad and then the nice old couple…I thought God was with us. Someone in a car waved at me so I went over to it. When I saw it was a bunch of guys, I knew I should've waited for you. But one of them seemed nice. He said he wanted to hear…" My voice caught. "He grabbed my wrist and did something awful to my hand."

Luke rose and sat beside me.

"And then…and then, I told him I wished he'd rot in Hell." I lowered my head. "I'm a horrible Christian. I don't think I can ever do this again."

Luke put his arm around me and tucked my head under his chin. His heart thumped in my ear. My body shuddered in relief.

He didn't have to say another word because for the first time in a long time, I knew where I belonged.

CHAPTER 14

VOICES FROM OUTSIDE interrupted us. Luke released me and we scooted a few inches apart. For the first time, I noticed his profile. His thin lips and straight nose reminded me of Pastor Steve, and like his uncle, he had a receding hairline. Someday he might be bald—would I still be attracted to him?

"Before the others get on, I want to say thanks for listening to me tonight."

"I'm glad you trusted me." He squeezed my arm and glanced toward the front of the bus. "Are you okay if I go catch up with Pastor Wayne? I'll wait for you when we get back to The Ark."

"Sure, go ahead." I gave him a little nudge.

The air hummed as students piled into the bus. Sheila skipped down the aisle, waving her arms in the air. She shouted, "Hallelujah," and tugged me up to join her.

We were blocking the aisle so I pulled her into my row. "You're so happy. Tell me about your night."

Sheila grinned. "You'll have to wait. It's the best part of the night—hearing the stories. We share them on the ride home."

I tensed and she patted my arm. "Don't worry. First-timers don't always share. It's okay to just listen."

Sheila left to join some students in the back of the bus. Luke and Pastor Wayne sat together in the first row. Part of me felt let down that Luke didn't sit with me, but I remembered what Mrs. Huffman taught in a recent class. *Do not disturb the men of God when they gather. Women can't be leaders. It would be chaos."*

No one told Ma that. She ruled our house and didn't take crap from anyone. One Memorial Day when I was thirteen, she took me, my sisters, and our cousin Erin to Martha's Vineyard. Erin was in college and seemed so grown up. I wanted to be her. After some sightseeing, we stopped for lunch at a little hole-in-the-wall place. Erin was on a diet and asked the waitress to hold the butter that came on her sandwich.

The waitress brought us our sodas, water for Erin, and a few minutes later she returned with our meals. Erin took a bite of her sandwich and put it back on her plate. She lifted the bread to show us a thick layer of butter.

Ma called the waitress back. "Excuse me, she ordered this with no butter."

"That's the way the sandwiches are made here." The waitress crossed her arms under her big chest. Ink marks outlined the side pocket of her stained white uniform.

"I understand," Ma said. She held Erin's plate in the air. "But she's on a special diet."

The waitress narrowed her eyes and spoke loud enough for

the other customers to hear. "If you don't like butter on your meat, go tell the cook, you skinny Jew."

Everyone stared at us. Ma rose from her chair in slow motion. The muscles in her jaw tightened. She held the plate an inch from the waitress's face. "How dare you?"

The waitress's smug look said *I dare you* back.

I felt like I was perched at the edge of a cliff. Pam's and BB's faces were big eyes and round mouths. Red blotches covered Erin's cheeks.

Ma gave us her *Don't move* stare and marched toward the kitchen. She barged through the swinging doors. Craning our necks, we could see through the square windows. The cook held a cleaver knife that he raised up and slammed down. His mouth moved, but we couldn't make out his words. Ma's back was to us. I rooted for her, but the cook's knife scared me.

"Are we Jewish?" Pam said.

"No. But that rude waitress thought so because Jewish people don't mix dairy and meat together," Erin said.

We let that thought sink in and watched the waitress seat some new customers. A moment later, Ma burst back into the room. All the diners watched her again. She stood in front of the waitress and dropped the plate. It broke into pieces that slid across the tile floor. "This is what I think of your food and your service."

Ma jerked her thumb toward the door. "Girls, get up. We're leaving this racist dump." We gathered our belongings. Ma didn't pay for anything, and I worried someone would call the police on us.

Before we got to the door, Ma spoke in a loud, cheerful voice, "Oh, you might want to call an exterminator to kill all those cockroaches crawling around in the kitchen."

Out on the street, Ma's hands trembled as she lit a cigarette. She walked fast down the sidewalk, and we ran to keep up with her. "Skinny Jew. Did you hear her?" She took a drag. "Who does she think she is? God damn Nazi. How friggin' hard would it have been to give us two new pieces of bread?"

Mrs. Huffman might've had a hard time dealing with Bobbi, but she'd have fainted if she'd met Ma.

Pastor Wayne's voice brought me back to the bus. He did a head count and asked us to pray for the driver and traveling mercies. Once we were out of the parking lot, he turned to face us. "Did we spread the good news of Jesus Christ tonight?" Cheers rang out. "Who would like to share first?"

"I'd like to start," Luke said.

I slumped down in my seat and twisted my watch around my wrist.

"It takes courage to witness on the streets for Christ. My teammate and I spoke with a father and his son. Even though it was her first night out, the Holy Spirit guided her to touch the hearts of this family, a family that had experienced a great loss. Everything we do in Jesus' name is important." Luke's confident voice soothed my nerves. "Our words, our compassion, our silent prayers—it doesn't matter whether we see immediate results or not, we give it all to God."

Luke caught my eye and I knew he meant what he said. I could trust him. It was like getting hugged from the inside out.

"Who would like to share next?" he said.

The scratchy voice of Denise quieted the bus. I tried to imagine her in the perfect way God saw her.

"I met a very lost soul tonight. This young woman was homeless. Worshipped the devil of alcohol. I took her hand and prayed for her. When I was done, she asked me for some money, but she wouldn't look me in the eye. I told her you can't escape life in a bottle. God knows I tried." Denise let out her sandpaper laugh. "She understood what I meant by that. We went for a burger, and afterward, she said she was ready to accept Jesus into her heart."

Someone shouted "amen," and we all clapped.

Others jumped up to tell their stories. The phrase *Warrior of God* became clear to me that night. My classmates overcame personal struggles and now, as Christians, fought spiritual wars to save others. I was humbled by it all. Sheila spoke last.

"I saw an old woman waiting by a bus stop. I felt led to talk to her and asked her name. She said, 'Leave me alone. It's none of your business.' She spun away from me. I walked around to face her again and asked her if she believed in God." Sheila imitated the woman. "'Listen, Missy, if there's a God, I'd like to know where he is. Where was God when my grandson was killed in Afghanistan? He was a wonderful young man. There is no God.'"

The bus stopped at a light. The only sound was the click of the turn signal.

"Her pain was overwhelming. I prayed to Jesus for words to comfort her. He answered me. I took her frail hands and asked her to tell me a story about her grandson. For several minutes, she spoke about him as a young boy. But then, she had to stop. Tears filled her eyes and rolled down her cheeks."

Sheila was a blessing who showed me the meaning of God's grace. My heart swelled with joy. I wondered if I could ever be a blessing to someone.

"Hazel will be on the senior bus Sunday morning. I can't wait for you all to meet her."

We shouted like our team just won the Super Bowl. This had to be the happiest day of my life. In total, ten souls were led to Christ. Ten people were not going to Hell because The Ark went out and told them about salvation.

Pastor Wayne strummed his guitar and led us in a round of "To God Be the Glory." The words had more meaning than ever before. When we reached the campus, Pastor Wayne and Luke departed the bus first. I lingered behind hoping they'd be done talking by the time I got off.

As I stepped down, Pastor Wayne beamed. "Kate, this was your first time out, right?"

"Yes, and it was much more than I expected."

"God is merciful and gracious. Then we'll see you again?"

He hugged me before I could reply, and he climbed back on the bus. I searched the lot for Luke. My heart sank. He was nowhere in sight.

CHAPTER 15

THE COOLNESS OF THE NIGHT made me shiver. So much for Bobbi's idea that I didn't need my sweater because Luke would keep me warm. I walked to a nearby pine tree, pulled off a cone, and shook it. Seeds rattled inside: It was a girl pine-cone—she'd never have to deal with guys who disappointed her.

I leaned against the tree trunk and replayed Luke's words. He specifically asked me to wait for him, but here I was, alone. What if he was kind to me on the bus because he's kind to everyone? Maybe he was just recruiting new people to go on the witness bus. A guy like Luke probably had a girlfriend. Oh God, the humiliation. Luke only felt bad for me. I sank down onto my butt.

Something moved above me in the tree branches. *Great. Probably a bat ready to swoop down into my hair.* I jumped up, put my arms over my head, and dashed toward the sidewalk. Could this night get any worse?

The sound of shoes running on pavement caught my attention. Luke. I quickly brushed off the back of my pants and patted down my hair. Little sparks of hope zinged in my heart.

"I'm so sorry," Luke said, a bit out of breath. "We all meet at the snack bar after the witness bus. I got us a table and waited for you, but then I realized you probably didn't know we did that."

I threw the pinecone at Luke, but he dodged it. "Hey, you were supposed to catch it."

He laughed. "Just basketballs. You look cold. How about we head over to the snack bar now and I'll get you something warm to drink instead?"

"Let's go." I wanted to skip with happiness.

We walked side by side with the inky sky above full of glittering stars. Luke reached for my hand and pointed out some planets and constellations. Tingles raced down my back, and they had nothing to do with the heavens.

At the snack bar, the buttery smell of popcorn filled the air. Most of the wooden tables were occupied with a mix of students from the witness bus plus a few couples on dates. We found a free table in the corner which I grabbed and Luke left to get our drinks. I hoped he brought back hot cocoa and not coffee.

While waiting, I watched a couple nearby intertwine their fingers and make goo-goo eyes at each other. Would Luke ever look at me like that? Before I could check out any other couples, Luke arrived with mugs of hot cocoa topped with whipped cream.

I blew out a sigh of relief. "How'd you know I wanted hot cocoa?"

Luke lifted his shoulders in a way that made my heart thump. I made an opening in the whipped cream for a sip of cocoa and burned my tongue. Luke tried the same thing, but I couldn't warn him in time.

"They should rename this chocolate lava," he said, and we laughed.

I wanted to get Luke to talk about himself, but wasn't sure how. Bobbi came to mind and I thought of what she'd do. She'd start with a compliment. "You were great tonight. You really know how to connect with people."

"Thanks." He hesitated for a moment. "I'd like to connect more with you. Tell me why you came to The Ark."

"Oh, no." I pointed a plastic spoon at him. "I've already shared tonight. Tell me something about your life."

"Well, I guess the best place to start is the beginning." Luke stared into his mug and then at me. He had a wistful expression on his face. "My dad left when I was a baby. Mom told me he wasn't ready to be a dad. There's a photo of him holding me when I was born. When I was a kid, I'd look at that photo and invent all kinds of cool stories about why he couldn't come back."

Luke stopped. I kept silent and nodded for him to go on.

"Back in those days, Mom and I lived in an apartment over a bakery. Man, I haven't thought of that place for years. It was in Woonsocket, Rhode Island. The best part of living over a bakery was Mom didn't have to spend money on heat during the winter. And for me, whenever I woke up from a bad dream, I'd smell bread baking. It made me feel safe, and I'd fall right back to sleep."

He closed his eyes for a moment. I imagined him as a lanky boy telling people he was from Woonsocket. New England had so many places named from Native American culture. My favorite one from Massachusetts was Chicopee. Even though it meant *raging waters*, to me it sounded like the sound a sweet bird would make.

Luke took a sip from his mug. "More?"

"Keep going." I noticed that Luke didn't change his personality when he spoke to a group or spoke to me. He offered his words like a gift—not the kind you rushed to rip open, but the kind you took your time to unwrap. I pulled my chair closer to the table, and he did the same. Our knees touched. Neither of us moved back. I hid my fluttering hands under the table.

"Another reason we lived in Woonsocket—have I said that enough times?" He laughed at himself. "We lived there because Mom's brother, Steve, lived there. Uncle Steve and Aunt Gail had two boys and their house was loud and fun compared to ours. We spent every Sunday with them. There was a Baptist church in town that we all went to. During the family service, we had to sit boy-grownup-boy-grownup because we couldn't stop poking each other." Luke traced a line carved into the table. "Without Uncle Steve, I don't think we would have made it. Mom would've cleaned houses her whole life. He got her a real job, with health insurance, answering phones at the car dealership where he worked."

My eyes popped open. *Pastor Steve sold cars.* Of course he wasn't born a pastor, but the image of him selling cars made me chuckle. I sucked my lips between my teeth.

"Why are you making that weird face?"

"I'm sorry. The car dealership. Pastor Steve." The word *Steve* came out singsong.

Luke grinned. "I hope you'll keep that fact to yourself."

"Sure." My knees bounced against his, betraying my efforts to keep cool.

"Uncle Steve always treated me like one of his sons. Praised me when I did well, reprimanded me when I got out of line. You know, my mom wasn't very religious. She did the whole Baptist thing just to keep me close to him." Luke glanced at his watch. "Wow. It's close to curfew. Shall we go?"

Luke took my hand. I shouted in my head—*Luke is holding my hand again!* He led me outside. The call of a whippoorwill caught our attention. Luke imitated it by whistling and it flew away.

"You scared the poor thing." I leaned into him.

At the steps to my dorm, Luke closed the space between us. My legs wobbled. I reached for his arm. When I looked into his eyes, I thought, *He's going to kiss me now.* I hoped he wouldn't be able to tell it was my first real kiss. Instead, he gave me a quick hug.

"Goodnight, Kate." He started to go and stopped. "Will you sit with me at morning service?"

"Sure." I waved goodbye. It was great he asked me to sit with him, but not as great as a kiss would've been.

I just had time to change before lights out. Telling Bobbi about my night would have to wait. She flashed me a thumbs-up, and I flashed her one back. As I rewound the night, I smiled thinking about Luke and our hot chocolate date. But another hot chocolate memory crashed through, a night when Ma really lost it.

It happened on a Christmas break when Pam snuck home a bunny she got from a kid in her second grade class. It looked like a cute stuffed toy. Pam was good with animals and wanted to be a vet. She knew how to put a baby bird back in its nest so the mama bird would find it.

"You have to tell Ma," I said.

"No. She'll make me give it back." Pam tucked the black ball of fur under her chin. "I'm going to name it Floppy."

"How are you going to hide it?"

"In the bottom drawer of my bureau. There's room for food and water and Floppy can sleep on my old clothes.

A few days later, I lay across my bed reading a Nancy Drew book when Ma yelled, "Pam. Get in here." I shot up straight, the book dropping from my hands.

Pam's room was across the hall from mine. Her footsteps pounded as she ran.

"What is this animal doing in your drawer?" Ma said in her scary pause-after-each-word voice.

Lying always made it worse. I watched Pam from my room and silently pleaded for her to tell the truth.

"I don't know how it got there."

Afraid to hear more, I shut my bedroom door and huddled on the floor of my closet. I pretended to be in my private sound-proof fort. My hand searched for the cookie tin where I kept my seashells. The smell of seaweed drifted out as I searched for the largest one to put against my ear.

Long minutes passed before I crept out of my closet. No voices. I opened the door a crack and saw Pam alone in the hall-way holding a shoebox. A black head pushed up the lid. With a gulp and sob, Pam looked at me. "I have to bring Floppy back."

Ma drove her to make sure she returned it. About a half hour later, the back door to the kitchen opened and closed. I ran down-stairs with BB behind me. Pam stood in the entryway clutching the empty shoebox to her chest. Her nose looked pink and cold.

"Did Ma make a big scene?" I said.

BB stood behind me mumbling, "Poor bunny. Poor little bunny."

"Where's Ma?" I said. "She still in the car?"

"Ma made me walk home," Pam said. Her whole body shook.

Pam wore no coat. Anger burned through me. How could Ma make her walk in the freezing cold without a coat? This was worse than any punishment Ma ever gave us for lying.

"BB, can you be a big girl and get Pam a blanket off the couch?"

Pam sat at the kitchen table and blew on her hands. "Is Floppy gonna miss me?"

Her crumpled expression choked my heart. "Maybe you can visit her at your friend's house. Want some hot chocolate?"

"Do we have any fluff?"

"I'll get the jar." Pam gave me a toothy smile. Hot chocolate fixed sad faces.

Dad came home a few hours later with two boxes of pizza. Ma must have called him because he didn't joke with us about who his favorite girl was, or go upstairs to change out of his office clothes. Even though it was our job, he set the table and filled our plastic cups with soda.

He didn't talk that much at dinner on a normal night, and without Ma there, he didn't say a word. Pam tore her slice into little bits. BB ate hunched over her plate. We took turns staring at him and each other.

Dad stood to clear his plate just as Ma banged the back door open. My sisters and I yelped, jumping in our seats. Ma's face looked shiny. She stretched her lips over her teeth and pointed her finger at us. "You friggin' kids are going to kill me."

I wanted to throw a bucket of water on her and make her melt like the wicked witch in Oz.

Ma turned to me. "I'm done. You're the oldest and now you're in charge. You watch after your sisters. Don't bother me unless you see blood or bones sticking out in the wrong places."

I hated her the most that day. No matter how hard I tried to keep my sisters away from her after that, she was never happy.

Now, Ma was gone, but a fear gripped me. The rage I felt at those guys in the parking lot, I'd learned that from Ma. With God's help, I vowed I'd never let that monster loose again.

CHAPTER 16

AS SEPTEMBER ENDED and October sped into November, Luke and I spent more time together. He saved a place for me at morning chapel and Sunday services. I paid close attention to Pastor Steve's sermons in case Luke asked me about them later. During closing prayers, I'd sneak a glance at Luke, and though I felt blessed, my body desired more. The most romantic thing Luke ever did was hold my hand. Once in a while, I'd get a close hug.

November was a busy month at Price Chopper, which meant Nick and I worked extra hours. He loved to talk about himself. I heard about what sports he played in high school, how he worked for his dad's painting company on school breaks, and when he'd be transferring to a state college to finish his business degree. But one night, he talked about his family.

"My mom makes the best lasagna in the world," he said. "I think that's why my dad married her."

My mouth started to water. "Can you bring some to work?"

"I have two younger brothers. We never have leftovers," Nick said. "Hey, got some customers."

The rush continued for the rest of the night and then Wanda announced, "The store will be closing in five minutes."

With no customers in sight, I bent left and right to stretch out my neck and sore back.

"So, where are you from?" Nick said. His mischievous brown eyes were so different from Luke's honest ones. "Where'd you live before you became an Arker?"

I hated that word. I'd heard other locals use it in the store. Nick came into my cashier space, and a quiver in my chest warned me to keep a distance between us.

"Salem, Mass," I said, backing away. He grabbed a stack of bags and moved to stock the end of the counter. I let out the breath I'd been holding.

"No way. I went there on a junior high field trip. That's where they hung all those witches."

I curled a finger at him. "Maybe they didn't get all of us," I cackled. "You better watch out or I'll cast a spell on you."

Nick tilted his head to the side. "Maybe you already have."

"Very funny."

"Time to round up the carts. Think you can handle the rest of the night yourself?"

I nodded. Nick winked and left. *Oh great, he winked. The one time I joke around with him and now he thinks I like him. What an ego.* Besides, I was pretty sure Luke and I were a couple. I'd never do anything to screw that up, especially with someone from outside The Ark.

The clock ticked nine and I brought my cash drawer to the

office. I walked to the breakroom to clock out. Someone—had to be Nick—liked to take my timecard and hide it behind someone else's so I'd have to look behind twenty of them before I could find it.

Halfway through the search, Nick came in, bringing the cold night air with him. He stood behind me and rested his chin on my shoulder. "Need some help? Can't you remember where you put your timecard?"

His breath tickled my neck. Sparks shot down my spine. I spun around, wanting to push him away but not wanting to touch his body. "You should know that I have a boyfriend at The Ark."

He stepped in closer, as if my words challenged him. For some reason, I didn't feel afraid of him. Our noses touched. I took a step to the side, and Nick did the same. His hand grasped the back of my neck. In an instant his lips were on mine. Stunned, I couldn't move. The kiss started soft and tender, and then grew demanding. My insides felt like they were falling. His tongue unlocked my teeth and searched my mouth. *Oh God, what am I doing?*

I regained control of my arms and pushed him away.

"Does your Bible boyfriend make you feel like that?" His smile teased me more than his words.

No one had ever made me feel like that.

"I didn't think so," he said.

"Go away," I said in a small voice.

Nick had tempted me, and I didn't stop him. What a weak hypocrite I was. How completely and utterly embarrassing.

He left and I ripped off my vest and threw it on a hook. Grabbing my jacket, I stormed out of the store to my car. Instead of praying for forgiveness during the drive, I wrestled with the way Nick made me feel. I wanted to feel like that when I was with Luke, but I couldn't make Luke kiss me like that. I couldn't make him kiss me at all.

There was only one place to go and one thing to do. Instinct must've returned me to the campus because I had no memory of the drive.

A good hour of prayer on my knees would help this sinner. I opened the door to the chapel and entered. The full moon cast a lone spotlight on the large wooden cross on the stage. The quietness welcomed me in.

"Psst."

I turned toward the noise. Bobbi sat up against one of the side walls. Other than the time we'd snuck out and broke curfew, I'd never seen her in the chapel at night.

"Is everything okay?" I said.

She rubbed her temples. "Just needed some time to think about things."

"Do you want to talk about it?"

Bobbi shook her head and patted the spot beside her. "Why are you here?"

I sat beside her and twisted my watchband. "I did something bad tonight."

She slid closer to me.

I covered my face with my hands and spoke through my fingers. "I kissed someone and it wasn't Luke."

Bobbi pulled my hands away. "Tell me."

My eyes searched the rafters for spies. "A guy at work. A worldly guy." There, I blurted it out. The roof didn't collapse and lightning didn't strike.

"Wow. How did that happen?" Bobbi laughed. "I mean I know how it happens."

The story about how Nick teased me tumbled out. "And when he kissed me, it took a full minute before I could even push him away."

"Now that's a good kisser." She tried to clap my hands together, but they fell limp on my lap. "Oh crap, Luke."

"You know him, he respects the rules. But that's not the point. I feel awful about kissing Nick."

Bobbi looked exasperated. "You know that old song?" She sang, "A kiss is just a kiss, a sigh is just a sigh."

My elbow found her ribs. She stopped singing.

"Listen to me. Luke never needs to know."

"I guess you're right." But God knew. I tried again with Bobbi. "Are things okay with your mom?"

Bobbi sighed. "Oh, just the usual stuff. Do you ever fight with your mom?"

My breath caught. "Before I came to The Ark, we had a terrible fight."

"What happened?"

"It was about coming here. My mother wanted me to go to Salem State College, but one night I couldn't hide it any longer. We were eating dinner. She knew I was fidgety and asked me if I had a beehive up my butt. Waiting for them to finish nearly drove me crazy and gave me the worst stomachache. I offered a quick prayer to God and blurted out that I wanted to be a missionary and train at The Ark."

Bobbi waited for me to go on.

"My mother didn't get mad. She just said, 'You're going to Salem State next fall. To a real college. And while you're up, turn the kettle on for some tea.' Well, I was furious. I banged my chair against the table and said, 'I am going to The Ark.'"

"Then my mother said, 'Fine job that'll get you.' So I told her that there's no finer job than to be called by the Lord. My sisters laughed."

"What about your father? What'd he say?"

"Oh Bobbi, no one says anything when my mother gets like that. She made me and my dad go into the den with her. I remember watching her light up a cigarette and hoping she'd catch on fire."

Bobbi let out a yelp. "Your mother smokes in your house?"

"Yes, and we're probably all going to get lung cancer." I took another deep breath. "Then she pointed her finger in my face. 'What's wrong with you? I should've never let you go to all those Bible study meetings.' I tried to tell her what I was doing was a good thing, but she wouldn't let me talk…told me to use my brains and to never mention The Ark again."

I locked eyes with my friend. "My dad finally put his two cents in about me being the oldest, an example for my sisters. The first one in the family to go to college. Blah, blah, blah. Oh my mother loved that."

Ma also swore and said 'you'll go to that cult over my dead body.' I couldn't share that with Bobbi or anyone ever.

My face crumpled. "We never fought again."

Through blurry eyes I saw Bobbi shaking her head back and forth. "Oh, no. Did she…?"

"Yes."

"I'm so sorry." Bobbi hooked her pinkie with my trembling one.

I leaned into her, and she hugged me tighter than anyone in my family had ever hugged me.

CHAPTER 17

ONE COOL NOVEMBER NIGHT, Luke asked me to join him for a walk. As soon as we were out of sight of the campus buildings, he reached for my hand. "Wow, your hand's so cold." He stopped and wrapped his warm ones over mine.

"You know the saying about cold hands," I said.

His face turned serious. "I already know you have a warm heart."

Luke's words heated up the rest of me. We continued down a path behind the chapel toward the gym. A few lights from the outer buildings lit our way, but otherwise we blended into the darkness. Alone and hidden, I hoped that Luke would finally kiss me.

"I've never walked here before," I said.

"Back when this was a boy's military school, the boys had to march around the campus to learn discipline. I bet they never saw how beautiful God's creation is. Here, come and look."

Luke guided me to a fallen tree trunk where we sat. The smell of wet grass mixed with the night air. "Close your eyes for a few seconds and then open them. Tell me what you see."

I shut my eyes and counted to five hoping to see his face close to mine when I opened them. But Luke hadn't moved. I let out a sigh as he put his hand under my chin and tilted my head up toward the sky to call out the constellations. *Here we go again, another astronomy lesson.*

"It's beautiful," I said, without much enthusiasm.

Luke scooted closer to me. "Can you believe God designed this all for us?" He put his arm around my shoulder. "You're my shining star."

Encouraged, I leaned in to give Luke a light kiss on his lips, but he turned away and my lips hit his cheek. Flushed with humiliation, I stood and rushed away.

"Kate." He caught up to me and I stopped. "As Pastor Steve's nephew, I have to set an example and follow the rules—hands and hugs."

We heard it all the time in chapel. Holding hands and hugging were the two allowable ways for unmarried students to show affection. I found it impossible to believe couples waited until they were married to have their first kiss. Of course, Luke didn't know how I struggled to erase Nick's kiss from my memory.

Luke reached for my hand and, after swatting his away a few times, I let him take it when we reached the steps to my dorm. He drew me close and held me tight inside his jacket. My face pressed against his shirt and strong chest muscles. I breathed in his clean scent and hoped he wouldn't pull away.

Feeling brave, I moved my arms up Luke's back, and he didn't stop me. That small gesture took us a step deeper and a sudden joy rushed through me. I couldn't deny it. I'd fallen for Luke and couldn't imagine us apart. We stayed entwined until our breathing calmed to the same rhythm.

Luke kissed the top of my head and let me go. "This has been a very special night."

"I loved it." I watched him closely to see how my words affected him.

He gave me his sweet smile. "Let's do it again."

We parted and even though I didn't get a kiss, I floated down the hallway to my room. My dreamy smile faded at the door where Sheila stood with her hands on her hips. "Sorry, the room is closed right now. You'll need to wait in the common area. I'll be by in a few minutes to explain."

Behind Sheila, an unfamiliar woman tossed clothes into a suitcase lying on Daisy's bunk.

Sometimes I forgot about Daisy. She moved so quietly. If she wasn't asleep, she was searching the hallways for the spirit of the dead boy. Recently, she'd started sleeping on the floor next to her bunk like a dog. Bobbi had to step over her to get into her upper bunk. She patted Daisy on the head and said, "Good girl." It was funny and at the same time it wasn't.

At first, Sheila knelt by Daisy praying and pleading with her to get off the floor. When that didn't work, she tried another approach. "You're creating a fire escape hazard. You must sleep on your bed."

Daisy's reply was the same each time. "As one who follows the Lord, I cannot do so. The early followers of Jesus did not sleep on mattresses. Am I more worthy than them?"

I went to the common room where Hannah and Alice sat on

the couch in silence. Bobbi paced back and forth. When she saw me, she pulled me aside. "Crazy Daisy's in the hospital."

My heart fell. "What's wrong with her? Is that her mom in the room?"

"I think she's been starving herself. Have you ever seen her eat?" Bobbi said.

"Now that you mention it, I've never seen her in the cafeteria."

"The way her clothes hang on her. She's all bones. And her stomach growls all night long."

Minutes later, Sheila burst into the common area with wild hair like she'd been pulling at it in all directions. "Ladies, I'm sorry about not letting you in the room. Daisy has left school to take care of some health problems. Let's respect her privacy."

Poor Daisy. She was the first roommate I'd met and now she was gone. I felt bad that I hadn't put much effort in trying to know her better. I vowed to add her to my prayers every night.

We filed quietly back into the room.

"Is anyone else taking her place?" Bobbi said.

"Not until next semester," Sheila said.

The next day, Bobbi converted Daisy's bed into an extended closet. She looped hangers through the metal bedframe to hang her blouses. Some still had price tags on them. The stained mattress disappeared beneath an aqua blanket while bracelets and rings lay in shiny piles.

I thought it looked like a mini boutique. One night later that week, Bobbi waved at me and pointed to the lower bunk. "I'd like to have a meeting with you in my office."

"Let me check my schedule." I pretended to look at my watch. "All clear."

We sat in our PJs and faced each other. Her blouses created a private fort around us.

"So…I saw you and Luke walking down the path by the gym," she said. "Did he finally kiss you?"

"No." I played with her stack of bracelets. "Just another hug."

"Show me a Luke hug."

Laughing, I pulled Bobbi to me and tucked her head under my chin the way Luke held me. Her hair smelled like coconut shampoo.

"Oh Luke, I beg you, kiss me now," Bobbi said, in a sexy voice.

Her words sent us into a fit of giggles. She was heavier than me, and I tipped back. My head fell over the side of the bed while Bobbi's face slipped down to my belly. With a sleeve draped across my neck and gasping for breath, I looked up and saw Sheila.

She shook her head and pointed at us. "Honestly, you two. This kind of behavior is sinful and not appropriate for God's Golden Women."

Bobbi wiggled her way off me and poked her head out. "Oh, loosen up, buttercup."

Poor Sheila, she couldn't tell the difference between silly fun and sinning.

CHAPTER 18

WITH THANKSGIVING a few weeks away, it hit me that other than the letters BB and I were exchanging, I hadn't spoken to my family since I arrived at The Ark. I couldn't blame it on being busy with Luke, work, and school. The truth was I loved my new life and thought of them less and less.

I waited until Saturday morning to call. With the dorm lobby to myself, I dropped my quarters in the pay phone with shaky fingers. I didn't realize talking to my own family would make me nervous. Just thinking about the disappointment in Dad's voice made my stomach hurt. If he answered, I'd hang up and call BB directly.

After a few rings, a sleepy voice said, "Hello."

I relaxed. "Hi BB, it's me." The short phone cord kept me close to the wall. I really missed my cell phone.

BB yawned. "Kate?"

"Sorry, I know it's early. How's everyone doing?"

"Okay, I guess. How's it going at The Ship?"

BB made me laugh. "Things are going great at The Ark." I wanted to tell her about Luke, but it didn't feel right. "It's so good to hear your voice. So Thanksgiving is in a couple of weeks. Do you know where dinner's going to be?"

"Gram had invited us to her house, but Dad's taking us to Disney World instead. He said he doesn't want to have a holiday here without Ma. We're staying at a hotel right in the park."

"Do you know if I'm invited?" A trip to Disney World sounded wonderful. We'd never been before.

"He said just the three of us."

Sadness and jealousy piled on top of me. "That's okay. I'll stay up here and have dinner with my friends."

"Maybe he'll be better by Christmas."

In spite of my wounded spirit, I stayed upbeat. "Have a great time in Florida. I've got to go now."

"Wait one sec." BB's voice sounded far away. "Yeah, I'm on the phone with Kate. You want to talk—" I heard a door close. "Um, sorry Kate. Dad's too busy to talk."

My heart crumpled a little bit more.

"I miss you," she said.

"I miss you too. Say hi to Pam for me."

The Bible didn't say how much being a disciple would ache. I slid down the wall and hugged myself. There wasn't anyone at The Ark to hold me together. Nobody would understand. Not Bobbi. Not Luke. What difference did it make if God forgave my sins? Dad would never forgive me for fighting with Ma.

But I didn't make her die.

CHAPTER 19

PASTOR STEVE CHOSE the Monday before Thanksgiving for a campus-wide day of fasting. That morning in chapel, he preached that fasting helped those who were struggling with temptation. I listened in shock as he spoke about the sexual sins of masturbation, pornography, and homosexuality. He shouted, "If anyone practices these sins at The Ark, you'll be found out. So pack your bags and leave now."

I don't think any student blinked or breathed during those two minutes of his sermon. He ended with the words from Matthew, "'If thine eye be single, thy whole body shall be full of light.'"

As we filed out of the chapel, no one made eye contact as if looking at someone might cause a sin. By the afternoon, my hunger pains reminded me of those who truly suffered, and in particular, I thought of Daisy. I tried to focus on Pastor Steve's sermon at work that night, but it was hard to focus on God while customers with food came through my checkout line.

"What's the matter with you? You've been throwing groceries at me all night," Nick said during our first break. He came closer.

I put my hands out to stop him. "Please. Just stay there."

"Let me know when you change your mind. I'll be out rounding up the carts."

The only thing on my mind was driving back to The Ark, going to sleep, and rising early enough to be the first person in the breakfast line. I clocked out at quitting time and headed to my car at the end of the lot. Even though employees had to park far away from the store, I always made sure to park near a light post.

Standing beside my car was a young guy dressed in a black shirt, jeans, and an army jacket with large pockets. His dark hair touched his shoulders.

I stopped several feet away from him. "Is something wrong?"

"I saw your *Jesus loves me* bumper stickers," he said. "Do you go to The Ark?"

Oh great, another jerk like the one from the night on the witness bus. I crossed my arms. "Yes, I do."

He smiled. "I knew I'd seen you before. So do I."

My tensed shoulders relaxed. *Good one Kate, don't pre-judge someone.* I stepped closer to my car, but his face didn't seem familiar—he must be a second year student.

"I'm Jessie. I don't think we've formally met." He stuck out his hand to shake. A gothic cross tattoo covered his wrist.

"Kate." His hand was as cold as mine.

"So the reason I'm bothering you is…see that car over there?" Jessie pointed to a car in the next row. "I wasn't paying attention and ran out of gas. So I'm waiting for a tow truck to bring me some. Then I saw all your bumper stickers and thought, hey, I bet this person goes to The Ark too."

"Sorry about your car. How much longer until the truck gets here?"

"Probably another fifteen minutes or so. Wouldn't be so bad but it's freezing out and the store's closed." He rubbed his arms and hopped from foot to foot. "Any chance I could wait in your car?"

"Sure," I said, laughing at his antics. "My car's old but the heater works great."

"Really? You're awesome."

"No problem." I got in my car and unlocked the passenger door. Jessie brought the smell of a laundry hamper in with him. Lots of the guys at The Ark didn't know how to wash their clothes and wore them over and over.

I started the engine and lowered my window. "It only takes a minute for it to warm up."

"Can I pick out some music?" Jessie searched through my CDs.

"Go ahead." I turned the heater to high. "So did you come to The Ark to be a pastor?"

Jessie was the kind of guy Bobbi liked: tall, lean, and with mysterious features. I'd have to tell her about him.

"No, I'm into music. I'm forming a band." He looked at me and smiled. "We need a singer. Do you like to sing?"

Of course, he looked more like a musician than a pastor. "Oh, that'd be an awful idea."

Jessie popped in a Christian Rock CD and tapped a beat on my dashboard.

"Are you a drummer?" I said.

He lowered the volume and turned to face me. "Do you have a boyfriend at The Ark?"

Thinking of Luke made me miss him. I nodded and noticed the white line of a scar along Jessie's jawline. "You might know—"

"Man, I really have to pee." Jessie pushed at his crotch. "I bet you didn't know that when a guy gets hard his urge to pee goes away."

Tiny bugs crawled up my skin. The space in the car got claustrophobic. I pasted on a fake smile and spoke in a strained voice, "Just go to the store. Knock on the door. The night guys will let you in."

"Have ya ever seen a guy's penis before? I'm guessing a sweet thing like you hasn't. Let me give you a little education."

I couldn't move. Daggers poked at my lungs. Sweat trickled down my armpits. Don't let him see fear. *Kate, stay calm.* He might have a knife in one of those pockets.

A zipper noise. My aching hands gripped the steering wheel so hard my knuckles turned white. I couldn't let go of the steering wheel and get out of my car. No matter what, I wouldn't give him the satisfaction of looking. *Dear God help me. Nick. Anyone, walk by. Save me.*

Seconds later, from a place deep inside me, Ma's voice erupted, "If you don't get the hell out of my car right now, I'm going to blare my friggin' horn and drive straight into the front of the store."

I heard the zip of his jeans and snuck a look at him. Jessie's face had become a mask of tight lips and slits for eyes.

"Don't forget, *you* invited me in." He opened the car door and a burst of cold air blew in. His last words before slamming it shut were "psycho bitch."

I punched the door lock button. Forgetting the engine was on, I grinded the ignition. *Remember how to drive: shift into reverse, shift into drive, turn on the headlights. Go. Get far away from here.* The tires squealed. I didn't look back.

"Why aren't you protecting me, God?" I yelled. "I fasted all day. Worked my shitty job. My family's going on an amazing vacation without me. Why did I even come here?"

I trembled as I replayed the scene of inviting Jessie into my car. He gave me an education, all right. He taught me what a stupid person I was. "Anybody else in the universe want to teach me anything? God, if this is a test, I'm done. No more tests."

I parked in a handicap spot in front of my dorm and didn't care. My rage followed me down the hallway and into my room. Sheila saw me first and got out of my way.

"Bad night at work." I kicked off my shoes, letting them fly into the back of our closet.

Bobbi jumped off her bed and took my arm. "Let's go for a walk." She pulled me down the hall to the lobby area. We stood side by side against a wall. "Okay, who needs to die tonight?"

I let out a deep breath and shuddered. Bobbi waited. With my arms crossed over my chest, the story in the parking lot unraveled. Then I sighed and said, "Really, what's wrong with me? Why do I attract sicko guys?"

Bobbi's face seemed to crumple. She swallowed hard. "You can't trust them. Not here, not anywhere. That's the one true thing in life I know."

We walked back to our room in silence. I nodded to Sheila that everything was okay. Falling asleep was hard. I thought about what Bobbi said and wondered what'd happened to her. More awake now, I prayed for everyone I knew. Finally, to get Jessie out of my mind and calm down, I conjured up images of sweet puppies playing in flower fields.

I'd forgotten to set my alarm and woke up too late for breakfast. In a mad dash, I made it to chapel on time and took a seat beside Luke. Tired and hungry, barely a word of Pastor Steve's sermon stayed with me. The hour dragged on. Finally, we closed with a prayer.

Luke touched my arm. "Are you okay? You don't seem yourself."

"Oh, I just need to eat."

His eyes widened. "Are you still fasting? You're a lightweight. You can't go this long without food. Let's go to the snack bar, and I'll treat you to a big breakfast."

Other than the cook and cashier, we had the place to ourselves. Luke guided me to a table. "Here, you sit. I'll bring you some pancakes." His kindness loosened my tears. He saw them and sat down on the bench beside me. "What's wrong?"

I dabbed at my eyes with a paper napkin. "It just seems like ever since I got here, I thought I'd be stronger, but I keep making mistakes. Sometimes…God feels far away."

"Oh, my dear." Luke let out a long sigh. "God is with us at all times, but doubt is a powerful force. Faith is believing even if we don't feel it." He put his arm around me. "Trust me. You're in the right place."

I snuggled under his neck. My stomach growled loudly.

Luke released me with a smile. "It's time to feed those hungry bears."

He went to the counter, and I silently thanked God that Luke didn't dig deeper. In a couple of minutes, he returned with two plates of pancakes. I almost drooled at the sight of them.

"I didn't want you to eat alone," he said.

"You're so thoughtful," I said, and meant it.

After covering each layer with butter and syrup, I cut into the stack. I must have groaned in delight because Luke laughed at me. Halfway through the meal, I realized each time I shoved in a mouthful, he matched me. The race was on. We ended in a tie.

"That wasn't my normal eating style," I said.

"Good," Luke said, raising his eyebrows. "Because if you aren't going home, I'd like to invite you to have Thanksgiving with my family."

"Really? I'm invited?" Happiness warmed my heart. My family abandoned me, but Luke wanted me to be with him and his family. "I promise I can eat like a lady."

"I know you can."

An unfamiliar lightness spread in my soul. *This is what it feels like to be loved.*

CHAPTER 20

THE DAY BEFORE THANKSGIVING, Sheila and I walked around campus kicking up the crisp brown leaves on the sidewalks.

"What are you doing for the holiday?" I said.

"I'm working—"

"What? You don't get Thanksgiving off?" Sheila had more seniority at the group home for disabled kids than anyone else.

"Well, I do, but I'll get paid a bonus and double time for working the early shift. I won't get home until late Thursday night. Mom said she'd hold off cooking the turkey until Friday."

"Your mother's amazing." Sheila's mom sent her care packages of homemade cookies that she shared with us. Her little sister drew stick figure pictures of her family holding hands with huge yellow suns. She taped them to the front of our closet door like it was a refrigerator. I'd never called Ma amazing and couldn't think of one time she did anything special for us.

I imagined Sheila's family in a Norman Rockwell poster. Her dad would be smiling at her mom as she placed the turkey on the table. The freckled kids would take turns patting their dog under the table. After eating, they'd get to pick out their favorite board game to play.

I'd love just one day in that family.

"What about you?" Sheila said.

"I'll be with Luke's family." I couldn't stop my smile.

"Praise God." Sheila took my hand and swung it up in the air.

We saw Bobbi near the entrance of the admin building. She raced toward us. "Kate, I need you."

Sheila shook her head and went on without us.

"What's the matter?"

"Well, you're finally going to meet the Queen Mum."

"Really? Your mother's coming to campus?" Despite Bobbi's complaints, I couldn't wait to meet her.

"Yes, she's on her way. And, she's invited us out to lunch before she kidnaps me for the holidays."

"Me too? Then you need to help me get dressed right."

In our dorm room, Bobbi opened my closet and took out a pair of gray pants. "Put these on and come to my office for a top." She picked out a smoky blue sweater and cut off the tags. "Here, try this. It'll look good with your eyes."

I put it on and ran my hand over the sleeves. "Wow, what's this made of? It's like cat fur, and it's not itchy or anything."

"It's cashmere." Bobbi's eyes lit up like she had a plan. "Tell you what, you can keep it. But there's a condition. You can't ask my mother any questions at lunch."

"Why not?"

"She just loves talking about herself. I can't stand it, so please don't encourage her." Bobbi pretended to stab herself in the heart.

I looked in the mirror for the tenth time. "Do you think your mom will like me? What if I say or do the wrong thing?"

Bobbi slid on a stack of silver bracelets. "I'm hoping that you will."

"You're not funny."

The Queen Mum arrived in a chauffeured black limousine. Bobbi's tight face relaxed when she saw the driver. It was Ricardo, the man who dropped her off on her first night at The Ark. He stood beside the driver's door.

"Miss Young." Ricardo tipped his hat at her. "Nice to see you again."

"Oh, Ricardo, have you missed me?" Bobbi reached out and touched his chest.

He bowed slightly and opened the limo door. "It hasn't been the same without you."

The scent of floral perfume greeted us as introductions were made. Please-call-me-Judith wore designer sunglasses, bright red lipstick, and spoke with a British accent. Now I understood why Bobbi called her the Queen Mum, but I couldn't figure out why Bobbi didn't have an accent too. Every detail of Judith's image was manicured: her nails, the highlights in her too-blonde hair, and her elegant outfit. Bobbi told me her mother took two hours to get ready for an outing. Now I believed her.

Judith had made reservations at a century-old inn famous for its view of the White Mountains. Pine trees decorated the brown base of the mountains, and an early snow painted the peaks white.

Being around Judith was like being with a movie star. I noticed Bobbi pouting when her mother attracted attention.

The tables were laid with white tablecloths, blue and white china, and polished silver. Crystal glasses reflected rainbows around the quiet room. The waiters startled me when they materialized out of nowhere to fill our water glasses.

Not wanting to make any mistakes, I followed Bobbi's lead and did whatever she did. I felt quite proper telling the waiter, "I'll have what she's having," after Bobbi ordered her lunch. We ate and discussed safe topics like the weather and the food. Bobbi rushed through the meal while her mother took a bite here and there.

As the lunch wore on, I forgot about the pact I'd made with Bobbi. Her mother was unlike anyone I'd ever met. "Judith, you have such a lovely accent. It makes everything you say sound beautiful."

"Oh, aren't you a dear girl." Bobbi rolled her eyes. Judith tapped her napkin on Bobbi's arm. "Roberta, making faces like that causes wrinkles."

"Mother, please. Call me Bobbi." She sat back and crossed her arms. "I've told you a thousand times that Roberta's an old lady's name."

Judith tucked a stray blonde hair behind her ear and a huge diamond earring winked at me. "By the way, is Kate a nickname?"

"No. I'm not Katherine or anything else. My mother named me after the musical *Kiss Me, Kate*."

"Oh, how charming. Cole Porter's best work. James and I must invite you to the Met when the season starts. Roberta—I mean Bobbi—make sure to remind me."

I'd never been to New York City, and now I had an invitation to the Metropolitan Opera. Bobbi's family probably sat in the fancy red velvet box seats.

"So how long have you lived in the US?"

Bobbi kicked me under the table.

"Let's see, I met James ten years ago and we got married shortly afterwards…"

I realized with a start that James wasn't Bobbi's dad. She'd never mentioned a stepdad. Bobbi had told me to not ask questions and after only one, I'd discovered something she may have not wanted to reveal. After that, I acted like everything was fine and focused on my crème brûlée.

When we finished, we walked outside and found the limo waiting at the curb. We got in and sat in the same lineup as before, Bobbi in the middle between Judith and me. Judith pulled a compact out of her handbag to reapply her lipstick and powder her nose. Satisfied, she closed her eyes, laid her head back, and said, "Ricardo, please put on some Chopin."

Bobbi held a pretend gun to her mother's head and pulled the trigger. Relieved she didn't point it at me, I made a silly face. Bobbi winked and pulled out an issue of *Vogue* from the seat pocket in front of her. The limo was full of secret compartments. I opened one near me and found a crystal dish of pastel mints. Bobbi's nod let me know it was okay to take one. The pillow of mint melted on my tongue. A few minutes later, we pulled into The Ark's parking lot, ending the luxury ride too soon.

"Go ahead," Bobbie said. "I'll meet you back in the dorm in a few minutes."

Ricardo opened my door. I extended my hand to her mother.

"It was so nice to meet you. Thank you very much for lunch."

Once I was out of the car, Judith rolled down her window and motioned me to her side.

"Kate, my daughter is fortunate to have a proper friend like you at this school." She looked past me and a stain of disapproval crossed her smooth face. As I walked away, she rolled up the window, but I heard her say, "Bobbi, are you staying out of trouble?"

My friend, you're full of secrets.

The cold made me shiver so I rushed back to the dorm room and sprawled on my bed to wait for Bobbi.

A few minutes later, Bobbi burst in with her hands in the air. "You'll never guess where we're going for Thanksgiving. Oh, don't even try. You won't believe it." She paced the room. "What's the worst place you could imagine? Try Montana. As if this place isn't God-forsaken enough."

"Yikes, Bobbi."

She glanced at the door. "Thank the Lord Saint Sheila didn't hear that."

"Or anyone else. Listen, I don't know how to ski or anything, but I've heard famous people go there to ski."

Bobbi pulled me off my bed. "I wish you could come with me. I know you'll be with Luke, but I'll miss you."

I wished my family had wanted me to go on vacation with them. "Do you need help packing?"

"Nope, Queen Mum brought all my ski clothes. All I need to do is pack my makeup." Bobbi slid it all into her oversized designer bag. She threw her arms around me in a tight hug. "See you next week."

When she left, all the energy in the room went with her.

I had just enough time to change for work and traded Bobbi's cashmere sweater for a gray cotton one. Since Nick now thought I liked him, I tried extra hard to be plain and uninteresting. It wasn't that difficult.

All ten checkout lanes were open. Nick and I worked our butts off. Shopping carts heaped with Thanksgiving food wound down every aisle. Since no one got a break, Wanda handed out free soda to keep us going. When the store closed, all the cashiers and baggers cheered. I scooted up onto the counter to finish my third Coke.

Nick jumped up beside me. Too tired to move, I didn't protest.

"Hey, a bunch of us are going out for a drink. Want to join us?"

I let out an exhausted groan. "Seriously, do you all have fake IDs or something? Plus you know I don't go to bars. Even if I did, I can barely move."

Nick put his hands on my lower back and dug his thumbs into the aching places. I wanted to tell him to stop, but my mouth wouldn't betray my body. His fingers kneaded their way up my back to my shoulders. When he reached my neck, I was so relaxed I almost dropped the can of Coke.

Nick leaned against me. "It feels a lot better with no clothes on."

I pretend punched him. "You're an evil person."

All the soda I drank required a visit to the ladies' room. The mirror reflected back a cracked-lipped, shiny-nosed, limp-haired mess. What did Nick see? There had to be prettier girls in his life. Did getting a girl from The Ark to sin give him some kind of cheap thrill? Still, his hands on my back had felt so good.

If only Luke touched me that way. Luke, Luke, Luke. I needed to forget about Nick and freshen up for Luke. He'd invited me to hear a visiting gospel band that was playing in our chapel.

Nick waited for me in front of the store. After I told Wanda that I'd seen a creepy guy lurking in the parking lot, she'd put up a flyer in the breakroom that all women on the night shifts should be escorted to their cars. Nick volunteered to be my personal escort.

"My lady." He offered me his arm.

I held back a smile, and purposefully ignoring his arm, walked beside him. "Are you having Thanksgiving at your house?"

"Yep, but probably not like yours. We have a big Italian feast. Turkey's more a side dish." He explained all of the dishes his mom cooked. "What about you? Do they let you go home for the holiday?"

I stopped and faced him. "Really, Nick?" He waited with a smirk on his face. "Since you asked, I am staying here of my own free will and eating with Luke and his family."

An awkward quiet fell between us as we walked the rest of the way to my car. I pulled my keys out of my shoulder bag and dropped them. Good Lord, I was tired. I bent down to get them and on the way up, Nick trapped me. His arms held me against the car door. A rush of heat raced through me.

"Thanks for walking with me, but I've got to go." I squirmed away.

Nick put on a sad face. "Geez. Can't I just give you a holiday hug?"

"Oh brother," I said. "Just a one-second hug."

We hugged, and I said, "Time's up" and tried to step away.

Nick embraced me tighter and nuzzled against my throat, up my neck, and behind my ear. My body leaned into him against my will. I was breathless and lost. When our lips touched, something inside me melted, and I kissed him back.

CHAPTER 21

BEFORE I FELL ASLEEP, I asked God for the strength to resist the temptation that Nick had become to me. I also prayed that Luke would kiss me so I could forget about Nick, but I knew you couldn't make deals like that with God.

The stillness and bright sun woke me on Thanksgiving morning. I stretched and reminded myself where everyone else was. Bobbi had gone with her mother on a ski trip, Sheila left early to work at the group home, and Hannah and Alice were probably chasing a turkey for dinner. And Daisy, I hoped she'd gotten the help she needed.

With two hours until Luke arrived, I took my time showering and getting dressed. Piles of blouses and turtlenecks covered my bunk. The winner was a beige pullover sweater and brown skirt. One look in the mirror and Bobbi's voice came to me: *"Moth girl, add more color."*

I opened her closet and spied a red and gold scarf that had fallen on the floor. I couldn't remember Bobbi wearing it, but she had so many of them. The scarf felt weightless and slippery in my hands. Her spicy perfume wrapped itself around my neck. After a few tries, I managed to tie it the way she'd taught me. With ten minutes to spare, I paced the room, too jittery to sit down.

Luke met me at the door to my dorm. He looked handsome in his white dress shirt, pressed khaki pants, and navy suit jacket. I wasn't exactly sure what swooning meant, but I think I was close to it.

"You look very pretty, Kate."

"You do too. I mean handsome, you look handsome." My face heated.

"Everything okay?" Luke said.

"Well, there is one thing. I feel empty-handed. We should be bringing something homemade with us."

"Don't worry." Luke helped me with my coat. "I brought something."

"Where is it? Did you drop it off already?"

He shushed me by putting his index finger on my lips. *Luke, put your lips there!* Thoughts of kissing Nick still lingered, but I pushed them away.

The brisk air calmed me as we walked to Pastor Steve and Elizabeth's home, a small two-story house. Like all the other campus buildings, it had been painted white with black shutters. A festive wreath of dried grape vines, plaid ribbon, and copper bells adorned the front door. Ma would've loved trying to make it.

"Wait. Don't knock yet," I said.

"What's wrong?" Luke took both my hands in his.

"Do they know I'm coming?"

"Of course. Just relax. This is a normal family having a normal Thanksgiving meal. Just be yourself, and they'll love you as much as I do."

Whoa, did he just say he loved me? I wanted to throw my arms around him, but Elizabeth opened the door. Her cheeks were flushed, and she wore a *Kiss the Cook* apron over her black jersey dress.

"I thought I heard something out here. I'm so happy to see you both." Elizabeth hugged Luke and gave me a squeeze, whispering, "After all the introductions, meet me in the kitchen. I could really use your help with the meal."

As soon as were inside, Elizabeth scooted off, leaving us alone in the foyer. Luke took my jacket and hung it on a hook near the door while I readjusted Bobbi's scarf in a lone mirror on a bare wall. To the left of the hallway, stairs led to the second floor, and to the right, we passed a long living room with minimal furniture and dark draperies.

I'd never been in a house without a knick-knack anywhere. Our living room was full of antique bargains Ma found at estate sales. I wondered if they'd just moved in but there were no boxes anywhere.

The smell of herbs and onions drifting from the kitchen made my mouth water. Luke's warm hand reached for my cool one, and we entered a den lit only by a large television screen. Everyone was so focused on a football game they didn't see us come in. I recognized Pastor Steve and his sons, Matt and Paul, but not the two women or the little boys playing with Matchbox cars on the floor. Luke squeezed my hand and imitated a turkey gobbling. I loved when he showed his goofy side.

Paul Carlson turned around to see us. "Well, it's about time you got here."

The adults stood up to greet us, and the boys tried to climb up Luke. I stepped back from the crowd as Luke exchanged hugs with each person. Then he turned to me. "For Thanksgiving, I brought some Katie Pie with me."

It took a second to realize that I was Luke's gift. It was clever and cute, and I put my hand on his arm as he introduced me to Paul and Matt, Paul's wife, Melanie, and their sons.

The boys stood like soldiers. "Nice to meet you, Katie Pie," they said, bumping their shoulders into each other. They added "pie" to the end of every word and cracked themselves up. My nerves eased away.

When that group returned to the football game, Pastor Steve and an older woman came over to us. They hugged Luke, and the woman kissed his cheek. This family touched each other more in one day than my family did in a lifetime.

"Katie Pie, nice to see you again," Pastor Steve said. When I put out my hand, he shook his head. "Shaking hands is for strangers."

Pastor Steve pulled me into an embrace that pinned my arms to my sides. My face squished into his crisp shirt. Thank God I didn't wear any lipstick. The hug grew uncomfortable as he crushed me tight into his chest.

"Steve, you're squeezing the life out of the poor girl. She can't move," the woman said.

"Sorry about that." He laughed and let go.

"Oh heavens, these men have no manners. I'm Beverly Carlson, the proud mother of this young man." She put her arm around Luke. "And sister to the human crusher."

Luke's mom? He didn't tell me she'd be here. I smiled inside knowing that Luke knew me well enough to save me from extra worry.

Beverly put her hand out. "Nice to have you join us."

I shook back. "Thank you for including me in your family celebration. I'm sure you miss Luke and want to catch up." I backed away from her. "I'll go see if Elizabeth needs any help."

"Oh no, you come sit with me." Mrs. Carlson took me by the arm and led me to a small round table and chairs in a corner away from the television. I'd lost Luke to playing with his nephews.

Luke's mother reminded me of Julie Andrews. Her pixie haircut showed some gray and soft wrinkles lined her eyes and mouth.

She motioned for me to sit and glanced toward the kitchen. "We'll both go help Elizabeth soon. But first, let's you and I chat a bit. Please tell me, how did you end up at The Ark?"

I tried to smile. "The short story is to train to be a missionary."

"And did your parents approve?" Beverly tilted her head. "I mean, you aren't spending the holiday with them."

"Well, I wasn't…" I trailed off. The room heated up. I searched the floor for an answer.

"Oh dear, you seem upset. I'm asking too many personal questions." She leaned in closer. "It's just that Luke's been very private about the two of you. Have you been dating for very long?"

"About three months. You must be very proud of Luke and how he followed in Pastor Steve's—I mean, your brother's footsteps."

"Oh, Steve's the father figure Luke never had. But my son, he's so smart. He could've been a lawyer, a doctor, or even an accountant."

Geez, that didn't go as expected. I'd much rather be with Elizabeth than Beverly and planned a way to escape. "Will you be staying for the long weekend?"

"Yes." She glanced over at Luke. "My son will be driving me back on Saturday."

Perfect. "Back to Woonsocket, Rhode Island?" I said as loud as I could without yelling.

Luke glanced at us. "Are you two talking about home?"

"Oh, yes. Your mom was telling me you're driving her home," I said. "Do you mind if I step away to help Elizabeth out for a few minutes?"

"Sure, go ahead," Luke said.

I rose and dashed into the kitchen. Elizabeth's back was to me. "Sorry I took so long. What can I do?"

"Everything." Elizabeth spun around with a pumpkin pie in her hands. Her cheerful expression faded into a look of shock—as if a ghost passed by. The pie tipped from her hands. I leapt forward and caught it. She stood with her hands raised, like in a stick up.

"I'm so sorry. Did I scare you?" I placed the pie on the kitchen table.

"That scarf." Elizabeth's voice squeaked. "Where'd you get that scarf?"

"This?" I picked up an end of the scarf. "I borrowed it from my friend, Bobbi. Do you know her—Bobbi Young?" Elizabeth didn't move. "Is something wrong?"

It took a few seconds before she spoke in her normal voice. "No. Nothing."

There wasn't time to figure out what caused her strange reaction because Beverly appeared at the threshold to the kitchen. My stomach tightened as she gestured to Elizabeth and said, "How's it going in here?"

Elizabeth gave her a huge smile and smoothed her apron. "We're in great shape. Dinner's almost ready. We'll call everyone in when it's time to eat."

"Well, then. Good luck ladies, I can't wait to see how it all comes together." Beverly made a harrumph noise and left.

Elizabeth picked up a wooden spoon from the counter. She pointed it toward the den. "Luck. We don't need no stinkin' luck. We've got talent."

My mouth hung open.

She laughed. "It's from an old movie. Let's go over what's left to do."

My jobs were to pour apple cider and light candles. The dining room lay tucked beside the staircase and off of the kitchen. Despite the plain room, the table, which sat ten, was festive with a gold tablecloth and a low centerpiece of yellow and rust mums surrounded by fall leaves. Two silver candlestick holders with white-tapered candles bordered the arrangement. A nostalgic tug pulled at me as I remembered how pretty Ma's table used to be.

In the kitchen, Elizabeth put some yeasty warm buns with shiny crusts into a wicker basket.

"Scratch?" I said.

"Bakery. Don't tell." Elizabeth winked. I loved that she trusted me with her food forgery.

Together we finished preparing the meal like we did this together every day. Next to the turkey, I counted the pies: the pumpkin pie I caught, two kinds of apple, and a pecan. I decided not to ask if she made any of them.

Ma made all her pies from scratch. Pam and BB thought cooking was a punishment and didn't help, but Ma let me peel and slice apples. Ma didn't like to talk when she cooked, but she didn't mind if I sang along when we listened to ABBA or The Beatles.

Elizabeth motioned for me to come close. She held a big pot. "I need you to guard the entrance to the kitchen. I am about to make the gravy. No one can come in here and watch…it's a secret recipe handed down from the pilgrims to my family."

She didn't have time to make gravy. I know because Ma made me stir it until I thought my hand would melt into the pot. Elizabeth reached under the sink and pulled out two jars of gravy. It was a struggle to keep my poker face. She poured them into a saucepan and hid the jars at the bottom of the trash.

"And now for the magic." Elizabeth scraped some of the pan drippings into the mixture. "Look, no lumps!" She took off her apron and smoothed out her dress. "Good work." She gave me a quick side hug and walked into the den. "Steve, it's time to carve the turkey."

Pastor Steve carved and Beverly took over as if it was her home, telling everyone where to sit. She put Pastor Steve at one end of the table where she and Luke flanked his sides. Paul sat at the other end with Elizabeth and me beside him. Paul's wife, Matt, and the grandsons were scattered in the middle seats. Beverly had broken up all the couples.

The meal was served buffet style from the kitchen. The line stretched into the den where Luke and I stood at the end.

"How are you doing?" Luke rubbed the side of my jaw with his thumb. "Looks like pumpkin pie." He licked it. "Tastes like pumpkin pie. How'd that get there? Oh, let me guess. You're really enjoying your nickname, Katie Pie."

His touch on my face made me melty inside. If only I didn't have to share him with everyone. "Yes, I'm a living pie. Seriously, though, I would've liked to sit next to you."

"Mom's a little bossy, huh?"

"It's okay. I guess she doesn't get to see you much."

"I'd sure like it if you got to know her better. And I'd love it if you'd come with us when I drive her home."

There was the word *love* again. Did Luke really mean it? I tried to keep my cool. Maybe it was the holiday. Even at my house, Ma got so excited about decorating, cooking, and having relatives visit that from Thanksgiving to Christmas she hardly ever got mad at us.

"...and after we drop her off, we could have lunch and take a tour of my hometown."

"Would your mom want that? She seems kind of possessive of you."

"That's my problem, not yours. It'll be a long day, but we'd get to spend a lot of time together."

I reached out for his hand and placed it on mine like a Bible. "Your mom has to agree. And you have to promise to tell me the truth."

He patted my back and motioned for me to go ahead of him in the line.

At the table, Pastor Steve waited until we were all seated and quiet. It was torture not to sneak a nibble off my plate.

"Everyone, please join hands."

I held hands with one of the boys and with Paul. Once my eyes closed, I started to wonder what Dad, Pam, and BB were doing at Disney World. To stop the images of swimming pools and parks rides from distracting me, I took a peek at Luke's family. Pastor Steve's face looked serene and kind. This would be Luke's face in twenty years. Luke caught me looking and smiled. I closed my eyes and thought of his touch on my face.

"...and we come together today to celebrate a day of thanks. We are thankful for our family and friends seated at this table. Lord, you have blessed us with your love and your grace. Make us truly thankful for these and all other blessings. And, before we have cold food to eat, we thank you for my lovely wife, Elizabeth, who made this meal possible. Through Jesus Christ we pray. Amen."

Everyone dug in and for several minutes, only the sound of silver clinking on plates filled the room. Later came bits of sentences like "great gravy" or "love the stuffing" or "another bun, please."

Beverly tapped the side of her glass. "I would like to make a toast." We all turned toward her. "To the cook. I must say, other than a few lumps in the mashed potatoes, you did a good job."

"To Elizabeth." Luke raised his glass. We raised ours with him, then I brought the glass to my lips and drank.

Elizabeth kicked me under the table mid-gulp and made me choke. To avoid a coughing scene, I left the table with watery eyes.

"Let me help her," Elizabeth said.

I went through the kitchen to the back door, stepped outside to try and cough in private. Elizabeth was right behind me. "You okay? Sorry, but I couldn't believe that backhanded compliment. She called me the cook, like I'm some hired help."

To settle my cough, I raised my arms over my head. "She's really something. But I'm glad I've got you alone. I need to ask you something." I glanced back to the kitchen. No one followed us. "So Luke's driving his mom home and invited me to go with him. What would you do?"

"Before I give you my expert advice, I just want you to know something. I've been married to Steve for three years. That's three years of family celebrations. And guess what? You're the first girl that Luke's invited to one. I see the way he looks at you. Do you feel the same way?"

I fumbled with the edge of my sweater and thought of the shivery exploding feeling in my heart that came when I was with Luke. "Yes, I think I do."

Elizabeth clapped her hands. "I'm so happy for the both of you. Now, your question about the drive." She lowered her voice. "On a good day it's a three-hour drive." She shuddered. "I couldn't stand her for that long."

I bet Elizabeth never sat in one of Mrs. Huffman's classes. She wasn't meek or submissive and said what she thought to me. The sun hung near the horizon. Inspired, I initiated a hug for the first time that day. "Elizabeth, what would I do without you?"

"Shall we get back to the dining room before anyone thinks we're plotting a conspiracy?"

After a round of seconds, Pastor Steve stood. "My dear family and Katie Pie, before we leave the table and break for dessert, if anyone would like to share what they are thankful for this year, now is the time. Who would like to start? You know that I could go on for hours if no one else has anything to say."

Everyone groaned and he sat down. I felt like I was shining inside and out. Pastor Steve—a man of God who preached sermons that shook me to my core, inspired me, made me weep—accepted me and shared his holiday with me.

The grandson next to me went first. He looked at his dad. "I'm thankful this meal is over. Can I go play now?"

"I am thankful I have such well-behaved boys. You may both be excused," Paul said.

They ran out of the room and we chuckled. I rolled my napkin ring between my hands. What would I say when it was my turn, that I was thankful I was here with them and not with my family? I watched a wax tear roll down the side of the candle.

Luke stood and we all quieted. His eyes lit up as he gazed around the table.

"I am thankful to have the people I love most in the world with me here tonight. There are those I have loved for a very long time: Mom, Uncle Steve, my cousins. There are the brave women who have joined our family: Melanie and Elizabeth." He paused and looked at me as if I was the only one in the room. "Then, there's my soul mate."

Oh my God. My heart raced. I couldn't swallow. Through blurry eyes, I watched him walk around the table. My hands shook as I wiped at my tears. He stopped and knelt in front of me. I grasped the hand he offered me.

"Are you feeling brave?"

CHAPTER 22

LUKE SLID A RING ON MY FINGER, and my heart soared as if a thousand doves took flight. A round diamond sparkled on the simple gold band. Luke's face beamed as he wiped away the happy tears rolling down my face. All the pain of the past year melted away. A wonderful man loved me and chose me.

Cheering and clapping reminded me that we weren't alone, and a hot blush rose up my neck to my face. All of Luke's family witnessed our private moment.

Luke stood and pulled my trembling body to him. My wet face pressed against his chest. The *thump-thump* of his heartbeat sounded like the words I wanted to say to the others: *Go away, go away.*

The boys bounced into the room and broke the spell. "What's going on?" the older one said.

Luke released me, but I clasped his arm like a pull bar on a roller coaster. "I've asked Kate to marry me." He lifted my hand to show my engagement ring.

"You and Katie Pie are getting married?" He made a grumbling sound and stuck his fingers in his mouth to pull both sides down. His little brother copied him.

"Boys, where are your manners?" Melanie said. "What would the good Lord Jesus say?"

They looked at the floor.

"He would say congratulations."

"Congrassuation. Can we please go play some more?" the younger son said.

Melanie touched his cheek. "Yes, you may."

They ran off and the adults surrounded us. Gazing at Luke's family, I saw joy on each face except one. Beverly's showed no emotion. *Please like me.*

Pastor Steve and his sons clapped Luke on the back while Melanie and Elizabeth huddled around me. "Congratulations," Elizabeth said. Melanie reached for my hand just as Beverly cut in and beat her to it. I couldn't meet her eyes.

"What a lovely ring." Beverly said. "I guess he really loves you." Her voice cracked as she spoke. She came closer and spoke in my ear, "Be good to him. He's all I got."

I touched her arm lightly. "I will." She nodded and walked away.

Melanie and Elizabeth each took an elbow and steered me into the kitchen. Melanie chirped nonstop. "I'm so happy for both of you. Paul and I met similar to the two of you. It was my daddy's idea to leave Texas and attend seminary on the East Coast, but I tell you, I thought I'd be graduating without my MRS degree. It wasn't until the start of my senior year that the good Lord Jesus bumped Paul on the head and opened his eyes."

She lowered her voice and shook her mane of hair. "Honey, now don't you rush into having any babies. We waited until I was twenty-five."

Good Lord Jesus. Babies were the last things on my mind.

"You just let me know if you need any help with your wedding plans. I do love weddings. Now, I'm going to give your fiancé a big ol' hug."

Melanie walked away as an "okay" and a "thank you" tumbled out of my mouth. I had a fiancé. It sounded so official.

Elizabeth took my hand. "Let's go someplace private." She led me into the bare living room. We sat on the only piece of furniture, a long upholstered sofa. "Kate, you look like a breeze could knock you over. Oh no, I'm starting to sound like Melanie." Elizabeth shook her head. "And what was she thinking, mentioning babies at a time like this?"

"Yeah, it's pretty overwhelming." I gave her a weak smile, untied Bobbi's scarf, and wrapped it around my wrist like a bracelet. *Wait until she hears about my day.*

Elizabeth blew out a sigh. "If I knew what Luke was planning, believe me, I would've tried to stop him. Meeting Beverly and the rest of the family is stressful enough. God love him that he decided this was the right time to propose."

I twisted the scarf and thought of Ma. She would've liked Luke if I hadn't met him at The Ark. Then again, no one at home would like him at first because they'd think The Ark sucked his brains out too. But once they spent a few minutes with him, they'd know how special he was.

Leaning close to Elizabeth, I said, "Do you think Beverly is freaking out over this?"

Elizabeth looked toward the hallway and then moved next to me so we touched hip to hip. "I've been through it with her too. As you saw earlier, she still gives me a hard time. But instead of getting mad, I try to put myself in her shoes. That helps me understand her better. I think she's lonely. So I try not to judge her." She put her hands over her heart. "And, when you love someone, when you find your soul mate, God helps you."

Her words sent goosebumps up my arms. If she could do it, I could too. Beverly would see how happy I made Luke.

"This is one Thanksgiving I'll never forget," I said. We both laughed.

Luke poked his head into the living room. "Hey, you two. Can I steal Katie Pie away? Uncle Steve wants to meet with us in his study. He'll be up there in a few minutes."

I stopped smiling. *Please, God. No more.*

Halfway up the stairs I tugged on Luke's shirtsleeve. He stopped. "What's wrong?"

"All of this, Luke. Meeting your family. Your proposal. And now a private meeting with Pastor Steve. It's too much. Too much for one day." I sank onto the staircase, exhausted. "I just want to be with you."

Luke sat beside me and put his hand on my back. When my breathing calmed, he touched my face like I might break. "I owe you an explanation about today. I wanted to wait for a romantic night when we were alone." He broke into a huge grin. "But once I got the ring, I just couldn't wait to ask you."

My eyes pleaded with him. "But we'll set the date together?"

"My sweet love." Luke moved down a step, making our faces level. A spark flicked between us. He leaned in and his mouth gently touched mine. His lips felt as soft and perfect as a ripe peach in summer. He broke the kiss too soon, but his face stayed close to mine. "Do you forgive me?"

I'd already forgotten why I was mad at him.

"Ready?" Luke stood.

"Do we have to have this private meeting now?" I said, tapping my fingers against the step. "It's Thanksgiving. Can't it wait?"

"Don't worry. My guess is that he wants to give us some advice or pray for us. Everyone here loves you. I promise."

Luke's sincerity kept me going, and I let him pull me to my feet.

At the landing on the second floor, the house changed from bare to beautiful. I saw Pastor Steve's office to the left and to the right, a hallway covered with an oriental carpet in rich reds and dark blues. Paintings and photographs of ballet dancers covered the walls.

"This is like a museum," I said.

"Go ahead and look around. I'll wait for you in Pastor Steve's study."

The photos of Elizabeth showed her in graceful poses and flowing ballet costumes. Despite her wonderful marriage to Pastor Steve, I wondered if she missed being on stage. Worried that Pastor Steve would come up any minute, I rushed back to Luke. Inside the study, the smell of old books filled the room and a large picture window framed a grove of pine trees. The setting sun bathed the room in a soothing light that helped calm my nerves.

Luke sat on an oversized leather couch and fumbled to switch on a lamp. I scanned the top of Pastor Steve's wooden desk covered with neat piles of notepads, a brass desk lamp, and photographs. I ran my fingers over the bindings of a couple of books. "Is it okay for me to look? I've never seen so many in one house before."

"Sure, it's a great collection." Luke yawned and rested his head against the back of the couch. "I might just shut my eyes for a minute. I'm turkey tired."

Ma said books told a lot about a person. Pastor Steve organized his collection by subjects. Two shelves were devoted to books about the Old and New Testaments. Another shelf held different versions of the Bible, including some ancient-looking ones.

Crossing the room, I stopped to watch Luke sleep, his face tranquil while his chest rose and fell. Someday we'd be married, and I'd be able to watch him sleep every night. The thought filled me with a tender glow.

The books on this side of the office were more intriguing: exorcism, cults, and healing. Mixed in with C.S. Lewis and Billy Graham, the red and white cover of *The Joy of Sex* stood out. Pastor Steve must counsel couples on sex problems. I couldn't imagine anything more embarrassing.

"Do you like my library, future Mrs. Luke Carlson?"

I jumped.

"Whoa there, didn't mean to scare you. Although, I understand I'm very good at that during morning chapel." Pastor Steve walked past me to hang his jacket on the back of his chair. "You're welcome to read anything you like, but some I can't let out of the room."

I felt like a naughty kid and scooted back to the couch. "Sorry, I didn't touch anything. Just looked."

Luke rubbed his eyes and stretched.

"Oh, that's not what I meant. They're just sentimentally valuable. Would you like to see my very first Bible?" Pastor Steve raised one eyebrow. I wondered if Luke knew how to do that.

"Yes, I'd love to," I said, honored he would share it with me.

He picked one from the shelf and opened it with care. "Sometimes, when God's voice is quiet and I need inspiration, I read my notes from the early days."

After a quick glance, I sat next to Luke. His weight made the cushion uneven, causing me to slide toward him. It was difficult trying to inch away from him with any dignity.

Pastor Steve covered his smile with a fake cough. "Now, since I've got this Bible open, let's talk about why I called you here. But first of all, Katie Pie, I am looking forward to getting to know you better. Consider yourself already a member of the family."

Luke intertwined his fingers with mine. *Kate Bennett, how did this happen to you?* The girl whose mother just died and who's been blamed by her father was now welcomed into the Carlson family by Pastor Steve himself. It was like being wrapped in a warm blanket.

"I consider Luke a son, and because of his relationship to me, others will be watching you closely. It will be a time of considerable testing. Most students will be happy for you. Others may be envious. Keep this in mind when you're in public together." He pointed at us. "Do not give anyone ammunition to use against you."

These were not the words I expected. I sat up straighter.

"If you treat each other with respect at all times, others will too. This goes for times you're alone as well. Physical temptations will be with you. Remember your bodies are God's holy temple. The marriage bed is sacred. There is no engagement bed."

I couldn't look at either of them and fixated on a loose thread on my sweater.

"Thank you, Uncle Steve. We appreciate your wisdom and advice." Luke squeezed my hand. "Before we join the others, would you pray for God to guide us?"

"Young man, you're going to make a fine pastor. Let me start with my favorite reading for a time like this." Pastor Steve flipped to the beginning of his Bible and read the story of Adam and Eve.

He finished with the verse, "'Then the Lord God made a woman from the rib he had taken out of the man, and he brought her to the man.'" Mrs. Huffman used the same verse in God's Golden Woman class. The idea of being subservient made me bristle. I wanted to be a strong wife like Elizabeth, but maybe not as strong as Ma.

Pastor Steve walked over to us and placed a hand on my head and Luke's. My nose was inches from Pastor Steve's pants, too close for comfort. I squeezed my eyes shut and said my own silent prayer. A loud pulse beat in my ears. I didn't hear anything until Luke and Pastor Steve said, "Amen."

"Let me help you up." Pastor Steve offered his hand. He pulled me into a hug and kissed me quickly on the lips. Shocked, I stiffened. Before he let me go, his nose grazed the side of my head and I felt him sniff my hair. *What the heck is going on?*

The two of them acted normal so I shook off my uneasiness and followed them downstairs. Elizabeth announced it was time for pie. I picked at my slice until everyone was done. When it came time to clear the dessert table, I volunteered and Matt offered to help me. He wasn't like the other Carlson men who left the women to do all the work. I liked him right away.

As we gathered the dishes, I noticed Matt wasn't much taller than me. *He must take after his mother.*

"Will you see your mom this weekend?" I asked him.

Sadness crept across his face. "You're the only person who's mentioned her all day. No, I won't see her. She lives in San Francisco. During the holidays, I miss her most." He looked down.

"I'm sorry about your mom." Before I could say anything, he was at my side. "Do you want to talk about her?"

The compassion in his voice changed the air in the room. I could breathe deeply for the first time all day. I paused and said, "I don't think she was saved."

Matt put his hand on my shoulder. "You'll learn a lot about the Bible here. But the most important thing to remember is this: God is love."

The heavy anchor of doubt rocked just enough for a trickle of hope to reach me. God loved Ma. "Thank you."

Matt smiled, and I could imagine what having a brother must feel like.

Luke entered the dining room. "How long does it take to clear a table?"

We all laughed and carried stacks of plates back into the kitchen.

Luke and I received a second round of best wishes as we said our goodbyes. It was late and bitter cold outside. We walked hand in hand as a light snow fell. The white flakes dusted everything they touched, and our breaths hung in the air like steam-filled clouds.

Before we reached my dorm, I turned to Luke. Tiny hammers beat inside me. "Luke, there's something I haven't had a chance to say." The words raced out. "I love you."

Luke opened his arms and pulled me to him. He tilted my head back, kissed my forehead and nose, and then lifted me off the ground. I wrapped my arms around his neck. Our lips met. His tasted sweet like apple pie. After our quick kiss, he said, "I love you too."

My heart hurt in a good way. A light shone on us, and Luke set me down. We turned to face the headlights of a lone car entering the parking lot. In undisturbed silence, we finished our walk.

Luke touched his fingertips to my face. "Goodnight, my future wife. Will I see you at breakfast?"

I answered with a huge smile. Soon, we'd be having breakfast together every morning. Heat raced through my body at the thought of us in bed together.

"Future husband, this has been the best day of my life."

CHAPTER 23

I FLOATED DOWN THE HALL to my dorm room and found Sheila sleeping. She'd put in another long day at the group home. As much as I wanted to tell her about my engagement to Luke, I couldn't wake her. She had to be up at dawn for her drive home. I really wanted to tell my news to Bobbi, but I had no idea how to reach her in Montana.

Stretched out in bed, I twirled Luke's ring and noticed it felt a little loose. I'd have to find a jeweler in town to resize it for me. For the time being, I wouldn't wear it at work and would keep it zipped in my wallet for safekeeping.

Bursting to tell someone, my body hummed with nervous energy. Luke's entire family witnessed his proposal, but no one in my family knew. I wondered if they thought about me during their Disney vacation. BB might miss me. My mind drifted from her to Ma and my breath caught. Ma would never meet Luke nor see me get married in the veil she'd made and saved from her wedding. *Ma, if you only took your medicine, you'd still be here. You'd see how happy I am and that going to The Ark wasn't a mistake.*

I woke up in the middle of the night with the remnants of a nightmare lingering. Luke had kissed me but when he pulled away, he looked old. I called out his name, and the voice that answered said, "I'm not Luke." The face had become Pastor Steve's. I jerked away in horror.

No one would believe that Pastor Steve sniffed my hair or care that he pecked me on the lips. It even sounded exaggerated in my mind, like a cry for attention. I had to let it go.

I slept through Sheila getting ready the next morning, but she'd left me a sweet note decorated with "God loves you" in air bubbles.

Hey sleepyhead,

Sorry I missed you. Hope your T Day was wonderful. I thank the Lord for your friendship. See you Sunday.

Love, Sheila.

P.S. You were mumbling in your sleep...hope it was a good dream.

Lazy clouds floating in the blue sky greeted me as I walked to the snack bar. When I opened the door, Luke was already in line. He pointed where Beverly was seated. She looked almost cheerful and waved me over.

"Please, come. Sit by me." Beverly's face had a softness I hadn't seen at Thanksgiving. "My dear, I have to apologize. I didn't know you lost your mother recently. I'm sorry if I upset you yesterday."

"It's okay."

"What was your mom like?"

I grabbed a napkin and rolled it in my palms, not sure how to explain Ma to her. "Well, my mother had a rough life growing up. Then she met my dad while working at the beach one summer. They fell in love. Got married. Then she had me and my two sisters all pretty close together. I think we wore her out."

Beverly sat still, and her kindness loosened more words.

"Being the oldest, I tried to keep my sisters away from her. Especially when she was doing her craft projects and wanted peace and quiet. But it was hard…" My voice broke. All those years being the good one, and I ended up being the one Dad couldn't look at.

"Sounds like you tried your best." Beverly patted my arm.

Luke joined us at the table with plates of pancakes, giving me the chance to dab at my eyes without anyone noticing.

When I finished my shift at work that night, Wanda pulled me aside.

"Kate, I hate to ask you this, since it's not your normal schedule, but half the cashiers have called in sick for tomorrow. I'm desperate. Would you be able to work? Any hours you can give me would be at time and a half."

"No problem. Whatever you need."

Wanda was so happy, she did a little dance and ended it with a high five.

Working on Saturday meant no driving to Rhode Island with Luke and his mother. Luke would understand that I couldn't say no to all that overtime money. Even though I was making progress with Beverly, she'd be happy to have Luke to herself, and I wouldn't have to watch my every word and move.

Back at The Ark, I parked in front of my dorm and walked down the dimly lit sidewalk to find Luke and let him know about the change of plans. I tried the snack bar first. A student I didn't know thought he might be at Pastor Steve's house. Since Beverly was staying there, that made sense.

I knocked on the door, and Luke answered. "Hey, there. Come on in."

"Can we walk for a few minutes first?"

"Sure." He came back out with his jacket. "Everything okay?"

Our shoes crunched on the gravel as we walked. "Yep, except… I'm really sorry but I won't be able to go with you tomorrow. My boss is in a jam and asked me to work—all overtime pay. I really could use the extra money. But there's a good part." I stopped to tug his sleeve. "You'll have lots of time to spend alone with your mom."

"Why that's so nice of you." Luke shook his head and smiled. Then he reached for my hands. "I was going to wait and tell you this on the ride back, but I'll tell you now." Even in the darkness, his eyes seemed to sparkle. "I've got good news. Your days of living in the group dorm room are almost over. Next semester, you'll be assigned to a single roommate on the second floor."

My hands twisted out of his. I backed away. What was he talking about?

He stepped closer and spoke like a passionate preacher. "The second floor is reserved for the chosen ones: those in training to be pastors' wives. You'll be paired with an experienced student. One who's finished God's Golden Woman training. This isn't a privilege many first years get. God has great things in store for you. Isn't his plan wonderful?"

"But I like where I live and the roommates I have now." I clasped my chilled hands under my chin.

"Of course you do, but in six months, I'll be a pastor. You'll be a pastor's wife. We need to get you ready. Accelerate your training so you'll graduate in one year. We know you can do it."

"One year?" My head spun. "And who is *we*?"

"Me. Pastor Steve. That's why I'm at his house. And more exciting news, we're also looking for a job for you on staff so you won't have to work at the grocery store any longer."

My confusion turned into an icy fury. I could barely meet his eyes.

"You don't seem happy about this."

"I thought *we* meant us."

"This is for us." Luke stretched out his arms to embrace me.

I put my hands up to stop him. "But you didn't ask me what I wanted." He didn't know I grew up being bossed around by my mother—in a place where my opinions never mattered.

A flicker of disappointment crossed Luke's face. "Isn't this what you want?"

I took a deep breath. "This is a lot to take in. Can we talk more about it when you get back?"

"Okay, I'll save you a seat at service on Sunday." His voice became softer. "And we can talk about it afterward."

I tried to put on a happy face. "Have a safe trip and say good-bye to your mom for me."

Luke hugged my stiff body. When he let go, I raced back to the dorm. A cold wind had picked up and blew right through me.

CHAPTER 24

NO ONE NEEDED GROCERIES two days after Thanksgiving and the hours dragged by. Nick told me he'd walk me to my car later and headed off to work in the stockroom. Then, Wanda let the other cashier and bagger go home. Alone up front, I cleaned every inch of my work area and then all the other stations.

I decided not to share my engagement news with anyone at work. Better to avoid the possibility of negative jabs thrown my way. When no one was looking, I flipped through some bridal magazines.

Wanda made the store-closing announcement a whole hour early, and I shouted "hooray." It was like being freed from boredom jail. After I punched out, I waited at the front door for Nick. Ten minutes passed. Anxious to leave, I headed back to the stockroom entrance. Even though the sign on the door said AUTHORIZED EMPLOYEES ONLY, I decided to peek in.

The rubber door weighed a ton and took all my strength to open. My eyes adjusted to the dull lighting just as the door swung back, hitting me hard in the butt. I slipped on some goo and clawed at the air to keep my balance just as Nick rounded the corner.

"What the hell?" He caught me before I wiped out and my face landed in his stomach. "That's why you're not allowed in here."

"You were late. That door attacked me." I giggled as I pulled myself up.

His hands tightened around my waist. Neither of us moved. Nick's woodsy smell tickled my nose. Danger signs flashed in my head, and I pulled away. I needed to find a new escort.

Nick opened the door like it weighed nothing and held it for me to pass through just as Wanda started shutting off the store lights.

"Let's get out before we get locked in for the night," I said.

"I can think of worse things."

I ignored him. Luke. I had to concentrate my thoughts only on Luke.

After Nick made sure no one was lurking near my car, I got in and turned on the engine. It cranked slower than normal. Nick heard it too and walked back to me. I rolled down my window. "Hey, does that sound funny?"

"Might be time for a new battery. Don't make any stops on your way home."

"Oh great. Are they expensive?" I hated car repairs.

"Probably all the money you earned today." Nick slapped the side of my car and headed over to his pickup truck.

My heart sank. If I worked at The Ark, I wouldn't need this old heap.

As I pulled out of the lot I noticed Nick following me. He continued until I turned into The Ark, and we waved goodbye to each other. He sure confused me, teasing one minute and protective the next. Sometimes I thought about him when I wasn't at work, and it dawned on me that Luke was right about me having a campus job. I'd be away from Nick and his worldly temptations.

Alone in my dorm room, I turned on the small light near my bunk. A long bath would've been nice, but we only had showers. For once, the hot water didn't run out and my aching bones were soothed. On holiday weekends, Pastor Steve only preached a Sunday evening sermon so I could sleep in. And my fiancé would be back and I'd be sitting with him. I fell into bed with a contented sigh.

When I woke, I rolled over to see the clock and smiled at the luxury of sleeping for twelve hours. I sat up and noticed something was wrong in the room. Bobbi's bed had no sheets. The lower bunk we called "the office" was also bare. How did I miss that last night?

I slid off my bed to flick on the overhead light. Bobbi's bureau was cleared off. Dust circles outlined the spots where her jewelry boxes and makeup used to sit. On the mirror, pieces of scotch tape marked where photos of "hot guys" had been. The drawers were empty too.

A going-to-the-dentist sick feeling hit my stomach. *Please God, let there be clothes in her closet.* A few metal hangers clinked together when I opened the door. What happened to all of Bobbi's stuff?

My heart skipped a beat. The edge of Bobbi's scarf poked out of my closet. I'd hung it on the doorknob after Thanksgiving. It was all I had left of her, and I buried it in my pajama drawer.

I had to find out what happened. Elizabeth would know. I

threw on some clothes, put on my ring, and headed to her house. Praying that I wouldn't interrupt anything important, I knocked on the door.

Elizabeth answered. "Kate, great to see you. Are you looking for Luke?"

"Oh, he's here?"

"Yes. Just arrived a few minutes ago. He must've left Rhode Island early this morning. He's upstairs with Steve. Come on in, it's freezing out there."

Hopefully they weren't discussing me. "I actually came to talk to you, but we can try another time."

"Stay there, I'll get my coat." Elizabeth came back in a second. "Let's go to the chapel."

It was so cold we almost ran the whole way there. Once inside, I waited for the holy feeling I always felt, but not a divine crumb reached me. Elizabeth found a light switch for the stage. She led the way to some seats near the front.

"Did something happen with you and Luke?" she said.

"We did have a misunderstanding. But that's not why I came to see you. I mean I'm worried about that, but there's something else. I didn't know who else to turn to."

Elizabeth touched my arm. "Tell me what's going on."

"It's my friend, Bobbi. You know, we talked about her on Thanksgiving. All her stuff is gone." I twirled my ring. "Nothing's left. No sheets, clothes, photos."

Elizabeth didn't say a word and stared at the stage for a minute before turning to me.

"This puts me in a difficult position. What I'm going to tell you, please promise me you won't repeat it to anyone."

"I promise. Is she okay?" A prayer started in my head, *Please God, let her be okay.*

She played with the zipper on her jacket. "You need to understand, I am telling you this in confidence."

I wanted to grab Elizabeth and shake out the words. "Yes, yes. I understand. Please, tell me. When will she be back?"

"She won't be coming back."

Horrible thoughts flashed in my head. Bobbi mangled in a car wreck. Bobbi buried under an avalanche. *God, I'm sorry. I'll be a good wife to Luke. I can be humble and submissive. Please, just don't let anything bad happen to Bobbi.*

"Your friend didn't choose to come to The Ark like the rest of us did. She was sent here because of her problem." Elizabeth's eyes darted around the chapel before stopping at her hands. "Shoplifting. And while she was at The Ark, she tried to steal something…something she couldn't have. I can't say more." She stood up. "I've got to get back. I'm sorry."

I mumbled a soft thank you and barely heard her leave. My body felt heavy like my blood had turned to cement. My mind, however, exploded as Elizabeth's words sank in. Bobbi wasn't a thief. Someone had made a huge mistake.

Bobbi's family had money and could buy her anything she needed. She didn't have to steal. Then I remembered the day of our fancy lunch. When I walked away from the limo, Judith had asked Bobbi if she'd been staying out of trouble.

What if her parents cut her off when she came to The Ark? A tentacle of doubt reached out, casting light onto other details I couldn't ignore. Bobbi told me she'd skipped classes to go shopping, and Daisy's bunk was draped with brand new clothes.

Another thought stopped me cold. If Bobbi didn't choose to come to The Ark—if she was forced to come here—maybe she wasn't a believer. I couldn't forget how she stood up to Mrs. Huffman in our first God's Golden Woman class. It was shocking then, but it was painful now.

The only other time I'd ever prayed on my knees was when Ma was in the hospital. I knelt again and pressed my forehead on the seat of the folding chair in front of me.

"Dear Lord, Thank you for all you've given me. I am worried about my friend, Bobbi. I pray that she's saved. I pray for Dad, Pam, and BB's salvation, too. Show me a way to find Bobbi, Lord, because I can't let her go like this."

Trusting Bobbi to God, I rose to leave the chapel. Someone stood against the far wall near the exit, a person I recognized. When I reached Luke, we took a couple of seats beside each other in the last row.

"I didn't hear you come in. Did Elizabeth tell you I was here?"

Luke nodded. "I'm sorry I made you angry."

"No, I'm sorry." I sighed. "Sometimes I'm afraid I'll be like my mother. She flew into rages. I don't want to be like her."

Luke took my hands. "I never knew your mother, but I can see your grief. You've had a huge loss. But to worry about being like her, it's like you're carrying her on your back. That's a heavy burden to bear. If you can let her go, just imagine how freeing that will be. Let God carry you."

Sometimes it seemed all I had left of Ma was her rage. My anger, my loss of control, they kept her alive in me. Luke pushed a strand of hair off my face and tucked it behind my ear. He kept his hand there and I leaned into it.

"Don't forget that I love everything about you. I don't want you to be anything but yourself."

His words were healing. "That's the nicest thing anyone's ever said to me."

"This is where you'll always be loved." Luke pulled me close. Tucked under his chin, feeling his chest rise and fall as he breathed, I wanted to believe every word he said.

CHAPTER 25

LUKE AND I MADE PLANS to meet for an early dinner before evening service. Back in my dorm room, I had forgotten how the sight of Bobbi's bare bed saddened me. Suddenly, a spark of hope hit me. Bobbi said she'd be back from her ski trip today. To reach her at home, I'd have to use the ancient pay phone in the lobby. Sometimes the no cell phone rule at The Ark was such a pain. Fishing in my wallet for change, I dialed information for Manhattan.

"Could I have the number for James Young, please," I said.

"That number is unlisted."

I kicked the wall. "What about a Judith or Roberta Young?"

"There are no public listings for either name. Can I help you with anything else?"

I hung up.

My backup plan involved sneaking into Elizabeth's office and looking in her file cabinet. The student files had to have home phone numbers. I prayed she wouldn't be in the office today and that God wouldn't punish me for my sin. If anyone did see me,

I'd clutch my stomach and pretend to be looking for a nurse.

With my jacket collar pulled up high, I ventured out like a spy. Only a lonely squirrel dashing up a tree noticed me. My last visit to the admin building was to hear Pastor Steve's call-in radio show and the first time I'd met Luke. *What Luke would think if he knew what I was doing now?* I leaned against the glass front door to open it, but forgot about the jingling bells. The racket made my heart beat double time.

In a squeaky voice I called out, "Hello, anyone here?" The only sounds were the creaks and groans of an old wooden building in the winter.

Elizabeth's office door stood open, and I tiptoed in. A vase of wilting roses perfumed the air. Pushing away my feelings of being a traitor, I sat in her chair and rolled over to the file cabinets.

I tried to pull open the first drawer. Shoot, it was locked. Of course she'd have to secure the student files. The jingle of bells made me jump. Dear God, someone was coming in. Too late to run out of the office, I dropped to the floor and crawled under the desk. The chair was askew, but I was too afraid to move it. Sweat trickled down my back. To be caught like this would be the most mortifying thing I could imagine.

"I always have to remember everything around here," a woman said.

The whiney voice and sound of nylons squeaking made me think it was Mrs. Payne, the school treasurer. Not the most loved person on campus—if she wanted to talk to you, it meant you owed the school money. Her favorite saying was "God doesn't pay the bills." I stayed hunkered under the desk. My ears strained at every sound.

When her footsteps tapped back down the hallway toward the front door, I heard keys jangle, the bells clink, and then quiet. I counted to ten and slid out of my hiding place on my butt. My eyes were level with a key left in the lock of Elizabeth's desk. This was such a stroke of luck that I pumped my fist in the air.

Elizabeth organized her hanging files with color-coded tabs. The blue ones listed titles of Pastor Steve's sermons dating back to the start of the school year: a literal God gold mine. Red labels indicated the different countries where The Ark had outreach ministries. The yellow ones looked like utility bills. I blew out a loud sigh. No student information in this drawer.

As a last resort, I opened her top center drawer and found a single file. Elizabeth had written *Pending* in pencil on the tab. My conscience warned me to stop, but I couldn't. God would forgive me if Bobbi was in trouble and she needed my help. A paperclip held a wad of receipts that I flipped through. Some were from doctors' offices, others were meal and hotel bills signed by Steve Carlson. Elizabeth must track all his expenses. A receipt for an expensive silk scarf caught my eye. It seemed too expensive for someone on a minister's salary to buy.

I lined everything back in order and found a ledger stapled inside the front of the file. My finger traced along each row of the five entries: a set of initials, a date, and dollar amounts. The first four entries also had the word *closed* written beside them. The last entry had the initials RY and a date: the day after Thanksgiving.

The hair rose on my arms. Those were Bobbi's initials and the date when her belongings disappeared. *What did this mean?* The other initials might belong to students who also had problems like

Bobbi. I took the file and crept over to the copy machine, made a copy, and stuffed it in the sleeve of my coat.

It was time to get out of here before anyone else came in. After double-checking that everything was back in its original place, I stood near the window that faced the front of the campus. The coast was clear. I used to say that to my sisters when it was safe to leave our rooms after Ma punished us. Pam and BB were too chicken to be a lookout so I'd listen at the top of the staircase. If Ma had her TV shows back on, it meant she'd calmed down.

Crouched like a hunchback, I pushed against the front door. It didn't budge. Mrs. Payne had locked it on her way out. *No, God, don't let me get trapped in here.* My panic soon transformed to relief—I just had to turn the deadbolt.

I raced back to my room and jumped on my bed. My body shook as it unwound from my unsuccessful crime. All that sneaking around and I never found Bobbi's phone number. The scarf receipt nagged at the edge of my mind. Elizabeth had freaked out when she saw Bobbi's scarf on me at Thanksgiving. *Could it have been the same scarf? If Pastor Steve bought it for Elizabeth, how did Bobbi get it?* Elizabeth said Bobbi tried to steal something at The Ark that wasn't hers. But I couldn't imagine she'd steal something from Elizabeth. I'd invented a new Nancy Drew mystery: *The Case of the Missing Scarf.*

When my breathing finally slowed to normal, I glanced at the clock on the nightstand that Sheila and I shared and almost whooped. It was so obvious. Sheila had asked each of us for an emergency contact during the first week of school. Bobbi's phone number was in the room the whole time.

Her clipboard lay in the top drawer with our names, addresses, and phone numbers. Daisy had a red line drawn through her name. I hoped she was getting better.

The last entry was Roberta "Bobbi" Young. I wrote all her information down on the photocopy I'd made in Elizabeth's office and raced back to the phone. While it rang, I tapped a beat to "please answer, please answer" on the wall.

"Good afternoon, Young residence." Of course, her family had a housekeeper.

"Hi, good afternoon," I said. "I'd like to speak with Bobbi. I mean Roberta."

"Who's calling, please?"

"I'm Kate. Kate Bennett. I'm a friend from The Ark."

"Oh, I see."

"Is she there? Can I talk to her?"

"Ms. Young is not available."

"Is she still on her ski trip?" That had to make me sound more official.

"I'm sorry, but I cannot give out any information about my employer or the family's whereabouts."

"Please, I need your help. All Bobbi's stuff is gone from school. Is she all right?"

"Miss Bennett, if you give me your phone number, I can have her call you when she's available."

"It's not that easy. Is Bobbi in trouble?" The operator asked for more money. *Stupid pay phone.* "Please don't hang up on me." I shoved my last quarters into the phone.

"Ms. Bennett, you sound upset. All I can tell you is, given the circumstances, Roberta is fine. Goodbye."

I stared at the phone and wondered if the circumstances meant Bobbi's shoplifting. I was so close to reaching her and had hit another dead end. There had to be a way to get past the housekeeper.

A few seconds later, Sheila burst through the door. "Oh Kate." She dropped her bag and wrapped me in a hug that mashed my face into her copper curls. "How was your Thanksgiving?"

"Great. How was yours?"

Sheila hooked her arm through mine and steered me toward the common room. "It's always fun to be home, hang out with my little sister. I love eating Mom's food. How'd it go at Pastor Steve's?"

My mind shifted gears to Luke and his proposal. I held up my hand. "This happened."

Sheila squealed. "Congratulations to you and Luke. Tell me all the details."

After she put some Tupperware in the fridge, we sat together on the worn couch. By the time I finished describing Luke's proposal, tears filled her eyes. "I am so happy for you. You know, you're going to be campus royalty now," she said.

"What do you mean?"

"Once word gets out about you and Luke, people will treat you like you are part of Pastor Steve's family. You're blessed. God found your soul mate." Sheila looked past me. "I hope someday God will find one for me."

I touched Sheila's arm. "I'm sure every guy here's in love with you. You're the best catch on campus."

Sheila smoothed her skirt and stood. "So did I miss anything else?"

I chewed on my lower lip. "Did you know that Bobbi left?"

"Did she run away?"

Good grief, Sheila. "No. When I came back from working a long shift on Saturday, all her stuff was gone."

"Aren't you her best friend?" Sheila wagged her finger at me. "Didn't Bobbi tell *you* why she left?"

The tone in Sheila's voice made me want to lash out, but I kept my cool. Elizabeth trusted me to keep her confidence, and now I wanted to protect Bobbi even more. "I saw her on Wednesday when her mom came to take her on vacation. I'm sure everything's fine."

"This is very unusual. I'm always informed in advance when something like this is going to happen." She shook her head. "That's two gone this semester."

We went to our room and I watched Sheila search Bobbi's area, opening and shutting all the same doors and drawers that I did.

"Well, it's going to be nice and quiet in here now." She wiped her hands together.

Her words stung. I pictured Sheila pulling out her clipboard and running a red line through Bobbi's name and that hurt even more.

CHAPTER 26

WHEN HANNAH AND ALICE returned from their visit home, I let them know Bobbi had left The Ark and we weren't sure of the reason. Unlike Sheila, they each embraced me in one of their strong bear hugs, said they were sorry, and would add Bobbi to their prayers.

I changed into navy slacks and a striped sweater and headed to the snack bar to meet Luke for dinner. From a distance, I could see him greeting students and shaking their hands like they'd been gone for months and not a four-day weekend. I could've watched him all night, but the crowd eventually thinned, and Luke smiled when he saw me.

"There you are." He reached for my hand. "Shall we go in?"

Luke didn't let go until he'd told each person at the snack bar about our engagement. "This is my soul mate…God blessed me with Kate…we haven't set a date yet…"

An older woman I'd never met before put her hand on my back. "Your face is glowing."

I felt it. A powerful light inside me reached out to each person that congratulated us.

Once we were alone, we ate the dinner someone had treated us to. Between bites, Luke filled me in on the ride with his mother. I was still feeling joyful when he said, "So I told my mother it was time for her to pack up my childhood stuff and haul it off to Goodwill."

My joy vanished. I couldn't believe I'd forgotten about Bobbi for even one minute.

"What's wrong?"

"Bobbi's gone. And all of her things too."

Worry lines creased Luke's forehead. "What do you mean?"

"The last time I saw her was Wednesday when her mom came and picked her up for break. We all had lunch together before she left for vacation…everything seemed normal. But sometime yesterday, someone packed up her clothes, her bed, everything."

Luke shook his head. "That's really strange."

"I know. I've tried to call her home, but couldn't get through. I'm really worried about her. If you hear anything, will you let me know?"

"I sure will." He reached over and rubbed my shoulder. "I'm really sorry. This must be very hard for you."

After dinner, we heard Pastor Steve's sermon about being thankful to God. I tried to pay attention, but I didn't feel thankful. My mind wandered from Bobbi and then to Ma. *Dear God, I can't lose anyone else.*

On Monday morning, when Luke and I entered the chapel, the air buzzed around us. Sheila was right. Eyes followed our every move. I held on tightly to Luke's arm until we found our seats. The rest of the week was similar. Students who'd never spoken to me before treated me differently. Some saved seats for me in class while others invited me to sit with them at lunch. Even the teachers hovered around me.

A downside to all the attention meant that Luke and I had no privacy, and I wanted to talk to him more about Bobbi. At the end of chapel on Friday morning, I grabbed Luke's arm. "Don't get up. Let everyone else go first."

He sat back and waited with me.

"Thank you. I feel like we haven't had a minute to ourselves all week."

"I know. I miss you too." Luke touched the side of my face. "I've got a full schedule all day, but I have an idea. You work tonight, right? What if I chauffeur you and we catch up in the car?"

"Why Jeeves, that's a dashing idea." I pointed my pinky in the air. "Pick me up in front of my country estate at 4:30."

"Yes, my lady."

"I shall need you to return for me at 9:05."

Luke stood and offered me his arm. "May I?"

Even though I'd wanted to talk now, I couldn't be mad at Luke. He was just too charming.

Luke arrived right on time to drive me to work. He got out and opened the door for me.

"I think this is the first time I've been in your car."

"You're right. You missed your big chance last weekend," he said.

"Do you know the way to the store?"

Luke gave me a thumbs-up and drove off campus. "How are you handling being half of The Ark's newest couple?"

"I'm trying to figure it out. Most everyone seems genuinely happy for us. I just hope I don't make any mistakes."

"Don't worry about that. Just be your wonderful self. Have you reached Bobbi yet?"

My shoulders sank. "No. Not yet. I tried a couple more times but couldn't get past the housekeeper. Have you heard anything?"

"The official word is that Bobbi had 'adjustment issues' and was asked to leave. Did she ever tell you why she came to The Ark?"

"When I asked, she said it was the same reason we're all here. What do you think?"

We stopped at a light, and Luke turned to me. "As much as I loved her energy and spirit, I don't think she wanted to be here."

Luke's words lined up with what Elizabeth had told me. *Was she sent to The Ark instead of jail because of her shoplifting problem?* I wished I could hear Bobbi's side.

"I still can't stop worrying about her."

"You're a good friend, but let's trust God to take care of her."

Luke was so in tune with his calling. Sometimes I wondered why he picked me. Most of the women at The Ark had been Christians for years and were more devout than me.

We pulled into a parking spot at the grocery store. "Can you say a prayer for Bobbi?"

"How about you pray?"

"Me?" I'd never prayed out loud in front of anyone before.

"Sure. As a pastor's wife you'll be asked to pray for the flock. This will be good practice." He saw my hesitation. "There's no wrong way to pray."

Luke took my hands. "Where's your ring?"

"It's a little loose. I didn't want to lose it at work. I've got it zipped in a safe place in my wallet."

"Let me take it back to the jeweler. They'll resize it for you."

"Thanks. Just half a size down should be perfect."

Luke put my ring into the inside pocket of his jacket and bowed his head. "Go ahead."

I closed my eyes. "Lord, we lift Bobbi to you in prayer. Guide her, protect her, and fill her heart with your love. Let her know we love her. Amen."

"Very nice. Praying is just like a two-way conversation with God. Remember to listen for his answer. Oh, I have something else to tell you." Luke grinned like a kid with a secret. "You know Caroline? She's the assistant at the high school. Well, she's leaving to have a baby soon. I told the principal all about you."

"I don't understand. What did you tell her?"

"They need to replace Caroline. I told her how you'd be perfect for the job. You're smart. A fast learner. And with a staff job, your tuition and room and board are all covered."

"I've never done anything like that."

"Working with the high school kids would be terrific experience for you."

My mind swirled trying to sort all these changes. "There's so much to think about."

"This is your decision to make. If you're interested, let me know, and I'll introduce you to the staff."

"Okay." He remembered to include me, and I loved him even more. "Thank you."

The rattle of shopping carts gave me a jolt. It was Nick, but he hadn't seen us yet.

"Time for me to go." I leaned over the console and kissed him on the lips. I hoped that being away from campus he'd try to really kiss me. We only touched lips for a few seconds, but the thought of Nick watching us made me feel a good kind of nervous.

Luke opened my door to help me out and wrapped me in his arms. I fell against him and hugged him tight before letting go.

Once in the store, I clocked in and went to my register. Nick stocked some paper bags at the end of my counter. "So, that your boyfriend?"

He did see us. I wanted to say *fiancé*, but held back. "That's Luke."

"That's quite a biblical name." Nick backed up a step. "Don't look so surprised. You're not the only one who's read the Bible."

"I'm sorry." Nick could be hard to predict.

"Maybe I've even been to a couple of your church services before."

I didn't believe him, but just then, a customer came through my line. I turned to say hello and jumped a foot. "Oh, you startled me." Luke had never shopped here before. "Is everything okay?"

Luke laughed. "Yes. Everything's fine. But you left something in my car, and I didn't know if you'd need it tonight." He pointed to my shoulder bag moving down the conveyer belt like a sack of potatoes.

"Oh, what a goof. Thanks for bringing it in." I stuffed it on a shelf under my register. The faster Luke left, the better. "I'll see you in a few hours."

"Hey, I'm Nick. I work nights with Kate."

Oh Lord, no.

"Nice to meet you. I'm Luke."

I held my breath while they shook hands. This was unbelievable. I prayed Nick wouldn't embarrass me.

"Nick, if you aren't going to a church in town, we'd love to invite you to worship with us at The Ark. We have two services every Sunday. Kate can fill you in on the details."

Luke had a self-assured way of talking about God without mentioning God's name. Someday I wanted to be able to speak that way.

"I'll sure think about it," Nick said.

Nick's buddying up to Luke made my stomach do a nervous flip. I watched them talk, nodding like a plastic bobble-head toy.

"Well, you two have a great night. And Nick, thanks for keeping an eye out for my girl."

"No worries. Kate's like a sister to me."

I wanted to pull Luke out of the store as fast I could, but stood motionless until he finally walked out to his car.

"I'm like a sister?" I shook my head.

"I've got work to do in the stockroom." And without another word, he left.

With Nick gone, I'd have to bag my own groceries. He confused me. It reminded me of a Bible verse in Corinthians about God not bringing confusion, but peace. Luke brought peace. I tried to keep that in my head instead of thinking about Nick.

The night dragged without Nick's help. He didn't come back until a few minutes before closing time. Tired and grumpy, I stretched side to side to get rid of the kinks in my back.

"Are you mad at me?" He spoke in a fake caring voice.

"Nope. I'm doing just fine." My arms burned from shoving groceries into paper bags.

"Oh yeah, Wanda gave me a phone message for you. It's from Luke." He stretched out Luke's name into extra syllables. "I got a little busy out back and forgot to give it to you."

Nick dug into the back pocket of his jeans and pulled out a folded piece of paper. "Just so you know, the answer is yes."

The paper was warm and curved like his butt. The urge to drop it was strong, but I resisted and read the note printed in Wanda's style of all caps.

KATE – SO SORRY. EMERGENCY PRAYER MEETING.
CAN THAT NICE GUY NICK GIVE YOU A RIDE HOME?
IF NOT, CALL ME AT PASTOR'S ASAP 603-234-1125
LUKE 7:00 PM

The note was written two hours ago. This wasn't Luke's fault, but I wished he'd just pick me up like we had planned. I shook my head thinking that if Nick and I were forest animals, he'd be the sly fox, and I'd be the dumb bunny.

Nick and his long eyelashes watched me. "Is that how it is there? You'll always be second?"

I hid my hurt. He wouldn't understand. "God always comes first." I smoothed my smock. "Both Luke and I appreciate your offer to drive me back to school."

"Meet you outside in fifteen minutes."

The walk to Nick's truck went in slow motion. He didn't open the door for me, so I got in and climbed up onto the long bench seat. In high school, the girls in PE class said bench seats were make out seats. I scooted close to the door. Nick started the truck and a song by Queen blared out of the radio. We reached for the volume at the same time, and Nick noticed my scratched wrist.

"Geez, is that from bagging groceries tonight?"

I gave him my best sneer and ignored the question.

Nick drove fast. I had to force myself not to tell him he was breaking the speed limit.

"So what's it like living there? The townies say it's a cult, you know. That whatever that Carlson guy preaches, you believe it like he's God." He glanced back and forth between me and the road.

That's what Ma said too. "The Ark is not a cult. We are devout. That is not the same thing as being brainwashed."

"So what happens if someone does something wrong? Do they get excommunicated back to the real world?"

That stopped me. "It's not a perfect place." My voice broke and the tears that came surprised me. I fumbled through my jacket pockets for a tissue.

Nick pulled over. "Whoa, are you crying? Shit. What'd I say?"

"I'm okay. You just made me think about a friend from school. Something happened and they made her leave." *Crap, why did I tell Nick that?*

"That sucks. Are you still allowed to be her friend?"

"Of course I am." I took a few breaths to calm myself down. "But I can't reach her."

"Why not?"

"I can't get past her housekeeper. She's like a guard dog." I sighed.

"I bet I can."

"How?"

Nick's face lit up. "If I can get her on the phone in five minutes, will you have a real drink with me?"

"Like in a bar? You know I don't do that, plus I'm underage."

"Don't worry about that part."

"And what makes you think you can get her on the phone if I can't?"

"I'm very persuasive." Nick radiated confidence. "So what's her name?"

"Bobbi. Her name is Bobbi." Saying her name out loud made me miss her more. "Okay, one drink, and I get to choose it. Then you drive me right back to The Ark."

This was a deal with a fox, but I didn't have to drink the drink. I'd show him. I wasn't going to be a stupid bunny.

CHAPTER 27

NICK DROVE DOWN A ROAD I'd never seen before. After a few minutes, he pulled into a dirt parking lot in front of a long wooden building. There were no signs on it except a neon one in the front window that flashed OPEN. Pickup trucks and motorcycles filled most of the spaces. Warning bells rang in my head—only tough guys rode bikes in the winter.

"I'm not sure about this…"

"Don't freak out. It's nicer inside. Half the place is a restaurant. Families eat here."

No families drove in on those bikes or ate dinner after nine at night. I followed close behind Nick, scanning the lot for potential trouble. When he opened the bar door, warm air and tinny country music welcomed us.

"What's the name of this place?"

"It's called No Name."

"Huh?"

"The full name is The No Name Bar & Grill."

I imagined a newspaper headline: *Missing Student from The Ark Last Seen at No Name*. It wasn't too late; I could still leave.

Nick must've seen me hesitate. "Ladies first. Pick wherever you'd like to sit."

"Can we sit over in the restaurant side?"

"Not if we're just drinking."

Great. Most of the bar tables were full of guys who looked like carnival roadies in need of dental work. One of them had the longest beard I'd ever seen and tattoos up both his arms. He caught me staring and winked. I kept my head down until we reached an empty table in a corner. Nick took the seat facing the door.

"Where's the pay phone?" I said, craning my neck in all directions.

"Pay phone? Are you a cavewoman?" Nick slapped the table. "Folks round here have cell phones." He looked toward the bar and waved. "We need to order our drinks first."

I wanted to point out that he hadn't called Bobbi yet, but a waitress was rushing over to our table. She wore a denim mini skirt, short cowboy boots, and a tank top that showed a mile of cleavage.

"Hi there. What can I get you?" She pulled an order pad and a pencil out of her bra.

My eyes must've popped out because she laughed at me like a honking goose. "Oh honey, you wouldn't believe what I can fit in here."

"I'll have whatever's on tap. Kate, what are you having?" Nick spoke like we were old drinking pals.

"Um." I looked up at the waitress willing her to card me, but she didn't. "Can you recommend something sweet that's not too strong?"

"Sure. Sounds like you want a pina colada."

After she walked away, I lowered my voice. "I can't believe what she's wearing."

"What's wrong with it?"

"It makes her look cheap and easy."

Nick sat back and stared at me. "Lighten up on the judgment. You know nothing about her. What do they teach you at that school?"

"You're right." Score one for the worldly guy.

The waitress rushed back with two glasses of water and pretzels. "Drinks will be up in a minute."

Nick stood up. "Okay, now let's go make that call."

I wrote Bobbi's number on a napkin and handed it to him. We left the bar area and wound our way to a table in the deserted restaurant.

"Make sure you ask for Roberta."

Nick pointed for me to sit and stepped away. After a few seconds, I could tell he'd gotten through and heard him laughing. I could hardly believe it. He was all smiles when he came back and we high-fived.

I took his phone and walked across the dining room for privacy. "Bobbi?"

"Kate, I can't believe it's you. Who was that?" I could hear happiness in her voice. I loved that voice. Frozen pieces inside of me started to melt.

"It's Nick from work."

"The one you kissed?"

"Forget about him. I've been trying to call you. Your housekeeper lady wouldn't put me through."

"My parents must've told her to screen all my calls from The Ark."

"Why? What happened? Why'd you leave school?"

"What's the rumor mill saying?"

"You had adjustment issues." I couldn't tell her what Elizabeth said.

Bobbi lowered her voice. "Oh, that's just like them."

"I miss you so much. We need to see each other."

"Listen, we'll be in Hartford next week. Can you come visit me there? It's only a three-hour drive. And stay the night. Please Kate, say you'll come." Her voice rose with excitement.

"I will, I will. Give me the directions." As I jotted them down, Nick motioned for his phone back. "Shoot, I have to go. I can't wait to see you."

"Kate, don't tell them you're coming. Please, promise."

"Okay, I promise." We said our goodbyes, and I wondered why she wanted me to keep my visit a secret. We had so much to catch up on. I didn't even get to tell her about my engagement to Luke.

Making our way back to the bar, I thanked God that I'd talked to Bobbi. Next, I had to thank Nick.

"I'd sure like to make you look that happy every day," Nick said as we sat down.

Typical Nick. "Thank you for reaching Bobbi. It means a lot to me. So how'd you do it?" I flicked my hair over my shoulders and leaned in. *Oh God, am I flirting with him?*

"Easy. I told the housekeeper that Bobbi had won a prize on a radio station."

I clapped my hands together. "That's perfect."

"Then," he paused. His dark eyes held my gaze. "I told Bobbi the prize was you."

Nick, don't you dare be adorable now. The word *sexy* tumbled inside my head. My face felt hot, and I couldn't look at him. The waitress saved me by setting down our drinks. Mine had pineapple on the rim and a miniature yellow umbrella in it.

"Thanks. This is pretty." I swirled the straw and asked God to forgive me in advance for the sin of drinking alcohol.

Nick held up his glass of beer. "To Bobbi."

We clinked and I took a sip. My drink tasted just like a coconut and pineapple milkshake. I didn't say anything, but the bartender obviously forgot to put alcohol in it. There'd be no sinning here tonight. In fact, the night was almost over and nothing horrible had happened. The people in the bar weren't too scary, and I'd spoken with Bobbi. Soon, I'd be back at The Ark safe and sound.

My drink gave me brain freeze, but I drank it as fast as I could. When it was nearly gone, it occurred to me that I hadn't checked the time for a while. If I didn't get back by eleven, I'd be breaking curfew. I couldn't tell Nick that. He'd call me a baby and laugh in my face.

"Damn. You drank that like a pro. Sure this is your first time in a bar?" He signaled to the waitress for another round.

"No. Please, no."

Nick ignored me. My body shivered at the thought of another cold drink, and I covered my shoulders with my jacket. The DJ played a set of Neil Diamond songs, and we sang along with the rest of the bar to "Sweet Caroline." The singing made me thirsty and without realizing it, I'd sucked down my second drink.

The clock over the bar read fifteen minutes after ten. "Nick, we gotta go."

"Let me pay up." He signaled for the bill, paid, and left a big tip.

I must've stood up too fast because my head felt woozy. I covered my forehead with my hand.

"Are you okay?" Nick said.

"My brain's frozen."

"Yep, that's what's wrong. Need help?"

My arms couldn't find the sleeves of my jacket, and I swayed. Nick came over to help me put it on. Then, he slid his arm around my waist. It felt good there as he steered me toward the door.

"Let's get you out of here."

Outside, I breathed in the cool air. The ground looked slippery. "Did it snow?"

"No. Just walk, we're almost there."

Nick didn't let me fall. What a nice guy he was. When he opened the truck door, I couldn't figure out how to climb in. My legs and arms didn't work right. *God, am I drunk?*

"Oh brother." Nick lifted me up off the ground like a child and placed me on the seat. He shut the door and walked away with his shoulders shaking.

"He better not be laughing at me," I said to the windshield.

A few seconds later Nick was in the truck. He didn't say a word as I fumbled with the seatbelt. I couldn't figure out how to get the metal part to click in. "I think it's broken."

He smiled at me. "That's not the problem."

"Well, then help me."

Nick slid across the bench seat and took the buckle out of my hand. Instead of belting me in, he let it go. His arm ended up around my shoulder and he pulled me close. He smelled of leather and the forest. I should've pushed him away, but I didn't.

He lips softly kissed mine. I reached up to touch his hair, the hair he ran his fingers through when he told a joke. Nick nuzzled against my neck, sending shivers down my back.

A rapping noise on the driver's window made us freeze.

The truck windows had fogged up, but I recognized the shape. It was Charlie, the janitor. I buried my face in Nick's chest.

Damn, shit, crap.

CHAPTER 28

"OH NO, I'M IN BIG TROUBLE. It's the janitor from The Ark."

Nick sat back. "Relax. I don't think he saw you."

I covered my face with my hands. "I looked right at him. What are we going to do?"

"Jump in the back and get on the floor. There's some tarp. Cover yourself."

"This is your best idea?"

"Just do it. Hurry up."

I hurled myself over. Nick opened his door and got out. "Hey, old timer. Can I help you?"

Covering myself with the stiff tarp wasn't easy. A paintbrush poked my neck and it stank like turpentine. The two of them had to be right outside my door because I heard them talking.

"Hey I saw the Russo Painting sign on the truck and was looking for your old man. Which son are you?"

"I'm his oldest, Nick."

"Well, I'll be. You look just like he did back when we played ball together. How is he?"

"He's doing fine. Business is a little slow in the winter. Mostly indoor work now…"

Enough chit chat, let's get out of here. I'm going to die of these fumes. It would serve me right. God should punish me. He gave me a wonderful man who wanted to marry me and what did I do? *I'm a bad person. A sinner who drank and made out with Nick. Now I'm going to get kicked out just like Bobbi.*

"…I'll tell my dad I ran into you."

"Tell him Knuckleball Charlie said hi." They laughed.

Nick got back in the truck and lifted the tarp off of me. "You're safe. He went into the bar."

Now I knew why Charlie had bad breath. I climbed back to the front seat. The truck clock was stuck on ten past seven. My watch read 10:30 p.m. "Drive, Nick. We've got to go straight to The Ark."

"You need to sober up."

"Then help me. What do I do?" My head felt like the slushy drink.

"Coffee would be a good start. My house is around the corner. If you promise to be quiet, I'll make you some."

"I promise." I didn't like coffee, but I'd do anything to feel normal again. A few minutes later we pulled into the driveway of his house, and Nick cut the engine.

"Now listen. Everyone's asleep. My dad gets up really early." He put his finger to his lips. I copied him. Then he got out and opened my door for me.

"My room is in the basement." His voice was just above a whisper. "I'll take you there, and then I'll go up to the kitchen and make you some coffee. But you need to be quiet. Do you understand?"

"Yes. I understand. I'm not stupid. I just drank too much." I thought my robot voice was funny, but Nick didn't react. He led me to the side of his house where some stairs went into the ground like the rabbit hole in *Alice in Wonderland*. I held on to the back of his jacket for balance.

Nick pushed open a small wooden door without making a sound. He switched on a light. I'd never been in a guy's bedroom before…maybe this wasn't a good idea.

"I'll be right back." Nick pushed piles of clothes off his bed onto the cement floor. "Go ahead. Sit down."

Posters of rock bands decorated the walls. A laundry basket full of folded clothes sat on the floor near his bureau. I bet his momma did his laundry. An odd smell filled the room.

"Is that licorice or something?"

"Yeah. I knocked over a bottle of Sambuca and it rolled under my bed."

"Gross, how long ago?"

"Can't remember." Nick shrugged off his jacket and tossed it on his bed. I wiggled out of mine. He smiled at me and sat on the edge of the bed. When he bent to pull off his boots, I beat him and slipped out of mine first.

Nick stood and lifted his shirt over his head. I made a squeak noise, but didn't move. His chest was smooth and toned. I wanted to touch it. He raised my arms in the air, and I let him lift my sweater over my head. A voice, softer than a sigh, told me this was wrong.

He pulled me to my feet. His fingers traced my spine and my back arched. Tingles rushed over my skin wherever he touched me. I wrapped my arms around him, and our stomachs touched. I could barely breathe.

Nick's voice was hot in my ear. "Do you want to do this?" I nodded yes. He undressed me and laid me on his bed. In a second, he was naked beside me. The booze fought my morals. Good and bad were confused. Good Kate was boring. Bad Kate wanted Nick.

The more Nick kissed and touched me, the deeper I fell. He turned from me and fumbled for something in his nightstand. I reached for him, not wanting to be separated for a moment.

I heard a ripping sound. Nick thought about protection. Birth control was the farthest thing from my mind. My body trembled for him. I was completely helpless, and Nick was completely in charge.

Afterward, when we both were panting and covered in sweat, Nick propped himself up to look at me. "That was great. Stay the night with me."

Oh, God. The runaway train of my night finally crashed. Guilt and regret spilled everywhere. It wasn't supposed to be Nick. Luke was the one I was supposed to marry. I'd given away my virginity so easily.

"Nick." My voice cracked. "What have I done?"

He wrapped me tight in his arms. "You've made me very happy."

"No, no. I'm engaged to Luke." My tears blurred his face. "Please, take me back. Don't ever tell anyone what we did."

Nick let go of me. I rolled away to find my clothes, not wanting to believe what had just happened, but the soreness in my body said otherwise.

We drove in silence back to campus. I got out of the truck without Nick's help, and he sped off without once looking back.

Alone in the cold night air, my shame weighed on me like a heavy cloak. *Please God, don't let this ruin everything. Please forgive me.*

I unlocked the dorm door with hopes of showering every trace of Nick off my body. Then I'd pray all night for forgiveness to get out of the sinful Hell I'd fallen into. Fallen. I was a fallen woman.

As I tiptoed away from the front door, Sheila sprang out of the common area, nearly scaring me to death. She wore her coat and held her Bible in the crook of her arm. The wrath of God shone in her eyes.

"I know I'm late. I'm really sorry."

"Where've you been? Luke's been worried about you." Her voice bordered on screechy.

"Look, I'm here. Everything's fine."

I didn't want to have this conversation with her and headed toward the hallway. She hooked her arm in mine like a square dancing partner and swung me around.

"Hey, I'm tired. Please let go of me."

"No. Luke asked me to bring you to Pastor Steve's house as soon as you got back."

This couldn't be happening. I looked at Sheila with begging eyes, but she seemed to be enjoying her role as the righteous one. Every part of me wanted to push her up against the wall and tell her to mind her own friggin' business.

"Let's go," she said. "They're all waiting for you."

CHAPTER 29

"WHO'S WAITING FOR ME?" I tried to pull away from Sheila's bossy grip.

"Pastor Steve. Luke. Elizabeth." She spoke as if I was one of the handicapped children from her job.

"Why?"

"You don't understand, do you?" She stopped and looked me straight in the eye.

Exhaustion made me snap. "Just tell me."

Sheila let go of my arm. "As unmarried Christian women, we have to be extra careful when we are out in the world. The worldly ones don't have our values. We are pure. They are unclean. You're connected to the Carlson family now. If anything happened to you tonight, the entire campus would be affected."

I tried not to flinch when she said unclean. The only way I'd get through this was by pulling myself together, staying strong, and not giving anyone ammunition to use against me. My sin was between me and God. Luke was the best thing that ever happened to me, and I couldn't lose him. I couldn't even think about it.

Sheila and I trudged along without speaking. As we approached Pastor Steve's house, the front door popped open without warning. Elizabeth stood there, her face wooden, and my heart dropped even more. Sheila turned and left us.

Inside, Elizabeth hovered but seemed afraid to touch me. I blew into my cupped hands and smelled pineapples. When she asked for my jacket, I shook my head. She might smell Nick. I willed myself to stay calm because I sure couldn't ask God for any help.

"Come with me," Elizabeth said. I followed her into the living room, and we sat on the couch. All the lights in the room were on. I missed the Elizabeth who joked with me, not this version who seemed afraid of me.

"I'm sorry for—" I said, but she put her hand up to shush me.

She studied me for a few moments before speaking. "Is there anything you want to tell me first before we go up to Pastor Steve's study?"

Oh, not his study again. I kept my hands in my lap. "Honestly, I'm fine. I'm sorry to have caused you all this worry."

Elizabeth crossed her legs under her long skirt and tugged at the sleeves of her top.

I looked her in the eye. "Luke knows who I was with. I haven't been harmed." *Oh God, forgive me for my choice of words.*

She let out a long exhale. "Thank the Lord. Let's go up. Poor Luke's a mess."

My pulse hammered in my ears. The last time I climbed these stairs was after Luke's proposal. It seemed like that happened months ago, not weeks ago. We entered the study where Pastor Steve and Luke stood, their faces lined with worry. I put that worry there.

"She's good," Elizabeth said.

I didn't have time to decipher her words because Luke rushed toward me. He wrapped his arms around me.

"You're my priority. I should've put you first. I'm so sorry." He trembled as he held me. "I was wrong to trust someone else to look after you. Please forgive me."

The way he held me filled me with a warm peace. God was peace, and God wanted us to be together. I'd made a mistake, but I'd be forgiven. I could go on. Pastor Steve interrupted and asked us to take a seat. He leaned against the front of his desk. Elizabeth kissed him quickly on the cheek and left.

"Kate, we are extremely relieved that you've arrived back to campus safely. Whenever one of our flock goes missing, we worry. When it is one of our young women, we worry much more. Please tell us why you're so late returning to campus tonight."

I looked at Luke for help. He reached for my hand.

"If we know what happened, we can guide you and pray for you. You can trust us, you're loved here."

Part of my night involved Bobbi. My head cleared enough to hatch a plan.

I spoke to Luke. "You asked if Nick could drive me and he agreed. During the ride here, we spoke about The Ark. The subject of Bobbi came up. I've had trouble getting hold of her so Nick offered to help and he was successful."

Pastor Steve lifted his arms and cracked his knuckles behind his head. "I don't understand why you'd ask a worldly person to help you contact Ms. Young. Why didn't you come to me?"

I shook free of Luke's hand. "Because she came here for help. And instead of getting help, she got sent away."

"While I admire your passion, Ms. Young was not here voluntarily, nor was she saved. We accepted her because we believed in the power of God to reach her. But when I discerned that she wasn't going to accept Jesus as her personal savior, we had no other choice."

I studied his face. "I thought only God truly knew a person's heart."

Pastor Steve gave me a slight nod. "This is true, but I met with Ms. Young weekly and she didn't believe."

Bobbi hadn't said a word to me about any meetings with him. All my energy drained away. "Luke, please walk me back to my dorm."

Pastor Steve interrupted, "I know this has been a long night for you. But we have more work to do here. I'll ask Elizabeth to make us some tea and give you two a few minutes alone."

After he left, I grabbed Luke's arm. "Please. I want to leave. I'm so tired. Can't we finish this tomorrow?"

"Oh Katie Pie, I know this is a challenging time for you, but it's during these times that we grow as Christians. When we feel we can't go on, that's when God reveals himself more fully to us."

I leaned back on the couch, crossed my arms over my chest, and tried not to hate the good part of Luke. He was a saint, and despite my sin, he needed me to be a golden woman.

"Please know that no one blames you for anything." He waited until I faced him before continuing. "I caused this. I should've picked you up. It's my fault and I take full responsibility."

Pastor Steve came back carrying three mugs of tea. Mint scented the air as he put them down on the coffee table. He pulled a side chair over so we were all at the same level.

The hot mug warmed my hands, and I shrugged off my coat. A prayer session loomed in my near future, and I hoped after that I'd finally be able to leave. It was creeping toward midnight.

Pastor Steve leaned forward. "As a servant of Christ and a shepherd of The Ark, I counsel, comfort, and care for the needs of the ministry. It's a job I love. Because the temptations of the world are many, it's important for my disciples to stay in the center of God's will. You are both blood-bought recipients of God's grace. Do you want to stay in the center of God's will?"

We said yes.

"God is speaking to my heart and telling me that we should not prolong your sacred union."

My hands shook and the tea sloshed around in my mug. I set it on the table.

"Until we set that date, Kate—for your safety and protection— if you have to leave campus, you should do so with a member of The Ark. I do not think it wise for you to continue your secular job either. Any financial obligations you have to the school will be cleared. You can start the position at the high school as soon as you'd like."

A hot spark flickered inside me at his words, but I had to control my anger. Luke pressed his warm hand on my tapping knee.

"Kate and I will pray together over your recommendations."

I put my hand over his. *Yes, Luke. Thank you.*

"Speaking of prayer, I'd like to do a laying on of hands to thank God for Kate's safe return and for his blessings on you both."

This was my first experience with laying on of hands, and I followed Luke's lead. We stood in the middle of the study and bowed our heads. Pastor Steve stood behind us gripping our shoulders.

"As I pray silently for you, imagine the pure light of God washing over you. Let that light fill your heart. Wrap yourself in God's love."

I prayed for my sin with Nick to be washed away and for God's forgiveness to clean my soul. After a few moments, the room seemed to tilt. I leaned against Luke for support, and he put his arm around my waist. My eyelids were too heavy to keep open. The next thing I knew, both Luke and Pastor Steve had me by my elbows.

"I've got her." Pastor Steve held me firm against his body as I struggled to stand on my own. "Grab a chair."

"Let me go. I'm okay," I said.

Pastor Steve pulled me tighter. I felt his nose in my hair and his breath on my neck. Was he trying to sniff out my sin? Luke put the chair in back of me, and Pastor Steve released me.

"Welcome back." Luke rubbed my back. If I had a spiritual experience, I didn't remember it.

"Luke, Kate, our work tonight is done." Pastor Steve faced me. "Kate, I know you're anxious to return to your dorm, but it's against campus rules to be out this late. You can spend the night in the workout room." He must've seen my raised eyebrows. "Don't worry, there's a twin bed in there. Elizabeth will get you something to wear. Luke, you're welcome to one of the couches downstairs."

"Goodnight." He patted my head and left the study.

A question floated back to me from before the laying of the hands. I stood up to face Luke. "If something bad had happened to me, if I had been violated, would you still marry me?"

His face drained of color. "Oh, Kate. I can't bear to think about that."

The moon shone through the sheer curtains on the windows. When I sat up, my dark reflection stared back from the mirrored wall. I wondered if Elizabeth still practiced her ballet poses in front of it. Sleep eluded me as my night with Nick kept replaying. The way my body wanted him scared me.

My thoughts careened in super-speed. Would Luke be able to tell I wasn't a virgin? Elizabeth said I was the first girl he'd ever brought to a holiday celebration. If he was a virgin too, then he might not know. But then Nick didn't seem to know either, and there'd been no blood.

Charlie's face in the truck window zoomed into my mind. What did he see? I wanted to blame Nick, but it wasn't his fault. He bought the drinks, but he didn't pour them down my throat. All of Pastor Steve's sermons against drinking made sense now. Alcohol was the devil's drink. If I took the staff job, I could give notice at Price Chopper. In two weeks, the Nick temptation would be gone.

My watch read two in the morning. Staying in bed any longer seemed ridiculous. The house was cold, too cold for just Elizabeth's thin nightgown, so I put my clothes back on. I'd just go down to the den, find a magazine, and bring it back to the room to read. When my eyes adjusted to the darkness in the hallway, I headed down the stairs.

I found a light switch for a table lamp in the entryway and flicked it on. Luke must have gone back to his dorm because all the couches were empty. He could leave, but I had to stay.

By the fireplace, I found a pile of magazines and took them to the couch to browse through. Just as I opened the first one, a creaking sound above startled me. It was too heavy to be Elizabeth. This night would never end.

"Guess that makes two of us who can't sleep," Pastor Steve said as he entered the den.

I was surprised to see him in dark sweatpants and a frayed white T-shirt, but of course, he didn't sleep in his shirt, tie, and dress pants.

"Sorry, did I make too much noise?" The informality of seeing Pastor Steve like this unbalanced me. *Breathe in, breathe out.*

"No. It wasn't you. I often get inspiration for my sermons in the middle of the night. Rather than fight it, I get up and write it." He laughed at his rhyme. "My night wanderings used to drive Elizabeth crazy. Now, she sleeps right through them. I'm going to make some more tea. Would you like some?"

I nodded and followed him into the kitchen. As he walked toward the stove, the resemblance to Luke hit me again. Even though Pastor Steve wasn't as tall, they shared the same bend of the back, muscular shoulders, and strong arms.

The best thing for me to do was act normal, except I didn't know what normal was at two in the morning, with Pastor Steve in the kitchen, and a screeching teakettle. It could've been a scenario from the Clue board game.

He poured the hot water, and I couldn't help think of Ma and all the times I poured her a cup of tea. She'd never once asked me if I wanted to join her.

Pastor Steve placed a mug in front of me. "Here you go. Pick your flavor from the tin."

While I sorted through the packets, he brought over a sugar bowl and some spoons. I noticed his bare forearm as he reached for a teabag. There was something too intimate about seeing it. His arm had swirly hair just like Luke's.

A cat-shaped clock on the wall swung its tail back and forth. "It's so quiet you can hear the clock ticking," I said.

Pastor Steve stirred some sugar in his mug. "It makes me think of Psalm 46: 'Be still, and know that I am God.'"

My mouth stayed still.

"This is good. Finding you up. I wanted to talk to you. Alone."

Oh, no. Here it comes. Charlie must've told Pastor Steve what he saw, and Pastor Steve didn't want to say it in front of Luke. I looked at the sugar bowl to avoid his eyes. He was going to kick me out just like he kicked out Bobbi. *Dear God, help me.*

"When Luke first told me about you, I knew he was in love. I wondered though, why did he choose you?"

I squirmed inside, not wanting to hear the next words. Wanting to bolt out the door and never look back.

"You look nervous. Don't be. I see what Luke sees, what a good match you'll make—your strength, your fighting skills, your intuition—these gifts will balance him."

What did he say? I'm a good match? My mind raced to catch up.

"Luke is fine pastor material, but I worry about how easily he trusts people. There are risks with that. One example is the risk he took letting that Nick character drive you home."

I stole a glance at Pastor Steve and saw a kind expression on his face.

"Maybe it was his mother. Beverly tried her best, but she made Luke her whole world. The way she doted on him. I thought she'd make him too soft." He stopped to sip his tea. "So I tried to be the father he didn't have. Encouraged him to try out for sports. Basketball stuck. Luke wasn't a natural, but he had the height and the discipline. How he practiced and practiced. He wanted me to be proud of him. And I was. I am." Pastor Steve wrapped both his hands around his mug. "Stand by him, but challenge him. You can do that, right?"

I met his eyes. "Yes I can."

His face turned solemn. "How are you and your family doing?"

"Not very good." I rubbed the handle of my mug. "It's my dad. He blames me for what happened to my mother." I hadn't shared this with anyone.

The clock ticked.

"Let's not give up on him. You may think he's given up on you, but I bet he feels abandoned. Two women he's loved dearly have left him. One involuntarily and one by choice."

A thin ray of light crept into the dark place where I stored my hurt. A single tear trickled down my cheek and I wiped at it. "I'm sorry."

"Don't be ashamed of your emotions. They're a beautiful part of being a woman, especially when they're full of hope."

His words touched me, and it felt like God touched me, all the way to my heart. If only Dad could've shown me that he cared about me after Ma died.

Pastor Steve stood. "I'll leave you with your thoughts. Oh, and you have permission to miss chapel in the morning. I know the guy who's speaking." He smiled and left the kitchen.

As I sipped my cool tea, I realized that Pastor Steve didn't try anything creepy with me, not even an awkward goodnight hug. Maybe I'd just overthought all those other times.

An image of two bridges filled my thoughts. The nearest one was the bridge to trusting Pastor Steve again. The other one was so far away, I could barely see it. It was the bridge to reconciliation with Dad.

CHAPTER 30

THE NEXT MORNING it took a few seconds for me to remember where I was. Then all the details of the past night tumbled back: my sin with Nick, being dragged to this house, my attempt to convince everyone I was fine, and the unexpected conversation I had with Pastor Steve.

For the third time in twenty-four hours, I put on the same clothes. I couldn't wait to go back to my dorm to shower and change.

The silence in Pastor Steve's house told me I was alone. Chapel had already started and for once I was glad to miss it. With a pounding headache and empty stomach, I headed for the kitchen. I craved bacon and eggs, but settled for a large glass of orange juice and a banana.

On my way out, I couldn't resist the opportunity to call Bobbi on their phone. If I got her housekeeper, I'd have to think fast like Nick. *Oh Nick, I can't think about you anymore.*

"Young residence. May I help you?"

"I'm trying to reach Roberta Young," I said.

"Who may I say is calling?"

"This is her hair salon. I'd like to confirm her appointment."

"Wait one minute."

A sleepy voice answered the phone. "Hello."

"Guess who? Me again. Are you still in bed?"

"Good one with the hair salon." Bobbi yawned. "You're still coming to Hartford, right?"

I hesitated. "I don't think I can. I caused a big commotion last night because I missed curfew. Sheila was waiting for me, and she marched me straight to Pastor Steve's house."

"First of all, she's a bitch, and second, were you having fun without me?"

"It's a long story that I can only tell you in person. But Luke and Elizabeth were there, and after a major prayer session, Pastor Steve pretty much laid down the law that I don't leave campus alone."

The phone stayed quiet. I heard a door shut.

"He doesn't control your life."

"I know. He wants to protect me, but forget about that for a second. I completely forgot to tell you my big news. Luke asked me to marry him over Thanksgiving."

I waited for her happy scream but only heard breathing. "Bobbi?"

"Wow, Kate. I knew he liked you, but that happened fast."

"I know, but it's so wonderful. We haven't set a date yet or anything. I should probably get off this phone. I'm at Pastor Steve's house, someone might come home."

"Why are you *there*?" Bobbi sounded freaked out.

"After the prayer session, it was too late for me to go to the dorm so I slept in their guest room."

"Holy shit. Listen to me. I'm telling you this as a friend who really cares about you. You can't trust him."

I wanted to ask her about her weekly meetings with Pastor Steve, but couldn't interrupt her.

"Kate, this is important. Promise me you won't marry Luke before you see me. Promise?"

In my mind, I saw her pacing and tossing her hair over her shoulders. "I promise. Are you doing okay?"

"We'll be skiing over Christmas week, call me before then."

After we said our goodbyes, I thought about how different our lives at The Ark turned out to be.

I took a chance and made one more call. The only way to get Nick out of my life was to quit the grocery store and take whatever staff job they offered me at The Ark.

"Price Chopper, Wanda speaking."

"Hi. I'm so glad I caught you. This is Kate Bennett."

"What's up? Did you forget your hours for the week?"

"No, it's not that." Christmas music played in the background. "I've got another job and need to give notice. I'm so sorry."

"Hey, relax." Wanda's voice softened. "You're not the first fish to jump out of the pond. But you could really help me out by coming in tonight. I've got a new gal starting and you can train her. If that goes well, you're off the hook for two weeks' notice." She laughed at her pun.

"Really? Great. Thanks so much for understanding."

"It's okay, hon." She hung up.

I licked my dry lips. That went great. But what if Nick was

there? The thought of seeing him made my stomach flip-flop. I couldn't look him in the eye or imagine what he thought of me. Ma would've said, "You screwed this up royally."

I got to my dorm, showered, and made it to my Old Testament class with a minute to spare. Repentance was the topic for today's discussion. I slid down my desk chair and listened to Paul Carlson speak.

"In Proverbs, Solomon wrote that we cannot receive God's mercy unless we confess our sins to him. But it is not just a matter of confessing our sins, we must also forsake the sin."

His words hit my soul like a branding iron. I couldn't wait for the class to end.

During a break between classes, I rushed over to the high school gym where Luke coached the boys' team. His face lit up when he noticed me. I wanted to run into his arms and hug him tight, but we weren't alone. A few boys leaned against the side of the building and watched us.

"How are you? Heard you had a late night." Luke's smile was infectious.

"I'm wonderful. I called the store and gave notice. My boss said I just have to work tonight and train my replacement." I clasped my hands together. "Can you drive me?"

"First, great news on work. And, not only will I drive you, I promise I'll pick you up right on time." He crossed his heart for emphasis.

A happy sigh escaped. Everything was going to work out fine.

By the time Luke picked me up for work, I'd rehearsed a bunch of conversations in my head in case I saw Nick. None of them seemed right. I couldn't exactly tell him he was a sin that I needed to forsake.

Luke noticed my quiet mood. "Are you sad about saying goodbye to everyone?"

"I'm not sure I was a good witness for The Ark."

"Don't underestimate how God uses us in the world. I'm sure, even though you've only worked there a short time, you've made a difference."

Oh, Luke, how do I deserve you?

He got out and opened my door. "Now don't be late and get fired." His goofy side was alive and well. "I'll be here ten minutes early to pick you up."

"I know you will."

Luke's goodbye hug was the best part of my day.

Inside the store, I could feel every muscle in my neck and shoulders tighten as I looked around for Nick. My nerves calmed when I realized he wasn't near the registers. I'd be bagging for the new person.

Wanda introduced me to Betty. She was an older lady who chattered nonstop. After a couple of hours, Betty seemed to have a handle on everything and I took a break.

As I walked by the warehouse doors, Nick came out pushing a two-wheeler stacked with produce boxes and stopped. *God help me.* I couldn't think about his body and mine together.

"You probably don't want to talk to me ever again." I stumbled over my words. "But, I'm leaving…I mean this is my last night here. What I'm trying to say is I've got a job on campus."

"Good for you." Nick shoved his hands into his jean pockets. "Is that your choice?"

"What do you mean?"

"Now you'll live, study, and work there."

I nodded.

"And you don't see anything wrong with that?"

"I'm weak. I need to be there all the time…to be stronger…"

Nick shook his head. "You'll be cut off from the rest of the world. Speaking of which, what does your family think about your engagement?"

I crossed my arms. "They don't know yet, but I'm going to tell them soon."

"You know, when love is real, you can't wait to tell everyone, especially your family." He took a step toward me. "And you aren't tempted by other guys either."

Nick's sharp words sent a bolt of heat up my neck to my face. Completely flustered, I turned and rushed away. I repeated "it will all be over soon" as I headed toward the breakroom.

I hid there until my break was over.

On our drive back to The Ark that night, headlights from an approaching car lit Luke's face. I loved his strong profile. After some small talk about my last night at the store, I grabbed the armrest.

"I haven't told my family about our engagement. I'm scared to call them. They're not going to be nice to me. I get the heebie-jee-bies just thinking about it."

We stopped at a light, and Luke reached over to touch my cheek. "I have an idea. Did you know that Pastor Wayne is ready to open his branch ministry? That warehouse he's been converting into a chapel is finally a real thing."

"That's such great news." I smiled remembering all the thrift shops Julie and I scoured trying to find items he needed for his office.

"Well, the building dedication is this weekend. Pastor Steve and Elizabeth are going. Why don't we go with them and make a side trip to your house? I'll meet your family. We can tell them together."

I leaned over and rested my head on Luke's shoulder. *Together.* I wouldn't have to do anything alone again.

"Thank you, Luke. You always know what to do."

Sprawled on my bed later that night, I searched in my wallet and found a photograph of me, Pam, and BB from an Easter long ago. Ma had dressed us in the yellow dresses she'd made, with white shoes, and bows in our hair. We stood perfectly matched in front of Gram's house. No flaws in the photo, only in real life.

Sheila came into the dorm. "What are you looking at?"

I handed her the picture.

"Is that you and your sisters? You're all so cute."

"Thanks." My voice cracked a little.

"Do you miss them?"

"I do. Luke and I are going to visit them this weekend."

Sheila rubbed her chin. "Do they know you're engaged yet?"

"No. I've haven't been able to tell them."

"Remember you've got Luke and God on your side. That's a powerful team. Why don't we pray?"

She placed the photo on the bed between us and put her warm hands around my cold ones like a prayer sandwich. I knew it was time to let go of the anger I'd been carrying against her. Blaming Sheila for something I did wrong wasn't what friends did to each other.

"Dear Lord, let us remember that you delivered your people from Egypt and you will deliver us from the burdens we entrust to you. Amen."

I leaned over and gave her a quick hug. "I'm going to call them right now."

It was close to ten, and someone would still be up. If Pam or BB answered, I'd tell them about Luke. If Dad picked up, I wouldn't. Once again, I plunked my coins in the lobby's ancient phone.

"Hello."

Dad. I took a deep breath. "Hi, it's me. Kate." Seconds passed. "Dad, are you there?"

"Yes. Anything wrong?"

"No. I'm good. How are you doing? How are the girls?" I never called my sisters the girls. It made me sound like a distant relative, or someone much older.

"Fine. We're all fine."

"The trip to Florida, how'd that go?"

"It was fine too. Why are you calling?"

Ma had trained me well. I couldn't lie. "This weekend I'll be close to home. I'd like to see everyone, and for you all to meet Luke, my fiancé."

I braced myself for the hurtful words. Nothing. His silence wounded me more.

"Dad?"

"Is he one of them?"

"Luke's a pastor-in-training at school."

I heard the rustle of his newspaper. "When are you coming and how long are you staying?"

"Saturday night. Just a short visit. After dinner, eight o'clock okay?"

"We'll be here. Is that it?"

His words pinned me against the wall. I'd wanted to talk to BB, but my mouth barely squeaked out, "Yes."

He said goodbye and hung up.

I reminded myself to breathe. Dad had agreed to the visit. It was a minor victory. He'd have a few days to prepare himself and my sisters. Whatever bad feelings they had for me, I could deal with them. But Luke, how could they not love him?

CHAPTER 31

LATE SATURDAY MORNING, I woke tangled in my sheets and remembered a vivid dream. I was inside my house searching for my bedroom. Nothing seemed familiar as I walked down endless hallways and passed unfamiliar rooms. I never found it or saw anyone from my family.

There wasn't time to figure out what my dream meant. Luke and I had made plans to meet in front of Pastor Steve's house at two o'clock, and I had a lot to do. After brunch at the snack bar, I showered, packed, and finished my term paper on spiritual gifts for my God's Golden Women class.

Even though I tried to be early, Luke beat me there. "Ready for the big day?"

I answered by dropping my bag on the ground and throwing my arms around him. His laugh vibrated in his chest.

Luke gently pried my fingers off his back and took my hand. "We can't tell your family about our engagement without this." He snapped open a black velvet box, took out my ring, and slipped it on my finger.

"Oh Luke, thank you." I shook my hand and the ring didn't move. "It fits perfect now."

Pastor Steve's front door was open and we could see him on the phone. He flashed his fingers for a ten minute delay so Luke went inside to get the car keys from him.

Without a word, he led me around the back where Pastor Steve's black Town Car was parked.

"Is something wrong?" I said.

Luke clicked the trunk open and tossed our bags inside. "This could be about Elizabeth. Last night she left to see her mom. Poor lady has been having memory problems."

Shoot, without Elizabeth I'd be stuck alone in the back seat for the whole ride. I stomped out my irritation and replaced it with a silent prayer for Elizabeth's mother. As I reached for the back door, Luke stopped me.

"Katie Pie, come sit up front with me until Pastor Steve comes out."

Luke started the car and fiddled with the heat controls. The dashboard gleamed like it just came off the lot, making me wonder how often Pastor Steve traded in his car for a new model.

A random thought of Elizabeth being a new model also flashed in my mind. "Luke, speaking of mothers, at Thanksgiving Matt told me his mom lives in California."

"And you probably want to know why." He paused. "Where to start? Well, in high school, Aunt Gail and Uncle Steve were sweethearts. They got married right after graduation and had Paul."

I tried not to show the surprise on my face. Did they have to get married? Then, without warning, the dark cloud of my sin with Nick descended on me. No matter how much I prayed, I couldn't forget his hands on my body and mine on his. I'd become convinced that only when Luke and I were physically husband and wife, could I wipe out Nick completely.

Luke touched my arm. "You know this was well before Uncle Steve was Pastor Steve. Soon after Paul, they had Matt. For many years, things were fine. But then Uncle Steve got the calling to become a pastor. He juggled his sales job during the day with night classes at seminary college. Aunt Gail and my cousins barely saw him. And Paul and Matt were a handful."

"No, I don't believe it."

Luke let out a belly laugh. "They weren't always Bible school teachers. Mom used to joke that the hospital staff was on a first-name basis with them because of all their broken bones and stitches." He stared out the window for a few seconds. "You know, I remember one night Aunt Gail sat next to me on the couch. She put her arm around me and said, 'It'd be so nice if my boys could sit still and read a book like you do.'"

I prayed silently that Pastor Steve would stay in his house longer. "Then what happened?"

"Aunt Gail's dream was to go to college and get her degree. She planned to go when my cousins started high school. But by that time, Uncle Steve had finished seminary and started preaching in our church. The ministry loved him, so he quit his job at the car dealership to serve the congregation full time." Luke glanced toward the house and back to me. "They lost their health insurance. Aunt Gail panicked. Uncle Steve wanted her to trust the Lord. Instead, she came to our house and cried to my mom.

Money was tight…the bills stacked up." He shook his head. "My mom worked as a front desk manager at the Holiday Inn then. She helped Aunt Gail get a management job too. But the only opening was the graveyard shift."

My God, that poor lady couldn't catch a break.

"When the opportunity came to start The Ark and move the ministry to New Hampshire, she didn't go with them."

"What?"

Luke shook his head. "She shocked us all. Paul and Matt were in seminary. She didn't want to be a pastor's wife. She chose her career over her family. Basically, she deserted them."

His words spun around my head. A part of me was shocked, but another part admired her courage.

Sorrow rested on Luke's face. "Uncle Steve was lost without her. The Bible says marriage is a sacred union. He prayed that God would change her heart. But in the end, she didn't embrace the Lord. She's a social worker or something now."

"How'd your cousins handle it?"

"Uncle Steve can be tough, but he's smart. He needed Paul and Matt to help build The Ark. As soon as they graduated from seminary, he gave them positions where he knew they'd do well."

I sat quiet for a moment. "And then he met Elizabeth?"

Luke nodded. "About a year after the divorce. This is a lot to take in, but the important thing to remember is that when you're doing the Lord's work, he blesses you." His eyes sparkled. "To be at the beginning of a ministry, to build it, and watch it grow, there isn't anything more rewarding."

I looked out the window at the gray skeletons of trees. Goose bumps rose on my arms as the "ifs" lined up in my head. Ma didn't love motherhood. What if she'd left us with Dad? What if she'd taken care of herself and followed her dreams instead? Would she still be alive? And would Pam, BB, and I have turned out differently?

"What did you think when Pastor Steve married Elizabeth?"

Luke lifted my hand to his lips. "God doesn't want man to be alone."

I didn't want to be alone either. Despite how different our families were, we'd all gone through a traumatic event: Luke grew up without a dad, his cousins went through a divorce, and my sisters and I lost our mother.

Pastor Steve appeared in the driveway. I opened the door, took my place in the back seat, and we set out for our drive to Massachusetts.

As they talked about Elizabeth and her mother, my mind wandered to my sisters and an old Christmas memory. I was seven and had asked Santa for a pound puppy toy. Pam, BB, and I sat in front of the TV and watched *Rudolph the Red-Nosed Reindeer*. The light of the screen flickered across my sisters' faces as Burl Ives sang "Silver and Gold." We danced and swayed like the pine trees.

At bedtime, Ma gave us new matching flannel nightgowns to wear. We stood over the metal heating vents on the floor and let the hot air puff them out and warm us up. She rushed us off to bed because "Santa won't come until you girls fall asleep."

On Christmas morning, we opened our presents. I waited to save my biggest present for last. My sisters watched as my fingers tore through the foil paper. When I saw my pound puppy's big eyes, I lifted her out of the box and hugged her tight.

Dad crouched beside me with his camera. "Kate, it's such a sad-looking puppy."

"I know. She needs someone to love her."

A few hours later, we arrived at Pastor Wayne's new church. The former warehouse had been decked out for the Christmas holiday. Inside, the place was packed with old and new faces. Luke and I were separated the minute we walked in.

Julia shouted out my name. We laughed and hugged like we hadn't seen each other for years. When she spoke to me, it was in Spanish.

"*Muy bien*, your classes are really paying off."

"My college professor says I'm a natural. And guess what? After the holidays I'm going to visit the mission team in Costa Rica."

"Oh Julia, I'm so excited for you, and I've missed you. But I've got some news too." I showed her my ring.

Her eyes grew wide and she gasped. "Is he the tall guy you came in with? I can't wait to meet him." We hugged again.

After a few more minutes of catching up, the volume in the room quieted. Pastor Steve had approached the podium, and we rushed to the closest seats we could find. I'd forgotten how exciting it was when he visited an offsite ministry. But try as I might, I couldn't keep a word of his dedication message in my head. My mind raced to the visit later at my house. Nervous sparks traveled over my skin, making it hard to sit still.

After the final prayer, I introduced Julia to Luke. The three of us filled our plates from the potluck dishes and found a quiet spot to talk and eat. The crowd started to thin out and Pastor Wayne came over.

"Julia, do you mind if I steal these two away?"

"If you have to." She smiled and we said quick goodbyes.

Pastor Wayne steered Luke and me to his sparse office in the back of the building.

"I still can't believe this place is real," I said.

"The power of prayer and rolled-up sleeves. But that's not the only exciting news. Wasn't it just a few months ago we were asking God to bless you as you set off for The Ark?" Joy burst across Pastor Wayne's face. "Now look what He has done."

Pastor Wayne spoke to Luke. "Friend, I've known you since seminary. I'm so happy you've found Kate. She's been a blessing to me and this ministry." He reached for our hands and lifted our arms in the air. "Praise the Lord for putting you two together."

Just then, Pastor Steve burst into the office. "So this is where you're all hiding. What do you think, Wayne? Isn't this wonderful—your Kate and my Luke?"

"I guess I don't have a chance officiating their wedding," Pastor Wayne said.

"You can be my best man," Luke said.

I thanked God for giving me this precious moment before my visit home.

We discussed plans for the evening. Pastor Wayne told us a generous new member of his ministry had offered us complimentary rooms at his historic inn. He offered to drive Pastor Steve there so we could keep the car for the visit with my family.

As Luke and I walked outside, an idea hit me and I stopped short.

"Are you okay?" Luke reached for my hand.

"I'm nervous about tonight. But since we're a little early to go to my house, what if we stopped to do some Christmas shopping?" I hoped giving gifts would make my family more generous to Luke and me.

"Sounds good to me. I need to get my mom something."

We drove into downtown Salem and found a parking spot in front of The Witch Shoppe.

"Who'd ever go into a place like this?" Luke said.

I hid my face from him. A few years ago, Pam and I had our fortunes read in that shop. My fortune teller wore a black cape. Dark liner rimmed her eyelids and lips, and stringy gray hair reached down the middle of her back. I'd almost chickened out just looking at her.

She led me into the reading room where a candle flickered on a round table. We sat opposite each other as she dealt out tarot cards, taking sharp breaths at certain ones. A card with the picture of an ice queen ended up closest to me.

"Ahh. Very interesting. This card tells me about a girl. She's outside…on a big lake. There are signs posted. Thin ice. The girl is not paying attention. If she gets too close to the thin ice, she will fall in and be trapped forever."

The room became still. I shivered, remembering the day on the pond with BB. "This is a card from my past."

She shook her head and lowered her voice. "This card represents the future. It is a warning. Do you understand?"

I nodded because she scared me and I wanted to get out of there as fast as I could.

"Very good. You must keep my words close to your heart. They are not to be shared with anyone else."

I never went near a witch or frozen water again.

With my arm locked through Luke's, we walked to a touristy gift shop where I found saltwater taffy for my dad and scented lotions and soaps for Pam and BB. Luke picked out a set of carved candles for his mother. When he wasn't looking, I snuck a bottle of earthy aftershave in my basket to give him later.

The gift bags crinkled on my lap as we drove to my house. The closer we got, the more my heart pounded. We pulled into the driveway too soon for me to calm down.

Luke shut off the engine and turned to me. "How are you feeling?"

I wanted to say, *Like I'm going to puke.* "I'm really nervous. Not so much about my sisters, but my dad. I don't know how he's going to react. I've never brought a boyfriend home before and now I'm going to introduce you as my fiancé." I took a deep breath. "If they ask, we haven't set a date, okay?"

"That's the truth." The kindness in his eyes gave me strength. "And whatever happens in there, remember that I love you and I'm right here with you. Let's pray before we go in."

I bowed my head.

"Lord, thank you for bringing us to Kate's home tonight. We ask you to open the hearts of her father and sisters and to bless the words we speak to them. May your spirit guide and direct us. Amen."

I begged God to hear Luke's words.

CHAPTER 32

LUKE STAYED CLOSE as we walked across the dark driveway. A curtain fluttered in the living room window, but I couldn't see anyone behind it. When we reached the front door, I hesitated.

"Geez," I said with a nervous laugh, "I don't know whether to knock or just walk in."

At that moment, BB opened the door. "Oh no, we forgot to turn on the light for you guys." She flicked it on and pulled me inside. "I've missed you so much."

I nearly froze in shock as BB wrapped her arms around me. She hugged me the way she used to when she was a toddler. I held her tight until she released me.

"BB, I'd like you to meet Luke."

He stepped inside and I saw her take in his height.

"My real name is Brenda. But you can call me BB if you want." I'd never seen her so bubbly. "Come on in. Dad and Pam are waiting in the den."

As we followed, Luke reached for my hand, but I shook my head no. If I held on to him I might not be able to let go.

The house smelled like Windex and Pledge. Thankfully, someone had cleaned for our visit. As we passed through the front rooms, I searched the wall with our family photo collection. Mine was still in it, and I let out the breath I'd been holding.

The den was quiet. The television that always buzzed in the background had been turned off. Pam and Dad rose from the couch to greet us. Dad's face sagged a bit, and he stood shorter than I remembered. Pam had dressed up for the occasion in a new outfit, and I noticed she'd gotten highlights in her hair.

My pulse beat overtime in my ears as I finished introducing everyone. Dad gestured for us to sit. Luke and I picked the two recliners, and my family took the couch.

"We did some shopping on our way here." I handed out the gift bags. "Just a little something from us for Christmas. You can open them now if you want."

As they opened their presents, I rattled on. "This is Luke's first time in Salem. We parked right in front of The Witch Shoppe. Pam, remember when we went there?" Shoot, I didn't mean to let that slip out. In my mind, I saw Luke's surprised face.

"How could I forget? She knew what was inside my closet. Did I ever tell you that?" Pam rubbed some of the lotion I gave her on her hands. "That witch really freaked me out."

"Thank you for the taffy." Dad's first words.

My sisters thanked me too and silence returned to the room. I stole a glance at Luke. His calm presence helped me to not fidget.

"So, Luke, what do you think of Salem?" Dad asked. He came to life one sentence at a time.

"The buildings are charming, Mr. Bennett. There's so much history here."

If Luke only knew how much history there was in this room.

Dad crossed and uncrossed his legs. "Where are you from?"

"I grew up in Rhode Island. Woonsocket, not too far from Pawtucket."

"That's where the Red Sox's minor league team is." Dad's face became a bit more animated.

Luke didn't miss a beat. "How do you think the Sox look for next year?"

Pam and BB groaned. Dad relaxed and spoke about his favorite players: Yaz, the Eck, and Big Papi.

When they ran out of baseball talk, Dad turned to me. "If you don't mind, I'd like to go for a drive with Luke. Have a little man-to-man talk."

Unprepared for this scenario, I looked at Luke for help.

"I think that's a great idea," Luke said. "Plus it'll give Kate time to catch up with her sisters. Would you like me to drive?"

Dad seemed surprised by Luke's offer. "Okay then, I'll get my jacket."

Luke reached over and patted my shoulder. His gesture and the smile on his face helped curb my panic. The last words I heard before the front door shut were Luke's. "You have a very nice home."

BB spoke first. Her hands danced along. "He's cute and so tall. Are you really marrying him?"

I showed them my ring, unable to hide my smile.

Pam took my hand and held the ring up to the light. "This is nice. But he seems much older than you. Just how old is he anyway?" She spoke in Ma's bossy tone.

"He's twenty-four. I know that might seem old, but I'm almost nineteen. Ma and Dad were five years apart."

"I can't believe you're marrying your first boyfriend," Pam said. "How do you know there isn't someone better out there?"

"We're getting married because we're soul mates."

"Oh brother." She rolled her eyes. "Well, at least you won't have to deal with Dad anymore."

"How bad is he?" I said.

Pam stood. "He is in his own quiet world. I tried once to cheer him up and cooked him his favorite dinner, but he only ate two bites. I even help grocery shop and still no thanks. Nothing makes him happy. You don't know how miserable it is living here. I can't wait to go to college. One more year until I graduate and get the hell out of here."

"You better have room for me to live there too. I'm not staying here alone with him," BB said. Then she smiled at me. "Or I could move in with you and Luke."

"Yes, that's just what newlyweds want," Pam said. "A full grown—" She couldn't finish because she made a snorting sound. Pam's pig laugh set us all off.

I bent over from laughing so hard. BB started hiccupping. After a few minutes, we all ended up on the carpet next to each other, worn out and breathing heavy.

"When was the last time we laughed that hard?" I said.

"I know. When Ma pushed you in that pool and boogers came out your nose," BB said.

Ma knew I hated going underwater, yet she'd snuck up behind me and pushed me in. When I surfaced with a snotty face and gasping for air, the three of them were roaring.

"No, no. Remember when Ma made us go to that Christmas Eve service? Dad farted and pretended it was one of us. I thought Ma was going to kill all of us that night." Pam wiped at her eyes. "She never took us to church after that."

I think we all had the same sobering thought. Ma did take us to church one more time.

"Speaking of Ma, it's already the middle of December. When are you guys putting up the tree?"

"Dad hasn't said anything about it," BB said.

Pam clapped her hands. "Let's just do it."

"Great," I said. "Let's hurry and we'll surprise him when he gets home."

BB and I followed Pam to the top of the basement stairs. The basement reminded me of a dungeon. Except for the laundry room, the rest of it was unfinished with dirt floors, stone walls, and cobwebs. We stood back and let Pam go first. BB held on to the back of my shirt.

"You two are such babies," Pam said over her shoulder.

It got colder each step we descended. BB practically choked me holding my shirt so tight. Once Pam found the light switch, our shadows moved with us along the stone walls. I pretended not to see the spider crawling across the floor.

"In here, slow pokes," Pam said. "The tree and boxes are over here."

My caboose and I caught up to her at the threshold of a room I'd never been in before. "How'd you know the decorations were in this room?" I said.

"This is where Ma used to hide our Christmas presents."

"You peeked?" BB said. "And you didn't tell us?"

Pam ignored her and moved a few boxes around. "Oh my God."

BB screamed. We all jumped. "Is it alive or dead?" I said, stepping back onto BB's sneakers.

"Really, you guys. I found some presents." Pam lifted two shopping bags off the table.

My heartbeat returned to normal. A single light bulb hung from the ceiling and the pull chain still swung.

Pam rummaged through the bag and found a receipt. "Geez, this one is dated in May."

We all could do the math, a month before she died.

"Well, what should we do with them?" Pam said.

"Bring it up with the tree and decorations," BB said.

After three trips up and down the creaky stairs, we got everything into the den. Poor Luke was still trapped in a car with Dad. I sent up a quick prayer that everything was going well for him.

The shopping bags leaned against the fireplace watching us as we put the tree together. Pam tested the lights, and like a miracle, they all lit up. As she wound them around the tree, BB and I took special care hanging the ornaments that Ma had made. When we were little kids, she'd let us sit at the dining room table with her and make our own. She'd end up fixing them the way she liked afterward, but we didn't complain. It was the only time of the year she didn't mind having us around. BB crowned the tree with a gold angel.

"That was fast," Pam said. "Let's take a break and see what she got us."

We sat in a circle on the den carpet while Pam rifled through the shopping bags like a pro. BB and I remained speechless. "I know her code. Our initials are on the price tags."

Pam let BB act the role of the elf. Soon piles of clothes grew in front of my sisters. I watched as they admired their sweaters, socks, and jeans. Pam put a beaded bracelet on her wrist. BB held up some sterling hoop earrings.

Ma bought me some clothes too, but most of my presents were gifts for a college-bound daughter: notebooks, pens, a backpack, and a sweatshirt from Salem State University. *Oh, Ma. You found a way to reach out from the grave and squeeze my heart.*

On our way to the basement with the empty boxes, we heard the front door open and close. I raced up the stairs ahead of my sisters.

Dad stood in the middle of the den. "What's going on?" He looked past me to Pam and BB. "You think everything's back to normal because Kate's here?"

No one said a word. He hated it, but something else seemed wrong.

"Dad, where's Luke?"

"He dropped me off and went to the inn. I've got your bag. He agreed with me that it would be best for you to stay the night with us."

Luke, how could you abandon me? I had to act like everything was okay. "Super. Let's finish decorating and hang the stockings."

"You might as well, *now*," Dad said.

"You were going to put the tree up, weren't you?" I said.

"I think it's too soon to celebrate holidays."

Now I knew what my sisters were going through, and why he took them to Disney World for Thanksgiving. He couldn't bear a family tradition without Ma.

I backed up to the recliner and sat down. "Dad, Ma loved

Christmas. By celebrating it, we honor her memory. It is a way to keep her spirit alive in our hearts."

"I don't believe in spirits."

"But we're all spiritual beings. It's what makes us different from animals. Our bodies are temporary, our spirits are eternal." Yikes, I sounded like Luke. If I made this too preachy I'd lose him, and for once, BB was listening. Pam decided it was a good time to crack her knuckles.

"I don't know how you can believe that rubbish," Dad said.

"How can I not? The alternative is awful. You die and that's the end. God didn't want us to be apes."

BB giggled. "Pam, your last boyfriend might've been an ape."

"Hmm, you're probably right," she said. "He had all that hair on his back."

Dad's eyes popped open.

Pam stumbled over her words. "I mean...I saw it when he was running track."

Good grief, Pam. I could've let her bungle along, but I saved her. "Dad, can you find a Christmas CD to put on?"

He sighed in resignation. "What do you want to hear?"

We used to play this game with Ma. I said, "Nat." Pam said, "King." BB said, "Cole." I saw the hint of a smile on Dad's face. Pam left to make hot cocoa while BB and I finished hanging the stockings. The den was pretty close to how Ma would have decorated it. Dad left the room and brought the last empty box down to the basement.

"O Holy Night" was playing when he joined Pam on the couch. BB and I sat on the floor in front of the coffee table sipping our mugs of cocoa.

"This is nice, Dad," I said.

"Well, I'm glad you said that. This is how it should be every night." His face softened. "Kate, I want you to move back home."

Stunned, I couldn't reply. My mouth dropped open.

Dad held up his hand. "Before you answer, I want you to hear me out. Sleep on it and make your decision in the morning."

Did he already have this speech with Luke? *Oh Luke, I need you here.* My sisters watched me carefully. I couldn't tell if they knew this was coming or not.

"Just give me two more years. You can go to any college near home and all the Bible meetings you want. Families need to stick together. I was wrong. I'm sorry about how I treated you." His eyes watered and he dabbed them with his handkerchief. "I can't do this alone."

Dad never apologized. The only time he cried in front of us was when the black limousine had pulled into the driveway to take us to Ma's funeral. I closed my eyes and let his apology find the place where I buried all his hurtful words. Could this mean he didn't blame me any longer for Ma's death?

The CD stopped, and I heard myself swallow. The anchor of guilt started to lift.

Dad put his hands on his knees and leaned forward. "This is your chance to do what your mother wanted."

A punch in the gut.

I'd already paid my dues to my sisters. It was his turn to step up and be the parent. My hands trembled, but my voice stayed steady. "Dad, you can do this. Pam and BB are doing fine." I couldn't look at them. "I'm engaged to Luke."

"You're eighteen. You're too young to know what you want."

I bolted from the chair. "I made a commitment to Luke. What did you say to him?"

Dad didn't flinch. "Unlike you, Luke is a good listener. You could learn a thing or two from him. He'll be back at eight in the morning, but if you leave with him, don't come back."

Invisible walls closed in on me. Pam and BB had become statues. The fight made my head feel too heavy for my neck and weariness poured over me.

"I'm going to bed."

At the foot of the stairs, Dad called out, "He'd wait for you. You can have a long engagement. If what you really have is love, two years won't be a sacrifice."

I wanted to scream. All he offered me was a boatload of guilt. All I wanted was a handful of love.

My overnight bag stood beside the front door. I carried it up the stairs to my bedroom where the moon lit up a patch on the floor. Peering out the window, I wished Luke were out there waiting to rescue me.

I kicked off my shoes, fell onto my bed, and grabbed my old pound puppy. When I looked up, BB's silhouette filled the doorway. Her arms were full of Ma's gifts to me.

"Thanks. Put them anywhere." I patted a space beside me. "Come. Tell me what's going on with you."

We scooted up against the wall side by side.

"You see how it is here," BB said. "So I joined the girls' basketball team. I don't score many points, but it's really fun. We practice a lot and hang out after games."

"That's great." I touched her arm. "You know, Luke coaches basketball. Will you be up tomorrow when he comes back? You can tell him about your team."

"You're not going to stay, are you?"

Even in the dark, I couldn't meet her eyes. "I wish I could make things better here, but I can't. Dad has to fix himself. Do you understand that?"

"Sort of." BB wiggled closer to me. She always smelled like baby powder. "What's it like being engaged?"

I closed my eyes and an image of Luke formed in my mind. "Oh, he's the most wonderful guy. He's caring and considerate. When we're together, I'm so happy." The more I described him, the more I realized how much I loved him. "More than anything, he's kind."

"If I found someone like that, I'd run away with him too."

I hit her with my puppy. "I'm not running away."

"Do you think I'll ever find someone like that?"

"Oh BB, when you get older, you'll meet that special person too. And whoever that lucky guy is, he's going to get a treasure."

We sat still for a few moments. I heard doors being locked downstairs. Soon Pam and Dad would be coming up. "Can you keep my decision to yourself until the morning?"

"On one condition."

"Name it."

"Remember when I was little and we had pajama parties in your room?"

"Shall we have one more for old time's sake?" I leaned against her. My shoulders shook and finally, the tears fell. They fell because I loved her and couldn't be her lifeboat. And more fell because Dad couldn't figure out how to love me without hurting me.

When I composed myself, I said, "Sorry about that. Go get ready for our party."

BB squeezed my arm. "That's what sisters are for."

I undressed in the dark, not wanting to see my room in the light, not wanting to uncover any more hidden memories. Still one came, from when BB was three. We were all in Dad's SUV driving to visit his parents. Pam and I played with our Barbie dolls. BB crawled around on the floor meowing like a cat. She wound her way into the corner between the car door and my legs.

The sound of the road surprised me. I looked toward the noise and saw a sliver of the pavement. My heart beat exploded as I yelled, "Dad, pull over. The door's opening!"

I wrapped my legs around BB and grabbed the door handle with both hands. It was heavy and wanted to open more. My arms burned. Dad stopped fast and got out. He came around to my side and knocked on the window. I heard him say let go, but it took a few seconds before my hands would unclench.

Ma turned around and faced us. "Get BB back into her God damn booster seat."

Dad ducked into the back seat. He patted me on the head and whispered, "You're my good girl."

I shivered and hugged myself wondering if Dad would ever feel proud of me again.

CHAPTER 33

THE SUN ROSE and I couldn't wait for Luke to arrive and take me back to The Ark. As quietly as possible, I dressed and packed my overnight bag. I stepped over BB, still sleeping on my floor, and left my room. We'd said our hushed goodbyes before we'd fallen asleep.

Dad's snores drifted into the hallway through his half-open door. A Keep Out sign hung on Pam's doorknob, making me a little sad. I loved my sisters and their quirky ways, but now my life was with Luke.

I left my bag by the front door and made a quick breakfast. The furnace kicked on, muffling the crunch of my Frosted Flakes. Pam must've bought them because Dad still thought we loved Cheerios. We'd only eaten them because Ma never bought anything else.

A copy of yesterday's newspaper lay on the table. It occurred to me that I hadn't read the paper, watched television, or been to the movies since I'd left for The Ark almost four months ago. I skimmed through the paper and stopped at the obituary section. The only obituary I'd ever cut out of a newspaper was Ma's. She was the youngest person who'd died that day. It said she was a loving mother, wife, and homemaker. One of my old aunts must have written it, and she probably believed it too. Ma was perfectly pleasant when the relatives visited. They didn't know Ma hated the whole idea of being a homemaker. She couldn't wait until we were old enough to cook and clean and give her a "friggin' break." Her obituary was tucked inside the front cover of my baby book.

Water running in the pipes above meant Dad was up. I rushed upstairs to Pam's room and barged in.

"Hey, what's going on?" Pam rolled over. She opened one eye. "You leaving now?"

"Luke should be here in about half an hour."

She stretched and yawned. "Okay. Have a nice life."

"No. I need you." I pulled at her puffy comforter. "Dad's getting up."

"God, you don't have to be afraid of him. What's that saying? His bark is worse than his bite."

"I know. I just hate leaving things messy with him."

"The things I do for you. Turn on my light so I can find something to wear." Pam picked clothes off the floor, sniffed them, and put on the ones that passed the test. "Okay, let's go down and see what's brewing besides coffee."

We walked into the kitchen together. Dad sat at the table in his weekend clothes: a flannel shirt and jeans. He glanced up from the newspaper. "Coffee's made."

"I need some." Pam's bare feet slapped against the kitchen floor. "Kate, you drink coffee yet?"

"No, still tea." My voice sounded calm, but panic was rising in me. I stood behind a chair and prayed to God for strength.

Dad turned a page of the paper. Then he took a sip of his coffee. He repeated the turn-and-sip routine a few times before Pam sat next to him. She found the sugar bowl and spooned half of it into her cup.

The waiting was torture. I strained to look out the kitchen window, hoping to see Pastor Steve's car, willing Luke to show up. Dad noticed.

"I saw your bag by the front door."

My words rushed out. "Dad, I'm sorry. I'm not staying. I just can't." I gripped the back of the chair.

He looked at me. "So I see."

And that was it. Pam shrugged. My hands fell to my sides. Dad returned to the newspaper as if neither Pam nor I were in the room. At the sound of a car door shutting, I sprang to life.

"Guess it's time to go." I gave Dad a few more seconds to acknowledge me and then turned to leave. Pam tapped the inside of her mug with her spoon. "Geez, Dad, you could at least say goodbye to her."

Nice try, Pam. I left the kitchen not wanting to see his reaction. She caught up with me in the hallway. "He can be such an asshole."

A gentle knock sounded on the front door. I opened it and pulled Luke in. The relief I felt seeing him made me want to melt into him forever. Luke seemed to know, and he hugged me tight.

"Good morning, Pam."

"Morning," she said. "Excuse me for not being in my Sunday best."

"You look fine," Luke said. His easy smile put one on Pam's face too.

I wrapped my arms around my sister. "Thanks for getting up with me." I spoke to the side of her head. "Listen, I'm not letting go until you hug me back."

"If I have to." Pam patted me a few times on the back before embracing me. It was the first time we ever hugged. Pam had so much of Ma's edge inside her, but thankfully I found her soft side.

When she backed away from me, Luke extended his hand to her. "I'm sorry I didn't have time to get to know you better. Maybe next visit."

"At your wedding?" We looked up. BB stood at the top of the stairs. Her hair was a tangled mess, but her sweet face made her beautiful. "Will that be the next time we see you?"

"Only if you'll both be my bridesmaids," I said.

"Only if you don't make us wear dorky dresses," Pam said.

I was one of the few people at The Ark who never had a family member visit the campus. If my dad and sisters came to my wedding, it'd be a miracle. But God had already given me Luke, and he might be my only miracle.

Luke and I said our final goodbyes with my sisters and walked to the car. I glanced up to the kitchen window to see if Dad was watching, but it was empty.

We drove for a few moments before Luke pulled over to the side of the road. "I'm sorry I left you last night. Your father gave me no choice. How did it go?"

I replayed my night for him, and Luke took my hands. "You're my brave one."

The last time Luke called me brave was when he asked me to marry him. The warm feeling filling my heart was proof that I'd made the right decision leaving home. It wasn't Luke's fault my dad made impossible demands.

Then it was his turn.

"We drove to a nearby coffee shop and talked for a long time. Your father started off telling me how hard it was for him to take care of your sisters. How your mother pretty much did all the parenting. He was the one who went to work, paid the bills. The way he went on and on about it I got to wondering something. Does your father have friends? Anyone to talk to?"

This brought me up short. I couldn't think of a single person. Dad had never talked about friends at work. A chill hit me as I thought about how alone he was. Ma might've been the only one he confided in. While my life improved at The Ark, his had worsened at home.

We were both quiet and then started talking at the same time. Luke let me go first.

"Thank you for letting him unload on you. By the way, I should tell you he did mention what a good listener you are."

Luke paused for a moment. "You know, I thought the reason he wanted to talk to me was to find out who I was. Who was this man that wanted to marry his daughter? But he didn't ask me anything about myself. It didn't take long to figure out why he was sharing all his problems with me. He was building his case. And now we both know he wanted you to hold the family together."

I winced at Luke seeing this side of my Dad. "Did he ask you to extend our engagement?"

"No, he realized I wasn't taking his side. So he asked me to at least let you spend the night there. I knew he'd be working on you. Pastor Steve and I prayed for you, for strength to endure the trial that you'd be going through. And then we prayed for your dad and your sisters."

I took his hands and held them. "I think God heard your prayers for Pam and BB."

"It was nice to see them at the door with you."

"My dad, he acted so detached this morning...like I was a stranger to him." I couldn't linger on the sadness of that thought because beside me was the man I loved.

"I don't know much about the stages of grief, but your dad seems very depressed. You can't take what he does or says personally. I tried a few times to get him to talk about his spiritual beliefs, but he cut me off."

"Thanks, Luke. Thanks so much for trying."

We drove the rest of the way to the inn lost in our own thoughts. When Luke went to get Pastor Steve, I took my overnight bag and moved to the back seat. Pastor Steve waved as he approached the car.

Once inside, he turned back to me. "My dear, I'm so glad to see you. I know you had a difficult night. Take some comfort in knowing that for those of us who love God, all things work together for the good."

"Thank you," I said, remembering the verse from one of his recent sermons.

On a Sunday morning with no traffic, we'd be back to the campus in less than two hours. I leaned against the seat and the murmur of their voices relaxed me. I thought I'd just close my eyes for a few minutes, until the jolt of the car parking shook me awake. We were in Pastor Steve's driveway, and I couldn't believe I'd slept the whole way back to The Ark.

Before we got out, Pastor Steve turned to me. "Kate, I have a big favor to ask. Elizabeth will be gone for a week taking care of her mother. Do you think you could work mornings in her office to cover the phones? You'll still be able to attend chapel and your afternoon classes."

"Of course I can. Whatever you need."

"You're a lifesaver." He patted the back of the seat and gave me a thumbs-up.

I couldn't believe he'd trust me with this responsibility.

On Monday morning, I met Pastor Steve in the admin building. We walked to Elizabeth's office where he explained how the phones and files worked. Some of what he explained I already knew from when I'd snuck into her office, but I paid close attention anyway.

"I'll be in my office down the hall if you have any questions. Mrs. Payne will be covering the phones after lunch."

Before leaving, he pulled me into one of his bone-crushing hugs. "I really appreciate you helping me out."

"Pastor Steve, I can't breathe." My face was crammed into his suit jacket.

"Sorry. I forget you're just a slip of a thing." He laughed as he released me.

The phone rang every few minutes and, in between, I did

some filing. Next thing I knew, it was noon. The day went much faster in an office compared to working at the grocery store. The offer of a staff position next semester seemed even better, and I hoped it'd be a busy job like this one.

With chapel at eight, work until noon, and classes in the afternoon, the week zoomed by. My last call on Friday was from Pastor Wayne. We caught up for a few minutes, and then he spoke with much more enthusiasm.

"I've been studying the early church. In the times of Jesus, he welcomed the outcasts of society: women, prostitutes, and lepers. But today, we've wandered away from being a welcoming place. It's time to embrace those who feel left out. We should open our doors to everyone who wants to worship God. God's love is unconditional."

I agreed and transferred him to Pastor Steve. A lightness washed over me as the words *unconditional love* became clearer in my mind. God's love wasn't a gift just for believers, it was for everyone.

A few minutes later, I heard footsteps in the hallway. Pastor Steve burst into my office. The worry lines etched across his face surprised me.

"Is everything okay?" I said.

"I'm calling an emergency meeting. You find Luke, I'll get my sons."

CHAPTER 34

I FOUND LUKE IN THE GYM, coaching the high school basketball players. When he saw me waving at him, he came right over.

"Hi there. What's up?"

"I'm not sure." A touch of alarm crept into my voice. "Pastor Steve just called an emergency meeting."

"Boys, put the equipment away," he called to them. "I'll see you at next practice."

On the way to the admin building, I told Luke about Pastor Wayne's call and how right afterward, Pastor Steve rushed to my office to request a meeting. We met up with Matt and Paul in the hallway.

"He's waiting for us in the conference room," Matt said.

I walked toward Elizabeth's office, but Paul stopped me. "Since you took Pastor Wayne's call, you should join us."

A ripple of excitement pulsed through me. I took a seat next to Luke at the conference table. Pastor Steve paced the room, filling it with nervous energy.

"Wayne has decided, on his own, to open his young church to anyone who believes in God. On the surface, this sounds inclusive, but his interpretation of the scripture will allow people in defiled relationships to worship there. He's completely ignoring God's commands in Leviticus." He pounded his fist into his open palm. "I can guarantee you this news will spread quickly, and it has the potential to cause a division in The Ark. We must proceed with caution."

Pastor Steve took a seat and looked at each of us. "We, as God's soldiers, must put on our armor of unity. I will revise my sermon on Sunday to further address this issue."

Paul slumped in his seat. Matt turned away from us. But it was Luke's ashen face that worried me. I didn't know what a defiled relationship was but it had to be something bad. As a new Christian, I didn't want to appear ignorant and stayed quiet.

"Kate, I'm sorry to ask you for another favor. Elizabeth won't be back until Sunday night. Can you come in Saturday for a couple of hours and type up my sermon notes?"

"Certainly."

"Good. I'll meet you here at two in the afternoon. Paul, can you close us in prayer?"

Paul bowed his head and we followed. "Dear Lord, we ask for your blessings in these trying times and to renew our faith in your strength. Faith does the impossible because nothing is impossible for God. God can move mountains, but faith and prayer move God."

After Pastor Steve dismissed us, Luke and I walked toward the cafeteria for lunch.

"I don't understand why Pastor Steve is so upset."

Luke let out a long exhale. "The best thing for us to do right now is trust in God and let the Holy Spirit guide us."

More confused, I let it go.

I met Pastor Steve the next day as planned. He sighed as he handed me his sermon.

"If you have trouble deciphering any of this, let me know." He wrote down a phone number on a slip of paper. "I'll be at my home office. You can call me there."

His face had lost some of its light, but I had no idea how to comfort someone of his stature.

Elizabeth had taken her laptop with her so I was stuck typing on an old electric typewriter. The sermon was titled: *Modern Day Lepers*. Pastor Wayne spoke about the early church and how Jesus allowed the undesirables of his time to worship. I couldn't wait to see how this was all connected.

Pastor Steve wrote in bullet format with Bible verses and key points. After a few words, I stopped typing and started reading. He wrote out Leviticus 20:13 in dark bold strokes: "'If a man also lie with mankind, as he lieth with a woman, both of them have committed an abomination: they shall surely be put to death; their blood shall be upon them.'"

The meaning of the verse swirled in my head. Was Pastor Steve calling gays modern day lepers? The Old Testament said they should be put to death. But in the New Testament, Jesus invited lepers to worship in the early church.

Then it hit me. Pastor Wayne wanted to open his ministry to

gays. Pastor Steve's fury jumped off the page. The two pastors I adored the most had interpreted the Bible so differently. I was ashamed that I'd never once thought about where gays might worship.

Pastor Steve went on to quote 1 Corinthians 6:9 and the list of sins that the verse included. The word *effeminate* was translated to mean perverts and homosexuals. He wrote, *The sexual desire for somebody of the same sex is sin.* He marked a verse in Matthew as a reference and went on, *It is not the way God designed things from the beginning.*

I imagined Pastor Steve shouting this sermon to a chapel full of people listening in stunned silence. *So is homosexual orientation sinful? I wouldn't want anyone to think that they are beyond God's mercy or forgiveness, but the Scripture clearly says to engage in that behavior is sinful.*

His closing point was, *So what's the answer? First, with God's grace, we are demanding that homosexuals live as celibates. Then, we pray for their healing. For their inner healing, which will transform their shame and sexual attraction to the way God originally made them.*

My mind churned in confusion. These words were from ancient times. Gay marriage was legal and it wasn't a choice that you could pray away. One of my favorite songs was about coming to God just the way I am. I wished I could talk to Pastor Wayne more about this.

After his sermon on Sunday, Pastor Steve warned against gossip and how divisive it could be. Nonetheless, word about Pastor

Wayne's open church spread. Students speculated on whether or not The Ark was going to cut ties with him.

When Luke and I met for dinner in the snack bar later that week, two groups had already formed. I dubbed them the Devoted and the Doubters. The Devoted group believed God spoke through Pastor Steve. The Doubters flipped through their Bibles and searched for verses to defend Pastor Wayne's move to a more open church. I listened to a heated discussion between a man who taught Sunday school and a woman who led us in worship songs.

"Pastor Steve is God's man." He slapped his Bible. "The scriptures back him up. Homosexuality is a sin. It is sodomy."

"But didn't Jesus welcome everyone to the church?" she said.

"God destroyed Sodom because of its wickedness." The man's face became covered in red blotches. "It is clear. No gays allowed."

The song leader shook her head. "Then where are they to worship?"

"Let them go through conversion therapy and then ask me."

"I'd rather worship with a kind gay person than a cruel Christian."

A few people said "hallelujah" and I turned to see if Luke agreed. Instead of seeing his kind face, I saw a stone cold one. He folded his arms across his chest and stood.

"I'm not up for this." Luke sounded defeated. "I'll walk you back unless you want to stay."

"No, I want to be with you." I searched for his hand, and we left to go out into the chilly night. After a few seconds, he shook off my hand. His pace was so brisk I had to run to keep up with him. "Luke, please slow down. What's wrong?"

"I can't believe what Wayne's doing. We just dedicated his new church and everything was fine. Now look at all the damage he's caused."

"Damage? Don't you think it's important that the church be more inclusive?"

Luke's body stiffened. "Don't be so naïve. This could split The Ark. I saw how hard it was for my uncle to build this ministry. This is my life."

"It's mine too. I started my spiritual journey with Pastor Wayne. I know how hard he's worked to build his ministry. You went to seminary with him. He wouldn't do anything purposefully to hurt The Ark."

"In my head, I know that. But I can't help feeling betrayed."

I wanted to ask Luke what conversion therapy was, but he started to walk fast again.

At the entrance to my dorm, he gave me a perfunctory hug. No one was out, so to distract him from his worries, I put my hands on the back of his neck and tried to kiss him.

He pushed me away. "Someone might see us."

Luke's rejection crushed me, but I answered the way God's Golden Woman would. "Of course, you're right."

He left without knowing how much he'd hurt me. I wanted him to feel passion for me. *The way Nick did.* My vow not to compare the two of them failed again.

I trudged to my room, feet scuffing the floor. Sheila was out. Hannah and Alice had already left for Christmas break. Alone, I flopped on my bed and hugged my pillow. Nick's words replayed in my head. *"Is that how it is there? You'll always be second?"*

CHAPTER 35

I NEEDED TO TALK TO BOBBI. She'd be skiing some-where with her family, but I had a plan to find her. In the dorm lobby, I dug into my wallet for change and made a call.

"Young Residence, may I help you?"

I gave myself an older-sounding voice. "Sorry to be calling so late. I'm trying to reach Mrs. Judith Young."

"She's not available, can I take a message?"

"I do hope so. Mrs. Young, well, she left her credit card at my boutique." I hoped that was the right word. "How do I reach her to get it back to her?"

"Oh dear, I'm afraid she's out of town."

"Mrs. Young mentioned skiing when she was in. Is she on her trip? She may need it there."

"Yes, they're up at the Sugarbush Trail Inn. Why don't you give me your number and I'll let her know."

"That's okay. I can leave her a message."

I hung up quick and did a touchdown dance. Vermont. Bobbi

was just a couple hours away in Vermont. Information gave me the number and a cheerful voice answered the phone.

"Happy Holidays, Sugarbush Trail Inn."

"I'm trying to reach one of your guests, James Young."

"Certainly. Let me connect you."

It was too easy. My spirit soared for the first time in a long while. After a few seconds of jazzy Christmas music on hold, I heard her voice.

"Hello."

"Bobbi, guess who? And, don't worry, I'm not married yet."

She laughed out loud. "Yes, Mom. Everything's okay. It's Kate. Sorry about that. How did you find me? Where are you?"

"I'm at The Ark. Everything's a big mess here. Can I visit you?"

"You're going to break the rules to see me?"

"Got any suggestions on how to do it?" I'd forgotten how much fun Bobbi was.

"Leave a note saying you have a family emergency."

"Great idea. I'll drive over first thing in the morning."

"You're really doing this?"

"Nothing can stop me."

When Sheila came into the room an hour later, I pretended to be asleep, afraid I'd give myself away. It took me a while to calm down from the excitement of the call and planning my escape. Lucky for me, Elizabeth would be back and both The Ark and the high school would be on Christmas break.

The next morning, I waited for Sheila to leave for her early shift at work before I got up. I wrote a note and placed it on her bed.

Sheila, sorry I missed you over the past few days. I have a family emergency and need to leave right away. Didn't have a chance to tell anyone else. I'll be back as soon as I can.

Love, Kate

I didn't like sneaking away from Luke, but I didn't want him to try to stop me either. A short break would be good for both of us. He needed time to deal with his anger over Pastor Wayne's plans, and I wanted him to miss me.

No siren sounded as I drove out the campus lot. I checked my rear view mirror a few times, and no one had followed me either. My hands unclenched the steering wheel, but the little kid in me who worried that lies could turn true prayed for everyone in my family to be safe.

According to Bobbi's directions, the drive would take a couple of hours. The GPS on my cell phone would've really helped on this trip. I wondered how much BB used it. With dry roads and light traffic, I'd be there before noon, in time for lunch with Bobbi.

The road out of town went by Nick's house. I tried not to look for his truck, but I did anyway. He was home. *Do. Not. Think. About. Him.*

I focused my wandering thoughts on Luke. Although he had many qualities that I loved, the one I didn't like was how strictly he followed all the rules. His refusal to kiss me last night still hurt, but I didn't want to spend the ride dwelling on that.

To lighten the mood, I put on a '90s station and sang along to the old hits. The ride went smoothly, and I passed a sign indicating only thirty more miles to go. The thought of finally seeing Bobbi again made me sing louder. All of a sudden, my steering wheel tightened up and barely moved. I shut off the radio. Silence. The engine had quit.

My heart raced as I tried to control my car. I prayed no one was speeding up behind me. *Please God, help me.* The car had enough momentum to make it to the shoulder of the road. What was wrong with my stupid old car? The tank was over half full, so it wasn't gas. I shifted into park and tried to start it again. Nothing. *Oh crap.* Nick told me to get a new battery and I'd completely forgotten. The engine probably needed a jump-start, and I couldn't even call anyone for help.

I stomped out and lifted the hood, hoping someone would stop. All around me was forest. How long had it been since I'd seen a house? Back in the car, I put on my hat and gloves. The cold chilled my bones. I tried to start the car one more time with no luck. BB's words came rushing back from when I gave her my cell phone. "What if you have an emergency?"

It didn't matter whether I had a cell phone or not because I knew this was God's punishment for my lying and sneaking away. No, I'd done worse. I'd sinned with Nick. God clearly wanted me to be in the chapel praying for forgiveness.

An occasional big rig drove by, vibrating the road before I heard them. Someone once told me that if you broke down you could trust truckers. I couldn't remember who'd said it, but I needed to believe they were right. I stood by my car and flagged down a long shiny gas truck. Its brakes squeaked as it came to a stop.

A guy wearing a red plaid shirt and dark sunglasses leaned

over his lowered window. "You need help?" he shouted over the noisy engine.

I stood on my toes and shouted back at him. "I think my battery's dead."

"How 'bout I radio in a tow truck for you?"

"Oh that'd be great." I smiled with relief.

"Probably take them 'bout half an hour to get to here. Get back in your car. It's not safe to be near the edge of the road."

He honked as he pulled away. Back in my car, my stomach growled. I found an ancient red and white hard mint in my glove box and spit out bits of the plastic that wouldn't peel off. *Yeah, Ma, I know. This is all my fault.*

Fifteen minutes later, a beat-up service truck came down the road toward me. I jumped out and waved him over. He parked so the hoods faced each other. Then, the skinniest guy I'd ever seen climbed out. As he walked over, I noticed he didn't look much older than me and wore a faded Red Sox baseball cap. His name, Slim, was embroidered in white thread on his gray jacket. I bit the inside of my lip so I wouldn't laugh.

"Hi. I'm Kate. Thanks for getting here so fast."

"Sure." Slim adjusted his cap. "So what happened before the car died?"

I hopped from foot to foot, trying to warm up. "Everything tightened up. Then it just shut down. I was able to roll to the side of the road, but couldn't get it to start again."

He leaned over the car engine. "You smell that?"

"That burning smell?" I hadn't noticed it earlier.

"Yeah, when's the last time you had the oil changed?"

Never. No one told me about oil changes. "I don't know."

"Well, let's try giving it a charge first."

I sat behind the wheel. We went through the charging routine with no success. Slim unplugged the cables and walked over to my window. He lifted off his cap and ran his grimy fingers through his hair. "Got some bad news for you."

I braced myself.

"Sorry to tell you this, but your car's shit the bed."

"It's dead?" This was the worst news ever.

"The engine's seized. No oil. Didn't you see the gauges were low?"

"I guess I didn't pay attention," I said, feeling like an idiot.

"You know, they should make *everyone* take auto shop class in high school." He shook his head. "Those gauges tell you more than just when you need gas."

I wanted to pound the dashboard. "So I guess putting a new engine in the car would cost a lot of money." Not like I had the money to do that anyway.

"Even a rebuilt engine would cost more than the car's worth. I can tow you to the garage. Then you can call someone to come get you."

I let out a frustrated groan. "How much will that cost?"

Slim scuffed the ground with his work boots. "It's a few miles up the road. How about twenty bucks?"

"Okay," I said.

"I just need to bang a U-ey and back up to your car. It'll only take a few more minutes."

Once Slim started to hook up my car, he let me wait in the truck's warm cab. I pushed aside a pile of yellow Juicy Fruit gum wrappers and considered my crappy situation. With thirty dollars in my pocket, a dead car, and a boyfriend who wouldn't kiss me, my life sounded like a bad country song.

All I wanted to do was visit Bobbi. Why did it have to be so hard? I hated the thought of calling her and asking to be picked up. Slim seemed like a nice guy. Maybe he'd take me to her hotel if I offered him my last ten dollars.

He got behind the wheel. "So where were you headed when you broke down?"

"To meet a friend over at Sugarbush Trail Inn."

"I heard there's some killer runs up there. What's your favorite?"

"Oh, I'm not a skier. She is. My friend is." I stumbled over my words. "Is it possible that I could pay you to drive me there?" I twisted my gloves in my hands. He didn't say anything. "I mean, on your lunch hour or something."

"Well, it's kinda slow today." Slim rubbed his chin. "I guess I could drive you up there. Just pay me for the gas. Maybe my uncle can come up with an idea of what to do with your car while we're gone."

"Your uncle owns the shop?"

"Yeah. He taught me all about fixing cars."

His CB radio crackled. "Excuse me." He picked up the microphone part. "Base, this is Slim. Come back, I didn't hear you."

A static voice replied, "There's a bear in the bushes two miles west of the shop."

All I could do was shrug and shake my head. I'd gone from sneaking out of The Ark to watching for cops hiding in the woods.

The process of driving to the garage and taking my car off the tow truck took longer than I expected. It was past lunchtime when

Slim pulled up to the entrance of the inn. With garland wrapped around the columns and lights on all the trees, the magic rush of Christmas poured over me.

"Wow, I didn't expect this place to be so fancy." I was under-dressed, but knowing Bobbi, she'd have the right clothes to share with me.

"These ski resorts sure do a good job getting into the spirit." Slim pulled a business card out of his pocket and scribbled on it. "Take this. It's got the number of the shop on the front and my cell on the back." He fidgeted. "You know, in case the shop's closed... so you can tell us what to do with your car."

Poor guy seemed nervous. "Thanks, Slim. You've gone out of your way for me. I really appreciate it." I took the card and handed him the last bill in my wallet. "Here's ten for the gas."

"No, it's the holidays, you keep it."

"Please. You've done a lot for me." I left the bill on the dash-board and got out. Slim grabbed my overnight bag for me.

We stood by the truck to take in the view of a brilliant blue sky and mountains covered in blankets of snow. The air smelled fresh and clean. Nearby, a strong horse clopped up a side trail pulling a sleigh that jingled with bells. As beautiful as it all was, I couldn't wait another minute to see Bobbi.

"Thanks for everything. I'll call soon about my car." I extended my hand. Slim didn't take it.

"I don't want to get your hands dirty with engine grease." He turned and got back into his tow truck.

Waving goodbye, I rushed inside the spacious lobby. This was nothing like the budget hotels my family stayed in on our road trips. A two-story Christmas tree decorated with shiny ornaments and cranberry garlands filled the foyer. An antique mirror adorned with a huge gold bow hung on a wall. Off to the right of the tree was a sitting area with festive poinsettia plants, leather couches, and low tables where servers carried drinks to guests. Ma would've loved this place.

I found the reception desk and, after a short wait, a young woman greeted me. She reminded me of a raccoon with white circles around her eyes and a deep tan on the rest of her face. This must be what they called a ski tan.

"Welcome to Sugarbush Trails Inn. Are you checking in?"

"No, I'm here to meet a guest. Could you ring her room?"

"I'd be happy to." She picked up her phone. "What's the name?"

"Roberta Young. She's with James and Judith Young. My name is Kate Bennett."

"Hello, this is reception. A Kate Bennett is in the lobby. Yes, I certainly will. Yes, I'll let her know. You're welcome." She hung up almost laughing. "Well, someone is very happy to see you. My instructions were to tell you not to move an inch. Ms. Young will be right down."

The thought of seeing Bobbi made me feel like I was thawing inside. Everything cold and tight started to unfold like a crocus pushing through the dirt in spring. I smiled with my whole body.

CHAPTER 36

JUDITH WOULD HAVE CRINGED at her daughter's entrance. Bobbi's hair flew as she barreled toward me like a puppy. We threw our arms around each other.

Bobbi whispered in my ear, "I can't believe you're here." She rocked me side to side for a full minute before letting go.

"I missed you too." A small crowd had gathered to watch us. "Can we go someplace private?"

Bobbi didn't miss a beat. "Everyone, this is my best friend, Kate Bennett. She has traveled from another planet to see me today."

I played along and took a bow. If she'd asked, I would've done the Macarena with her right then.

"So, are you hungry for some real food?"

"Starving."

"Great. I know just the place. And we can charge everything to the room." Bobbi signaled for a bellman. "Please be a dear and take this bag up to room 510." If she only knew she sounded just like her mother.

"I'm sorry I'm dressed in this old turtleneck and jeans." Bobbi wore a stylish red sweater and black leggings. "I've never been in a place like this."

"Don't worry. It's fine for the day. Tonight, I'll dress you up. Just like old times."

She led me to a restaurant with a roaring stone fireplace. Wood-paneled walls and iron chandeliers made the room quiet and dark. As soon as the waiter came, we placed our orders so we'd have time to talk without interruption.

"Are both your parents here? Do they mind that I've dropped in like this?"

"They're both here and thrilled you are too. We've got a suite. You'll stay in my room."

"That's awesome. Oh, Bobbi, I have so much to tell you. How long until you have to do something with your parents?"

"It's we. Until *we* do something. We're free until dinner. How'd the drive go?"

I sagged back into my seat. "My stupid car broke down on the way." I told her the whole story and when I got to the part where Slim came to rescue me, Bobbi choked on her soda.

"It may sound amusing, but now I have no car."

Bobbi clapped. "Great, you can stay with me and never go back."

"Remember Luke?" I showed her my engagement ring.

"Do you really love him?"

"I do." My stomach flip-flopped. "But I did a terrible thing."

Bobbi watched me closely. "The night you broke curfew?"

I looked down at my lap and then back at her. "It was with Nick."

"The one who kisses great and who called me? He sounds like a lot of fun."

"That night he called you, I'd made a crazy deal with him. I was so frustrated when I couldn't get past your housekeeper." I took a deep breath and let it out. "Nick said if he could get you on the phone, I had to have a drink with him. It was the first time I ever drank, and I ended up getting drunk."

Bobbi's eyes popped. "You're kidding, right?"

I shook my head. "It gets worse."

"Worse how?"

"We had sex." I cringed and glanced up to see if God was going to strike me dead with a falling chandelier.

Bobbi grabbed my arm. "Seriously, Kate. There's no one from God's headquarters up there. The important question is who do you want to be with?"

She didn't judge me. I loved her so much for that.

"You know how Luke is. He's seen me lose it and that didn't scare him away. But he always follows the rules and there are so many at The Ark. The whole campus watches our every move. And even when we are alone, he barely kisses me." I rolled the napkin ring between my palms. "Then there's Nick. He makes me feel things…" I blushed. "If only I could meld them together, I'd have the perfect guy."

"In a million years, I never would've thought that you'd be in a love triangle."

Sinning and love were not the same, but I didn't correct her. The waiter dropped off our sandwiches. After a few bites, I blurted out, "Why did you leave?"

Bobbi flinched and took a long gulp of water. "Let's finish

your stories first. What else's been going on since I left?"

"Well, you remember Pastor Wayne?" She shrugged. "He was my youth leader in high school. He just started his new ministry and wants to open his church up to everyone, like the early church did. It's created a huge panic."

"What's the panic?" Bobbi said.

"He's welcoming gays."

Bobbi's mouth fell open. "Oh, Pastor Almighty must be having a fit. Remember that morning chapel service when he went off on the sexual sins tirade? I always wondered who got caught doing what."

No one would ever forget that sermon, but what stuck in my head now was that she called Pastor Steve Pastor Almighty.

"Is that why you're here? Are you a lesbian on the run?" Bobbi reached for my face and pretended she was going to kiss me.

"You goofball." I swatted her away. "The Ark could split over this. I've never seen people argue like this before. Some are for the open church, but others are talking about something called conversion therapy. Do you know what it is?"

"Yes, and it is horrible and illegal almost everywhere. The sneaky ones still doing it torture the gays straight until they hate themselves. Or worse."

I shuddered at her words. "And then there's Luke. He and Pastor Wayne are friends from back when they went to seminary. But Luke believes whatever Pastor Steve believes."

Bobbi arched her eyebrows. "What do you believe?"

The waiter interrupted us and slid a small silver tray on the table. While Bobbi signed off for the room charge, a warm shiver touched my heart. Something about her question brought back

Matt's simple words from Thanksgiving, "God is love."

Love should include everyone, but The Ark didn't.

We finished lunch and toured the inn. I let out a kid-like yelp when Bobbi showed me the steaming outdoor hot tub with a spectacular view of the resort grounds.

"Can we go in there?" I said.

"Definitely. Let's go back to the room and change."

Minutes later we stood at the door to Bobbi's hotel room. In her rush to meet me, she'd left her key in the room. Just as she raised her hand to knock, I grabbed her wrist. "Are you sure it's okay I'm here?"

"Could you relax for one minute?" Bobbi's mouth twisted into a smirk. "With you here, they know I won't be sneaking off with some hot ski instructor."

"Have you met one?"

"Oh there's enough here for both of us."

Some things never changed.

Bobbi rapped on the door, and a tall man with wavy brown hair opened it. His clothes looked both casual and polished. Behind wire-framed glasses, he had gentle gray eyes.

"Please, come in."

"You didn't believe me, did you, Dad?" Bobbi play-punched him on the arm. "I told you she'd come. Kate Bennett, this is my dad, James Young."

Bobbi called her stepfather *Dad*. I still didn't know a thing about her real father.

"Kate, it's a pleasure to finally meet you."

"Same here, Mr. Young."

"Please, call me James." He shook my hand with a strong grip and lowered his voice. "I prefer Jim, but I think you know Judith."

We followed him into an airy living room decorated in shades of white and pale green. Classical music played from hidden speakers. Beyond the wood-framed windows, a chair lift and some ski trails lined the mountain.

At first I didn't see Bobbi's mom. In her ivory sweater and matching pants, she blended into the sofa.

When she rose, I approached her. "It's so nice to see you again."

"Thank you. It's a pleasure to have you join us." She air-kissed my cheeks and the heavy scent of flowery perfume lingered. "You're our guest for as long as you can stay."

"I'm sorry for the short notice."

Bobbi huffed behind me. "Mom, Dad, Kate and I are going for a soak in the outdoor hot tub."

"You two go ahead and enjoy," Judith said. "We've got massages scheduled in a few minutes."

Double doors to the left of the suite opened to the master bedroom. On the right side was a single door. Bobbi took my wrist and led me into that room. Heaps of clothes covered one twin bed. The other was made up.

Bobbi pointed to my overnight bag. "Let's see what we've got to work with."

I dumped my clothes onto the neat bed, and Bobbi's silk scarf slid out. "Oh, I've got something of yours." I threw it to her. "I borrowed it to wear on Thanksgiving."

Bobbi froze. The scarf floated to the floor.

I bent to pick it up. "You know, you look just like Elizabeth did when she saw it on me. Man, she almost dropped the pie she was holding. What's the deal with this scarf?"

"So you have it." Bobbi backed up to her bed and sat down hard. "I thought she took it."

"*Elizabeth?* Why would she take it?"

"Because he bought it for me," Bobbi said, looking past me.

I was completely confused. "Who? What are you talking about?"

"Pastor Steve."

CHAPTER 37

"PASTOR STEVE BOUGHT you that scarf? I don't understand."

Bobbi shook her hands as if they were wet. "I'll need a drink for this."

I wanted to protest, but instead watched her pick up the phone on her bedside table and order us each a Hot Chocolate Anti-freeze. Anything made with hot chocolate sounded harmless enough. We went into the living area of the suite just as her parents were leaving.

"We will be back in a couple of hours. Shall we all dine together this evening?" Judith said.

"Yeah. Sure," Bobbi said. She rolled her eyes at me. "'Shall we all dine together?' You see why I call her the Queen Mum."

"Bobbi, I need to tell you something. I saw a receipt for an expensive scarf in Elizabeth's files. Is that it?"

"You went through her things?" A look of disbelief covered her face.

"It's a long story, but I was looking for your phone number. I found something else too. An odd list with initials, dates, and amounts. Your initials and the date you left were on it."

"Must be his dirty list."

"What do you mean?" I was so lost. Bobbi could've been speaking another language.

"Do you have it?"

"I made a copy of it. It's in my bag. Wait a sec." I rushed into her room and rummaged through my shoulder bag until I found it.

Bobbi patted a spot for me to sit beside her, and I handed her the list.

"Holy shit. There's one almost every six months. That's close to one a semester for the past three years."

I flopped back against the couch. "Bobbi, I have no idea what you're talking about."

A knock on the door interrupted us, and Bobbi jumped up to open it. The waiter set a silver tray with our drinks on the coffee table. Without looking, she signed the receipt. I peeked at the price and couldn't believe how much it cost. I'd make sure to drink every drop.

Bobbi took a chair opposite me and the scent of peppermint swirled between us. When I took a sip, the mint flavor burned my throat. *There must be a strong candy cane melting in the bottom of my mug.*

"I guess I should start with why I went to The Ark." Bobbi stared across the room for a few seconds before she spoke again. "I got arrested for shoplifting."

Oh God, what Elizabeth told me in the chapel was true. I said nothing and hoped my neutral face didn't betray either of us.

"You're probably thinking, why would I shoplift? My parents have money, and I could've paid for the stuff I stole. It was a cheap thrill, that's all. Like driving really fast. The more I got away with it, the more daring I got. The first time I was caught, I got off easy. But by the third time, my parents had to hire an expensive lawyer and a therapist. The therapist told the judge that I wasn't a criminal. Told him some mumbo jumbo about how I had low self-esteem and other stuff. Can you believe it?" She swung her hair over her shoulder. "Anyway, to avoid getting a record, the judge agreed to let me attend a religious school."

"The Ark."

"Yep."

Oh, my poor friend. *And what a secret to carry around.*

"When I got to The Ark, I was okay for a while. But after a few weeks with no cell phones or internet, I thought I'd die. And it was God, God, God all the time. I might've made it except for Mrs. Huffy and all that submissive woman crap." Bobbi rolled her eyes. "I couldn't buy it. Without you, Kate, I might've gone nuts."

My heart crumpled. Bobbi was lost in so many ways.

"Wasn't long before the urge or sickness, whatever it is, came back. I skipped classes and went to the mall." Bobbi exhaled deeply. "I got caught stealing again. Pastor Steve and Elizabeth had to come and get me. He vouched for me, and the store dropped the charges. To try and fix me, Pastor Steve recommended counseling sessions with him twice a week. That's how I got the scarf. He went back to the store and bought it for me."

I set my mug on the coffee table. "As a gift?"

Bobbi didn't answer. She stood and went to the window. The low sun framed the back of her head, leaving her face in shadows.

"He wanted me to meet him in his home office. Said it would protect my privacy. I hate to admit it now, but there was something about him, his power, his strength…I had a crush on him. During those sessions I flirted with him to see if he liked me too. When he prayed for me, I sat close. Sometimes, I'd fake cry just so he'd console me."

"Stop." The air in the room thickened. "Pastor Steve's a married man and the founder of The Ark."

Bobbi covered her face with her hands. "I know, but I'd never met anyone like him. It was a crush at first, but then I fell for him."

The room swayed. Shoplifting was bad enough, but going after Pastor Steve?

"He seemed so happy when I arrived for my sessions. He made me feel special."

I knew that feeling too and a part of me softened at her words.

"But in the end, he didn't love me back."

A thousand spiders raced up my back. "The end?" My voice squeaked. I grabbed a toss pillow and hugged it tight.

"There's more…why I had to leave…but you have to promise you'll keep it a secret."

I didn't want to know more, but she'd taken me this far. The sun slid behind a mountain, dimming the room. I fumbled and found the lamp switch.

Bobbi waited for me to say "I promise" and then she turned away from the light toward the dark window.

"The last time we met, he said he had something special for me. We went into the room with the mirrored wall. He reached into his jacket pocket and pulled out the scarf."

Sentence by sentence, she pieced together a time bomb. I held the pillow in front of my body like a shield.

"He stood behind me and tied it around my neck. Told me I was beautiful. I leaned back into him. He wrapped my hair in his hand and smelled it. I was so happy he finally felt the same way I did. I looked into the mirror to see his face." Her voice caught. "It scared me. No smile. And his eyes. Dead eyes."

I barely breathed.

Bobbi placed her palms on the window and leaned against it. "I tried to laugh. Told him this was a mistake. That I didn't want him to touch me anymore. When I tried to break free, he tightened his hold on my hair. He groaned and rubbed himself against me. The more I tried to pull away, the harder he twisted my hair. I told him he was hurting me. He said 'I like the fighters.'"

Her voice rose. "I begged him to stop but he wouldn't let go. He knocked me to my knees. 'Look in the mirror,' he said. 'That's what a stealing whore looks like.'"

An explosion went off in my head, nearly drowning out Bobbi's words.

"I told him to let go of me or I'd scream. He said, 'Go ahead, Jezebel. No one's going to hear you. You're getting just what you deserve.'"

My mind didn't want to believe her, but memories of Pastor Steve sniffing my hair, kissing me on the lips, and hugging me too long and too tightly came back like a spark of lightning. Whatever Bobbi's faults, she wouldn't make this up.

"I managed to get my arms free and I swung at him. He laughed. It was the meanest sound I've ever heard. Then he said, 'It's me or jail.'"

Bobbi faced me. Her hands curled into fists.

"He played me and he blackmailed me. I never saw it coming." Tears streamed down her face.

"Oh, Bobbi." My whole being went out to her.

She kept talking as if she hadn't heard me. Her words raced out. "He dragged me to the bed and pinned me down. I lay there like a ragdoll with my eyes shut. I prayed he'd have a heart attack. That God would strike him dead." Hate filled her voice. "But why would God listen to me? When he finished, I rolled over and dry heaved."

I stood to go to her, but she put her hand up. She let out a sigh. It was the saddest sound I'd ever heard.

"A few days later, Thanksgiving break came. When we got home from Montana, there was a letter from The Ark. It was a copy of a letter sent to the judge. It said The Ark was recommending I finish my probation at home. My record at the school was exemplary. Someone packed up all my stuff and shipped it back." Bobbi wiped at her eyes and came to sit beside me on the couch. "Do you think I'm a bad person?"

I shook my head and took her hands. "He raped you. Nothing you did would make you deserve that. Bobbi, you have to press charges."

She hung her head. "I can't. You know who'd win."

It was her word against his. The shoplifter versus the holy man. His lawyers would exalt him, and they'd crucify her.

Pastor Steve said *fighters*. A sour wave rolled through my stomach. "What if we could find the others, the ones on the list?"

"I just want to forget it ever happened. I never want to see him again. Never want to talk about it again."

My friend, whose soft laugh reminded me of liquid bells, was broken. She leaned her head against my shoulder, and I wrapped my arm around her.

"I'm so sorry this happened to you. It makes me sick, Bobbi. You *are* a good person. He's a monster."

"I'm so glad you found me."

CHAPTER 38

BOBBI PLEADED WITH ME not to let her secret ruin our two days together. Because I didn't know how to ski, we stayed busy with soaks in the hot tub, horse-drawn sleigh rides, and fancy meals with her parents. At night, we'd kick back and watch newly released movies in Bobbi's hotel room.

But when the lights went out, no luxuries in the world could keep thoughts about Pastor Steve away. I'd felt so special during the private times he spoke to me. His sermons had touched my heart and made me weep. With all the wonderful people at The Ark, how could he have gotten away with such a crime?

Each night, I'd tossed under the blankets from the weight of it all. I wanted to beg Bobbi to report Pastor Steve. He couldn't get away with what he did. Her secret was too great for me to keep buried inside. My mind wandered everywhere. I didn't understand Elizabeth's reaction to Bobbi's scarf, but now it was obvious. And, the list of names I found in her desk made me think she knew exactly what was going on. How could she stay with Pastor Steve?

Always itching at the edge of my thoughts was my sin with Nick. I'd visualize Luke's face and realize how much I needed him. But deep down I was worried about the way he idolized his uncle and how difficult it would be to convince him to leave The Ark. Maybe after our wedding, Luke and I could go on a mission in a faraway country.

On our last morning, James knocked and opened the door a few inches. "Your mother and I are heading down for breakfast and then to the slopes. Let's catch up at lunch."

"Thanks, Dad," Bobbi said. He closed the door and she fumbled for the bedside clock. "God, it's only seven. Let's sleep in. We can get room service later."

"Perfect." I yawned and fell back asleep.

We got up two hours later and Bobbie ordered a feast of eggs, bacon, bagels, smoked salmon, fruit, juice, and coffee. I didn't know what to eat first.

"Merry Christmas Eve, Ms. Young," I said in a snooty voice, raising my glass.

Bobbi touched her glass to mine and spoke in a perfect British accent. "Why the same to you, Ms. Bennett."

I stopped smiling. "I know you don't want to talk about it, but how do you get through each day?"

"You know, telling you helped me." Bobbi pulled back her hair. "But, maybe I shouldn't have."

I reached across the table and touched her arm. "You're my friend. You had to tell me. And last night, I made a decision. If Luke and I are going to stay together, it will have to be away from The Ark."

Bobbi locked eyes with me. "If he won't leave, you know there's always a place for you in New York. My parents love you, and after The Ark, we could be roommates anywhere."

We loaded our plates and ate in silence for a few minutes. I wanted to drop it, but so many things still nagged at me. "What do you think the numbers by the initials meant? Is it tuition? Did you pay extra to come to The Ark?"

"Not that I know of."

I jumped up and paced the room. "If it's not tuition, could they be—"

"Payoffs?" we said together.

"How do we stop him?" I said.

"We can't." Bobbi's voice filled with panic. "You promised. Kate, please."

I nodded and returned to the table.

Bobbi finished eating first and went to take a shower. Once I heard the water running, I pulled out Slim's business card and called to let him know I'd see him after lunch to deal with my car. My next call was much harder. I punched the numbers for The Ark.

"God bless you. You've reached The Ark." I recognized the voice.

"Elizabeth, it's Kate."

"Oh, Kate." There was a long pause. "Yes. It's her... Sorry about that. Are you okay? Where are you? We've been worried sick about you."

"I left a note with Sheila. Didn't she tell you?"

"You can't just leave like that." Elizabeth covered the receiver, but I could still hear her side of the conversation. "I know. I'm trying to find out."

"Can you hear me? Everything is fine." Now we were all liars. "I'm in Vermont. My car broke down. It's at a service station. Can Luke meet me there at two?"

"Vermont? What are you doing out there? I thought your family was in Salem. She said she's fine… Sorry. Give me the address, Luke will meet you there. And please, stay where you are."

I hung up as Bobbi came out of the shower. She wore a hotel robe and her hair was wrapped in a towel. "Who was that?"

"I called The Ark. Luke's coming to get me."

She clutched the belt of her robe. "You don't have to go back there."

"I've got to figure stuff out with Luke."

Bobbi crouched beside her bed. She pulled out a pair of short lace-up boots. "These are too big for me. Try them on."

I slipped my bare feet into soft fleece. The boot ended just above my ankles. As I laced them, I ran a finger over the buttery soft leather. "Thank you. I can't believe how warm and beautiful they are. Like dream boots."

"Good, think of me whenever you wear them."

I hugged her and inhaled her vanilla-scented lotion. "You know I'll think of you more than that."

After lunch with her parents, James arranged for a hotel driver to take me back to Slim's shop. I'd never be able to repay this family's generosity. We walked out together to say our goodbyes.

Judith motioned with her gloved hand for me to come close. "When Roberta got in trouble, all her friends in the city abandoned her. You are a true friend. One who's always welcome in our family."

Her words warmed my heart. "Thanks again for everything. I hope I'll see you soon."

Judith's face softened and she lowered her voice. "Are you going to marry him?"

I took in a sharp breath. We hadn't talked about my engagement, but she must have seen my ring. "I've got some stuff to sort out."

"You're not my daughter, but if you were, I'd say enjoy life as much as you can before you settle down." She air-kissed my cheeks.

James smiled and hugged me next. "Don't be a stranger."

Bobbi pulled me away from her parents. She slipped an envelope into the front pocket of my overnight bag.

"What's that?"

"It's a surprise. Open only in case of emergency." She winked.

"You know I hate leaving you. I'll call you soon." We walked the final steps to the waiting car. "What if I try to get to the city for New Year's Eve?"

"Oh yes." Bobbi's eyes lit up. "We have the best parties. I've got the perfect dress for you too."

The driver stood by the open back door. "Are you ready, miss?"

"Yes, thanks." I rolled down my window and shouted to my New York family, "Merry Christmas!"

With cheerful faces, James and Bobbi waved at me. Judith held her hand up in an elegant gesture befitting of her nickname. My spirits sank a bit, but I remembered Bobbi's envelope. On it, she'd written in red and green markers:

Kate,

For Your Next Adventure
You've got the boots to run in
Open this when you need $$$ to run with

Love, Bobbi

Oh, Bobbi. What have you done? I smiled despite myself as I tucked the envelope away.

All too soon, the hotel car approached the service station. I could see Luke in the office. He'd probably already made friends with Slim, so I needed to be extra careful about my details.

"There you go, miss. Need any help getting out?" the driver said.

"No, thank you." As I opened the door, Luke rushed outside. Deep worry lines creased his face.

"Kate." Luke wrapped me inside his jacket. Cocooned against him, I felt the rise and fall of his chest. "Is everything okay?"

I couldn't resist the comfort of his arms. "I'm fine. Thanks for coming to get me."

"When Sheila said you had a family emergency, I called your house to find out what happened. When you weren't there, I imagined all kinds of horrible things. But here you are. Thank God. He answered my prayers."

I stepped back. "You called my house? What did you say to my family?"

"Your father said you hadn't mentioned coming home. I tried not to alarm him. But what are you doing here? Why were you at that fancy inn?"

"A friend was there. I needed to see her. The note I left, I wrote it too fast."

"You know we're a team and you can tell me anything. Please don't leave like that again."

"I'm so sorry that I worried you." I searched his face until he smiled.

Luke hooked his arm through mine. "Okay then, let's deal with your car. Slim has a good idea."

As we entered the garage office, Slim stood to greet us.

"Hi Slim, good to see you again. You have an idea about what to do with my car?" I said.

"Sort of." He scuffed the floor with his work boots. "Well, since repairing your car costs more than it's worth, I told Luke that the local high school shop teacher is always looking for engines to take apart. Luke thought it was a great idea and that you'd like to donate it."

I couldn't speak. How could I forget that the men at The Ark made all the decisions?

Luke took a pen out his jacket. "All that's left to do is sign the title over to the shop."

He'd gone through my glove box without asking. I signed the document without looking at either of them.

"It was nice meeting you, Slim. If you ever make it out to Lincoln, come visit one of our services." Luke shook his hand. "Thanks for helping out my girl."

"Yes, thank you. And have a wonderful holiday." I managed a genuine smile and Slim tipped his cap.

"Well then." Luke took me by the elbow and guided me outside.

A familiar black Town Car was parked facing one of the service stalls. *Just freaking great.* Pastor Steve let Luke borrow his car. Now I'd have to smell that man's cologne the whole way back to The Ark. Luke opened the back door and slid my overnight bag on the seat. I started to walk around the car.

"Wait. You're back here too," Luke said.

"That's not funny. I'm sitting up front with you."

"No, you can't. Pastor Steve's sitting there."

I couldn't breathe.

CHAPTER 39

THUNDER STRIKES CRASHED in my head. *No, God. Not him. Not now.* Bobbi's secret was too close to the surface. I backed away from Luke.

"What's the matter with you?" Luke reached for me and got the edge of my coat. "You look like you've seen a ghost."

"My car. I left something in there." I broke free and spun away.

He called after me, "But I cleaned it out for you already."

Of course he did.

I burst into the garage office. Slim dropped some paperwork he'd been holding.

"Where's my car? I need to get something."

"It's around back. Want me to show you?" He reached for his jacket.

I shook my head. "Is it locked?"

"No. Remember, it's dead. No one can steal it."

"Right."

As I sped to the back of the lot, I saw Pastor Steve standing by his car with a hand on Luke's shoulder. The sight of him made me want to throw up. *Luke, can't you do anything without him?*

My old Subaru was parked next to some other broken-down heaps. I jumped in. The cold seat numbed my butt. I rested my forehead against the steering wheel and the silent swearing began.

I swore at Pastor Steve for what he'd done to Bobbi and those other girls.

I swore at God for letting it happen.

And I swore at Ma for dying and being right about The Ark.

A knock on my driver's side window startled me. Luke pressed his palm flat against it. I put my hand on the glass to match our wrists together. My fingers barely reached the start of his. I heard him say, "Can I open the door?"

I nodded.

"What's wrong, Katie Pie?"

His nickname reminded me of Thanksgiving when everything was still good, before Pastor Steve ruined it all.

"I'm so confused. I don't understand anything anymore."

"What's going on? How can I help you?"

My voice tightened. "Why'd you bring him here with you?"

"You're a member of his flock. You went missing. The shepherd always searches and gathers the lamb in his arms."

Oh no, not a Bible lesson now. "Oh Luke, I just want to be with you."

"Come out. I know you're freezing in there." He spoke in his most encouraging voice. "You can sit up front. Pastor Steve can sit in the back this time."

"Is that allowed?" My words came out mean, and I didn't care.

"Please, tell me what you want."

How could I put into words what I wanted? Luke couldn't undo the past. He offered me his arm and with each step toward the Town Car, my body tensed. I forced myself to breathe. To stay strong for myself and for Bobbi.

"There you are. We are so relieved to see you." Pastor Steve started toward me with open arms. Luke shook his head no.

"Pastor Steve, if it's not too much trouble, I'd like Kate to sit up front with me."

"No trouble at all."

I couldn't believe it. Luke actually put me first.

From behind the plate glass window of the office, Slim watched us leave. I wondered what he thought of these two church men who'd come to get me.

Once in the car, I vowed not to make a scene.

"Slim seems like a nice guy," Luke said.

"He is."

"And your engine seized?" Pastor Steve said.

"Yep," I said.

"How did you like the resort? I hear it caters to the rich and famous." Pastor Steve wouldn't shut up.

"Yep." The car heated up. I unzipped my coat and slid out of it.

"Kate, you left The Ark so suddenly. We were very worried." Pastor Steve's words sounded hollow to me. "Now that you're with us, you seem very angry and defensive. When you're ready to talk, know you're in a safe place with us."

He went on and prayed for me. I tried not to listen to his voice, but words like *mistakes*, *forgiveness*, and *confessing our sins* reached my ears. In my mind, I spun in my seat and spat out what a fraud he was.

For the next half hour, the only sound was the whoosh of cars driving by. When we missed the exit for Lincoln, I sat up straighter. "Wait. You're going the wrong way."

"We're not going to The Ark. We're going to a camp by Squam Lake." Luke turned quickly to smile at me and then focused back on the road. "You'll love it. It's a Carlson family tradition on Christmas Eve. This year we've got it for four days. We'll get back on Sunday in time for evening service."

There was no way I was spending four days with Pastor Steve in some cabin near a *God-forsaken lake*, as Bobbi would say. "I've got to go back to campus. Please, drop me off first."

Luke looked over. "Don't be silly. This is our annual tradition. No phones. No television. Just family."

"That's right, and you're part of the family," Pastor Steve said. "We're making good time too. I bet we'll be the first ones there."

I crossed my arms as dread spread through my bones.

"If anyone sees a white boulder with an arrow on it, give a shout out. That's our landmark," Luke said.

Pastor Steve found it, and we headed down a narrow dirt road.

"What happens when another car comes?" I said, trying not to cringe.

"There are a couple of turnouts. One car has to back up into the closest one. But I don't think we'll see anyone else this time of year. This is mostly a summer place," Luke said.

We'd be isolated in the middle of nowhere like a slasher horror movie. Maybe if I kept my mouth shut, no one would have any reason to hurt me. *Lord, please help me. I'm losing it.*

Luke parked in front of a tired two-story house with mismatched paint. The front steps sagged like they'd given up on the world.

"We beat everyone else. I'll go in and air it out." Pastor Steve opened his car door. "Luke, why don't you show Kate the lake and then bring in some firewood."

A couple of faded rowboats rested behind the house. Luke took my hand in his warm one and led me down a path. My heart ached because I didn't know how to tell Luke what I needed without telling him what happened to Bobbi.

Except for our boots crunching down the path, it was quiet and peaceful. We cleared the trees and I stopped short at the sight of a frozen lake. It stretched out as far as I could see. The words from the fortune teller in Salem murmured through the trees: *"If she gets too close to the thin ice, she will fall in and be trapped forever."*

God help me.

Luke stood close beside me. "We might not be alone again this weekend. I have something difficult to ask you."

A chill ran through me even though the setting sun warmed my face.

"Did you really see a girlfriend, or is there someone else? Is it Nick?" He faced me with watery eyes.

I blew out a breath and spoke with conviction. "I told you the truth about visiting a girlfriend. I saw Bobbi."

Relief broke over Luke's face. "My sweet Kate, I'm sorry I doubted you. The devil filled my head with thoughts of… Never mind." He pulled me into a hug.

Oh Luke, I don't deserve you, but I can't lose you.

We walked until we came to a woodpile stacked between two tree stumps. Luke hoisted logs into a rusted wheelbarrow, and I gathered the skinnier branches. In the distance, a white-tailed deer skipped off, leaving a puff of snow behind.

Inside, the house was clean and cold. Luke and I carried armfuls of firewood into a spacious common room that served as the den, dining room, and living room. Dark paneling covered most of the walls. The best feature was the picture window with a stunning view of the lake.

Pastor Steve crouched in front of the fireplace. My pulse beat loud in my ears as I lay my branches as far away from him as I could. Over the mantel hung the head of a moose—God forgive me, I wanted it to fall on him.

Luke listened to Pastor Steve's lecture on fire-making. Soon, the flames crackled and started heating up the room. Near the stairwell, I found a place to hang my coat and slip off my new boots. *Thank you, Bobbi.*

I sat down in one corner of a long couch and wrapped a blanket around me. The roaring fire made me drowsy. I'd just close my eyes for a minute…pretend I was somewhere else.

The weight of someone sinking onto the couch woke me. I blinked and screamed. Pastor Steve sat inches from my feet. The blanket tangled around my legs. I couldn't get up.

"Sorry, I didn't mean to frighten you." He reached out to me.

"No. Don't touch me."

He stood and backed away.

I kicked free of the blanket and jumped up. "Where's Luke?"

"He just went outside to… Are you afraid of me?" Pastor Steve wore a hurt expression.

I moved toward the dining room table.

"Listen," he spoke slowly, "you stay there. I'll stay by the fireplace. Have I done something to upset you?"

I watched a lone ember fly up into the air and land on the hearth.

"Did someone else upset you?" He used a softer, comforting tone.

No eye contact. I would not let him pull me in.

"Before you judge, remember there are always two sides to a story." Pastor Steve's long pause made me look at him. He'd moved to the other end of the table. "Ms. Young's envelope fell out of your overnight bag when I carried it into the house."

I grabbed the edge of the table. *Liar.* He probably found it in the car and didn't say a word about it for the whole ride to the camp.

"That envelope is none of your business." This was Ma's voice, and I needed her.

"Everyone and everything in this ministry is my business. You ran off for two days. You weren't with your family... Luke was sick with worry over you. And, on top of all that, your car broke down." Pastor Steve laid his palms on the table. "What if someone dangerous got to you before the tow truck guy?"

I looked him in the eye. "There's danger everywhere."

Pastor Steve stopped. "The flesh is weak, isn't it, Kate?"

The hair rose on my arms as if an icy wind blew in. If he knew about Nick, why didn't he tell Luke?

"You look pale. Let me help you." Pastor Steve came toward me.

"No. Stay away from me." I put my hands out to stop him. They trembled. "I know what you did."

"I don't know what Ms. Young told you, but if you think I would risk my reputation, my ministry, or my family to lay one hand on her... Be careful who you trust, Kate." He shook his head. "I feel sorry for her and worse for you. I don't know what she told you, unless..."

"Unless what?"

"Unless she's so lost that she'd say anything to get you to leave The Ark. Just so you'd follow her path instead of the one God chose for you."

I hesitated. Judith told me I was Bobbi's only friend. Bobbi had pleaded with me to go to college with her and be her roommate. Wasps of doubt tried to sting, but I squashed them.

"What about the other girls? The ones on the list?"

Pastor Steve froze. A vein throbbed on the side of his forehead.

Ma's confidence filled me. "I found it in Elizabeth's office when you asked me to cover for her."

He switched to his comforting voice. "It's been a very hard year for you, dear. First, your mother's death, and how your father's blamed you for it. You aren't thinking clearly. Let me pray for the demons tormenting you."

"You hypocrite." I glared at him. "Step down. Have Paul take over the ministry."

"I will not step down."

"I'll expose you."

"Are you willing to lose your soul mate?" His eyes tried to pierce me. "And hurt a lot of good people. Is that what you want?"

"I didn't start this, you did."

"What in the world is going on here?" We turned at Elizabeth's voice. "Kate, come with me. Steve, there are groceries in the car."

The ice cracked.

CHAPTER 40

I DIDN'T KNOW HOW MUCH Elizabeth heard, but the way she stomped up the stairs, she'd heard enough. If it wasn't for the railing, I might not have had the strength to follow her. She stopped in front of an open door and gestured for me to go inside. Her face was unreadable.

Double bunk beds and a pullout sofa crowded the small room. My overnight bag lay on the sofa and I raced over to search it for Bobbi's envelope. A small miracle, it was still sealed.

I turned back to Elizabeth. She stood in front of the closed door with her arms crossed over her long red sweater. It was like we'd never met before.

"Do you want to tell me what's going on?"

I didn't flinch. "You know what he did."

"What did he do?"

"To start, he bought Bobbi that scarf."

"So, you've been with her." Elizabeth's index finger fluttered for an instant. "But you're wrong. She's a thief. She stole it."

"I saw the receipt in your office."

"How dare you go through my things?"

My voice stayed calm. "Pastor Steve asked me to fill in for you while you were away with your mother."

"She's a wicked temptress. She was in love with him. When he didn't love her back, she tried to seduce him and steal him from me. You can't trust her."

I stepped toward her. "This isn't about Bobbi. This is about what your husband did to her. He's supposed to be a man of God."

The cords in Elizabeth's neck stood out. "You don't know a thing."

She opened the door and left.

I fell back against the couch and hugged myself. How could Elizabeth know what he did and still protect him? It took a few minutes for my nerves to steady. I had to get out of this place and convince Luke to take me.

With my bag slung over my shoulder, I crept down the stairs. Pastor Steve and Elizabeth stood at the window overlooking the lake talking softly to each other. I slipped into my boots and coat, eased open the back door, and left without a sound.

A few moments later, I found Luke heading down a path with an empty wheelbarrow.

"Luke, wait up."

He stopped near some dead branches and wiped his brow. "Hi. What's up? Why are you lugging your overnight bag around?"

I paused to collect my breath. "Something's happened. I can't explain it, but it's really important that we leave." *God, please let Luke understand me.* "I thought we could go visit Pastor Wayne in person. You and he could try to work things out."

Luke shook his head. "You're not making any sense. You want me to leave my family for the holidays, but you can't explain it? And then visit Wayne? Honestly, Kate. Enough about him."

The hard look on his face shocked me.

"How naïve are you? Why do you think he opened up his church to homosexuals?" He waited. "That's right. And, we're never going there. I certainly don't want anyone to think I'm one of them."

His words fell on me like sharp rocks. Even if Pastor Wayne was gay, I couldn't believe the hate in Luke's voice. The way he said *them* sounded nothing like the kind person I knew.

I reached for his arm. "I don't understand your feelings about this."

"You don't have to. Your job is to respect me."

My job? I didn't know this Luke. He was cutting off a friendship, speaking like a bigot, and demeaning me. Less than an hour ago, he'd wrapped me in his arms and called me Katie Pie.

"When you get back to the cabin, let Pastor Steve know I'll be a few more minutes loading up some firewood."

Numb and wounded, I trudged back to the cabin just as a faded blue Honda pulled up.

Luke's cousin, Matt, smiled and waved, but when he got out of the car and saw me, his expression changed. "Are you okay?"

"I need to walk for a few minutes."

"Do you want some company? There's a neat boathouse down the path."

"Yes. Please." Matt took my bag. He put it in his car and led me up a small hill away from the house. Icicles sparkled on twigs and clumps of snow dropped off tree branches without a sound.

At the crest of the hill, I spotted a weathered shack near the water. "Is that it?"

"Yep, but watch out, it can be icy here."

Just as he'd warned, I slid several feet before reaching out for a tree trunk to slow me down. A shower of pine needles fell on my head. Matt rushed over, a huge smile on his face.

"Go ahead, I know I look ridiculous." I pulled at the sticky needles in my hair.

He let out a laugh. "Oh, it's not your hair. It's the way you slid. You looked like a panicked surfer."

Matt gave me his arm and we took baby steps the rest of the way. The front of the boathouse had a large opening with hanging double doors. He slid them open to reveal a red boat docked on the sand floor.

"Your ship awaits," Matt said, with a sweep of his arm. "I'll grab some blankets."

I looked around. The faint odor of fish hung in the air. The walls were just planks of exposed wood with no insulation. In a corner, a mummified rat lay caught in a trap. I scrambled into the boat and sat on the bench.

Matt stepped in and handed me a blanket. He arranged his as a seat cushion while I wrapped mine around my legs. Facing each other, Matt reached down to drag out a toolbox from under his bench. He opened it up and took out a new pack of menthol cigarettes and a lighter. After a drag, he offered it to me.

"No thanks. But you go ahead." I tried to act cool. "How long have you been hiding this habit?"

"Being a pastor's son isn't as easy as it looks."

"I don't think it looks easy at all." And he didn't even know the worst of being Pastor Steve's son. *Oh God, how can I live with this secret?*

"Do you want to talk about what's going on?" Matt said.

I smoothed out the blanket and chose my words carefully. "I have to leave The Ark."

Matt raised his eyebrows. "Leave? What about you and Luke?"

"You've known Luke your whole life. I've only known him a few months. All that time I thought he was the most accepting person I'd ever met."

"And now you're finding out he's not perfect."

I was too miserable to smile. "Luke's changed. Ever since he found out Pastor Wayne's gay and what he plans for his ministry...I've just seen this hateful side of him come out. I'm so confused."

Matt coughed as he exhaled. "Whoa. Just because Wayne opened his ministry to the gay community, don't assume he's gay. But that's not the point here. It's really about Luke and his relationship with my dad. It was painful for him growing up without a father, so he'd do anything to please the one man who did love him. And the way he's done that is by agreeing with whatever my dad preaches."

Poor Luke, I didn't realize what he'd been through.

"But on this issue, I'm with Wayne." Matt's face brightened. "And he's offered me a position as his youth minister. I'm thinking about taking it."

"You'd be a great youth minister." I wondered what Pastor Steve would think of his son's choice.

Matt put his hand on my arm. "You should know that Luke's like a brother to me. And as much as I'd love you to be part of our family, maybe you should take some time to think about what you really want." He buried his cigarette butt in the sand. "We should head back. They'll be wondering what happened to us."

He offered me a piece of mint gum on the walk back. When we reached the house, I stopped quickly as if it was haunted.

"I can't go in there."

"Is this about more than Luke?"

Elizabeth's face appeared in the front window. Her ghostly expression chilled the blood in my veins.

"I've got to go back to The Ark." My voice cracked. "Please help me."

Sadness filled Matt's eyes. "You'll be alone on Christmas."

"Can I borrow your car? I'm a really safe driver. I'll fill it with gas."

"If this is what you really want, I can hitch a ride back with someone." He opened the trunk and took out a small suitcase. "Do you want to go in and say goodbye?"

"No, no." After a quick hug, Matt handed me his keys. "Thank you for doing this. You'll never know how much it means to me."

"Okay. Be careful. It's almost dusk. That road's tough even in daylight."

I got in and lowered the window. "What will you tell the others?"

Matt looked past me toward the lake. "The truth. You need some time to be alone with God."

My hands shook so much I needed both of them to guide the key into the ignition. I glanced up just as Matt reached the front door. Elizabeth's face disappeared from the window.

I prayed for traveling mercies and to never see her or Pastor Steve again.

With a tight grip on the wheel, I made it to the main street without having to deal with anyone driving in. A few miles down the road, I passed Paul Carlson's car. His wife sat in the front with him and Luke's mom and the boys were in the back seat. They didn't see me and I thanked God for timing. If they had arrived ten minutes earlier, I wouldn't have been able to sneak away as easily.

Free at last, I found a safe place to pull over and opened Bobbi's envelope. She'd wrapped two crisp hundred-dollar bills inside a blank sheet of the inn's stationery. I put the cash in my wallet and held the envelope against my heart.

On the hour-long drive to Lincoln, I never switched on the radio. My mind tried to grasp what had happened during my four months at The Ark. How long would I have tried to be God's Golden Woman if Bobbi hadn't told me what happened to her? All the times Pastor Steve had made me feel special, now made me feel like a fool. I'd believed his words were anointed and trusted them without question.

Matt had told me to think about what I really wanted. On the night of our big fight, Ma had said, *"Use your brains."* They were both right. I couldn't believe how little thinking I'd done for myself since I'd arrived at The Ark.

But Luke hurt in a different way. He'd seen my anger and still loved me. Now, he'd shown me his dark side. Could I accept him the same way? Wrapped in his arms, my face against his chest, I'd found a place to be loved. I might never find another person like Luke.

Then there was me, Kate Bennett, training to be a missionary so I could save people from Hell. Not only did I go to a bar with a worldly guy, but I drank and sinned with him all while being engaged to the man I'd thought was my soul mate.

A question hovered at the edge of all these thoughts. If Pastor Steve knew about Nick, why would he let Luke marry me? Nothing made sense anymore.

It was five-thirty when I pulled off the highway.

I drove through The Ark's parking lot toward my dorm. The car's headlights bounced off battered trashcans, broken fences, and grimy mounds of snow.

Some students still hung around the empty campus. "Fools!" I shouted at them from inside the car. "Pastor Steve is not who you think he is. Don't believe him. He is not a man of God."

In my head I heard Ma say, *Who are you yelling at, Kate? Them or yourself?*

Goosebumps rose on my arm. All the times I heard Ma's voice telling me what to do, what if it was really my own voice?

I spun the wheel of Matt's car and sped away.

CHAPTER 41

MY STOMACH GROWLED, reminding me it was dinner-time. Bobbi's money was for an emergency, but I decided it would be okay to use some for a meal. After driving around a bit, the only place I found open was the No Name Bar. God's humor was endless.

I planned to get a table on the restaurant side and avoid the bar scene. Just as I headed in, a motorcycle guy with a fluffy white beard came out.

"Merry Christmas, little lady."

His resemblance to Santa made me smile. "Same to you."

Inside, holiday-themed country music played. I stood by the empty hostess station perusing a menu.

"Hey there," said a familiar voice. I looked up and Wanda waved to me from the bar.

I'd never seen her outside of the store. She looked younger

and pretty in her sparkly silver sweater and dark pants. She even wore bright red lipstick and nail polish.

"Wanda, it's so wonderful to see you again. You look so nice. Merry Christmas."

"Same to you. What's that on your finger?"

I looked down at my hand. "Oh, my engagement ring."

"Honey, you don't sound very excited."

"It's been a long day." I couldn't even remember the beginning of it.

Wanda's face fell. "Tell me you didn't have a fight on Christmas Eve."

"Something like that."

"You know, the restaurant side is closed tonight. Just bar food. Would you like to join me? I'm about to order."

Why not? Nothing else had gone as planned. "That would be great, thanks."

I sat on the stool next to her, and she whistled. A friendly-looking older guy hurried down the bar toward us. "Hank, this is my friend, Kate."

"Hi there. What are you drinking tonight?"

"Just a Coke." I liked that Wanda called me her friend and not an ex-employee.

Hank brought me my soda and Wanda a glass of red wine. We ordered burgers and fries, not quite a traditional holiday meal, but just the kind of food I needed.

"How are things at the store?"

Wanda told me stories about customers going crazy when they ran out of hams. Her impersonations made me laugh. I'd never seen this side of her before.

When our meals arrived, we dug in. The salty fries were extra crunchy. The burger came on a toasted buttery bun I could hardly hold on to.

"If you want to talk about anything, folks tell me I'm a good listener," Wanda said. She dunked her fry into a pool of ketchup.

A shiver ran down my back. A lifetime ago, Elizabeth had told me the same thing.

"It's a complicated story. How about you? Is there a nice guy in your life?"

"There was. My George and I were married for a long time. But cancer got him. He died a few years ago right around this time of year." Wanda's eyes misted. "I never did find anyone like him again."

"I'm so sorry. How did you and George meet?"

Wanda's face brightened as she told me how he stole her away from her high school steady. And then, on graduation day as she received her diploma, he jumped up on the stage, knelt in front of the entire class, and asked her to marry him.

"Sounds like he was a great guy," I said.

The bill came and I wrestled Wanda for it, saying it was my treat for her sharing her night with me. I pulled one of the hundreds out of my wallet.

Wanda slapped the bar top. "Did you rob a bank on your way here?"

"No, a gift from a good friend." It felt nice doing something generous on Christmas Eve.

As Hank counted out my change, I glanced into the mirror behind the bar and flinched. Luke was in the bar and heading toward us.

"Oh, Wanda. He's here."

A second later, Luke stood beside me. He put a heavy hand on my shoulder. "Is this where you go to get closer to God?"

"It's not what you think," I said. The burger tossed in my stomach.

"What should I think? You keep running away from me. To Bobbi. And here, where you were that night with Nick. I've been searching all over town for you. I prayed you wouldn't be here." Luke scanned the bar. "Where is he?"

"I'm not here with him. I'm having dinner with Wanda. Remember her? We worked together."

Wanda offered her hand to Luke, but he didn't take it. It felt like a slap in the face.

"You're at a bar. What's happened to you?" Luke took his hand off me and ran it across his forehead. "I feel like I don't know you anymore."

"We need to talk. Let's go outside." He started toward the door and I turned to Wanda. "I'm sorry about all this."

Her face softened with concern. "Do what you have to do. I'll be here for a little while if you need anything."

In the parking lot, Luke paced beside Matt's car. I unlocked the doors. "Please. Come sit in the car with me."

We got in and I started the engine. As the heater chugged, Luke stared out the windshield, his breaths heavy. Finally, he turned to me. "Do you realize who you are associating with? Bobbi, Nick, Wanda...none of them are believers. There are so many better choices—your roommates, the students at The Ark— yet you choose not to fellowship with them. Have you lost your faith?"

"No. But something bad has happened, and I don't know what to do."

Luke's jaw tightened. "It's Nick, isn't it? What happened the night you were here with him?"

Of all the secrets locked up inside me, my sin with Nick was the last one I wanted to tell Luke. The truth would change him. Change us. Luke's warm hand would never hold mine again. His face wouldn't light up when he saw me. But to lie to him wasn't an option.

I summoned the strength to speak. "That night I made a deal with Nick. I was desperate to reach Bobbi. He told me if he reached her, I had to have a drink with him. I didn't know what I was doing. I got drunk and scared and didn't want to go back to The Ark like that."

Luke's lips barely moved when he spoke. "Have I ever done anything to make you think I wouldn't take care of you?" The ache in his voice stabbed at my heart.

"No."

"What happened after you left?"

"He told me he'd make me coffee at his house. I wasn't thinking straight. I shouldn't have gone there." Tears filled my eyes. "Luke, I didn't mean to hurt you. I'm so sorry."

"You went to a man's house alone." Luke raised his hand. "I don't want to hear the rest." The light had left his eyes. "I loved you unconditionally. And you were so easily tempted. Like any worldly girl."

Hurt swirled through me at the unfairness. I wanted to scream out what his uncle did. I wanted to beg Luke to forgive me. But I couldn't do either. Luke didn't want this defiled version of me. I pulled the ring off my finger. "Goodbye, Luke."

He took the ring and closed his hand around it. Without looking at me, he said, "I thought you were the one," and got out of the car.

Our love snuffed out so quickly, I didn't know what to do. I watched him walk to Pastor Steve's Town Car and drive away. After all we'd been through, I thought I'd wail, but instead my body locked up. My thoughts jumped from how wonderful Luke was to the times he dismissed me and tried to control me. Worst of all was his lack of passion when we were alone.

A voice deep within my soul asked, *Did he love me or the idea of me?*

Numb, I went back into the bar and found Wanda putting on her coat.

"Want to have some dessert at my place?"

My yes came out as a sigh. I followed Wanda's car to her apartment, thanking God the whole way for her friendship.

Wanda lived on the top floor of a triple-decker. I was out of breath by the time I reached her door. She waited there for me with a grin. "Try climbing them a couple of times a day. You get used to it."

She unlocked the door, and we slipped out of our boots and coats. Wanda's den was decorated with fuzzy throw rugs and bright curtains. On a side table a ceramic Christmas tree with white lights reminded me of one Ma made for our holidays.

"I'll just be in the kitchen getting the coffee ready. Make yourself at home."

"Do you have tea by any chance?"

"Sure do."

I crossed the room to her bookcase. Instead of books, it was full of Christmas cards and picture frames. One shelf held photos of Wanda and a man that must've been her husband. The other shelves were filled with family photos. A set of frames with girls in their graduation caps and gowns caught my eye.

Wanda came up beside me. "High school graduation. My girls, all grown up."

My eyes grew huge as I counted. "You have five daughters?"

"Not all at the same time." She chuckled. "I was a foster mom."

Beside me stood a woman with an enormous heart. And Luke called her a non-believer. He knew nothing about her. I dropped my head and stepped back.

"Oh, dear." Wanda put her arm around my shoulder. "Were you a foster kid?"

"No. But you, you're a special lady."

"There's nothing special about me. The good Lord didn't give me my own babies, so I took care of ones who needed a mom."

The teakettle whistled. "Come, help me." I followed her into the kitchen where she handed me a plate of sugar cookies. "Let's sit at the dining room table."

Wanda carried a teapot-shaped like a gingerbread house. She motioned for me to sit, and then she set out china plates and teacups.

"This is fancy," I said.

"Aren't we worth it? It's Christmas Eve."

"Oh, Wanda, I'm such a jerk. Am I keeping you from other plans? Are any of the girls coming to visit?"

"They'll start coming tomorrow. Right now, this is exactly what I want to be doing."

While we munched on cookies and sipped tea, I asked her to tell me about each of her daughters. By the time she finished, their personalities filled the room. I admired how she loved generously, not the miserly way Ma loved us.

"You've let me talk all night," Wanda said. "But I see you've already made a decision." She glanced at my ring-free hand.

"I did, but there are a few more things I need to take care of." I stood up and hugged her. "Thank you for your hospitality and sharing your family with me."

Wanda followed me to her door. "Take care of yourself, hon. Now you know where to find me if you need me."

CHAPTER 42

"WILL YOU ACCEPT A COLLECT CALL from Kate Bennett?"

"Yes, I will," Dad said.

I pressed a palm on my heart. "Merry Christmas, Dad."

"Same to you. Are you okay? That Luke fellow called here thinking you were with us."

"Sorry if he worried you. He misunderstood." I lightened my voice. "What are you doing today?"

In the background I heard BB say, "Let me talk next, Dad."

"We're going over to Aunt Linda's house. Okay, okay. BB is jumping like a pogo stick over here. Let me put her on. You know you're welcome home."

His words lifted half my burden. "Thank you. Bye, Dad."

"Hi. It's me." BB's voice was breathless.

"Hey, little sister. How are you?"

"Are you coming home? I heard what Dad said."

"Very soon, I promise. How is he?"

BB muffled the mouthpiece. "He might have a girlfriend."

"What?" I almost dropped the phone. "You're kidding me. How do you know that?"

"Pam saw lipstick on his shirt collar in the laundry pile."

"Wow, that's fast," I said. "Isn't there a rule about not dating for a year?"

"Well, according to what Pam heard, if a man dates soon after his wife has died, it means he loved her very much and wants to replace her. But, I don't know. It seems soon to me."

Dad had a girlfriend. I guess he was handsome in an older guy kind of way. *If she makes him happy, that'll be good for everyone.*

"Speaking of Pam, how are things going with her?" I shifted the phone to my other ear.

"She keeps trying to discover herself. Been researching colleges and taking personality quizzes. I think maybe she wants to jump out of airplanes because she's reading a book about what color your parachute is."

I loved BB's view of the world. She took life so literally. Pam must've been in hearing range because she shouted, "I don't want to be a skydiver, silly. It's a book about careers."

"You don't have to yell. Did you and Luke set a date for the wedding?"

"No." I looked down at my bare hand and wondered how I'd tell them.

"Okay. I hope you're visiting soon. Pam wants to talk now. Bye."

After a phone shuffle, Pam said, "Hey, Dad's pretending to be a cash register, so I'll be quick. I've been reading and found this perfect job for you. You can take all that Bible stuff you've been learning and work with old people who are dying. They need people to sit with them. You help them pass peacefully to the other side. It's called a grief counselor."

I cleared my throat. "Well, I'll think about that." It was the most depressing career choice imaginable. "What about you, what're you thinking about for college?"

"I can't pick a college until I know what I want to do. I think I'm driving my guidance counselor crazy. She told me not to worry about any of this until next year and to take time to heal over Ma."

"That's probably good advice." I paused. "You know, I think about her more than I thought I would. How about you?"

"Yeah, I guess I do too. But there's *someone* who still won't sleep in her room at night. You've got to come home and give me a break." We both laughed. "I'm glad you called. I should probably go now."

"Can you tell everyone I love them?"

Pam sang out, "Kate loves everyone," and hung up.

Even though no one said they loved me back, it felt like the best call home since I'd been at The Ark. I hugged myself and thanked God for each one of them.

With all the Carlson family snug in their cabin by the lake, there wouldn't be a service at The Ark until the Sunday after Christmas. For those left behind, we could attend a singalong of traditional carols in the chapel on Christmas night. I went over extra early, cringing with each dark corner I passed, as if Pastor Steve might jump out at me.

I walked onto the stage and looked out toward the empty seats. Would he dare preach here again? Bobbi's silk scarf lay inside my shoulder bag. I looped its slippery fabric around the wooden cross on the altar. To hold it in place, I clipped a verse to it from Matthew 7:15. In bold letters, I had written, "Beware of false prophets, which come to you in sheep's clothing, but inwardly they are ravening wolves."

From the back of the chapel, the red in the scarf stained the cross like blood.

CHAPTER 43

THE DAY AFTER CHRISTMAS, I found myself in the near-empty lot of Price Chopper. I parked Matt's car next to Nick's truck. Without having one good reason to be there, I finger-combed my hair and went to find Nick.

A lone cashier with no bagger manned the front of the store. I glanced up to the manager's desk, happy to see that Wanda had the day off. Casually, I strolled toward the back of the produce section near the warehouse doors. A pyramid of lemons caught my eye. Half paying attention and half looking for Nick, I picked one and caused a yellow avalanche. I swooped in over the display to stop as many as I could with my body.

There wasn't a customer in sight to ask for help. I probably looked like a lemon-hugging freak. After a minute, the store intercom crackled, "Clean up in produce."

I counted to thirty before the warehouse doors burst open. Nick came out carrying an empty box. His mouth twisted into a smirk when he recognized me. My insides turned into slush.

"Well, miss. What's happened here?" He said each word as slow as he could.

I couldn't hold my position over the lemons much longer. "Come on."

Nick walked around me as if he was analyzing the most complicated problem in the world.

My arms cramped. "Hurry. What should I do?"

"*You* don't do anything. I'll just take them and put them in this box." He stood behind me and rested his chin on my shoulder. "Did you miss me or were you going to make a couple gallons of lemonade?"

A shiver ran down my back. Nick reached around and pulled lemons from each side of me. The clean smell of citrus filled the air.

"Hey, people are going to see us."

"Let them." He nuzzled my ear.

The front door whooshed open and Nick stepped beside me. The customer walked by us to another aisle. The only lemons left were in front of my chest. Nick removed them one by one, handling them like fragile eggs.

"Can you go any faster?"

He ignored me. When it was finally safe to move, I stepped away from him. Some fruit lay on the floor. I crouched to pick them up.

Nick crouched too. "Why are you here? Isn't this a big week at your place?"

What am I doing here? I sat on the floor and Nick joined me.

"Oh, Nick. You were right. I thought The Ark was where I belonged. That everyone was godly and caring. But I've learned a terrible secret about Pastor Steve. Now it's all a huge mess. And Luke, he won't marry me because I'm not a…because of that night we were together."

Nick locked eyes with me. "You told him?"

"There were too many secrets. But it's more than that. I was never to question him. He didn't like me having friends outside The Ark, and his attitude about gays." I shook my head.

"Like what?"

"One of the branch ministries opened its doors to gays. Pastor Steve had a fit over it, and because Pastor Steve is Luke's uncle and he believes every word he says, he hates gays too. It's awful."

Nick slid closer. "You know that saying about a person who protests too much. It could mean they are afraid of that thing in themselves."

"What do you mean?"

"Remember the first time I kissed you?"

I nodded and felt my face get warm.

"I'm curious. Has Luke ever kissed you like that?"

My chin dropped. "We have rules."

"And people in love have physical desires."

"You think he didn't desire me?"

"I'm no expert, but my gut tells me Luke might be hiding his own secret."

It took a few moments for me to understand his words. And when I did, I almost bent over in shock. Each of the times Luke rejected me replayed in my head. His cruelness toward gays… what if it was actually fear?

I grabbed Nick's arm in a panic. "Oh my God, I think I'm falling apart."

He put his arm around me until I stopped shaking.

"Thank you, Nick. However this turns out, can we still be friends?"

"Shall we get a drink for old time's sake?"

I punched him in the side. "I think I'll pass this time."

"Seriously, what are you going to do?" Nick's voice tickled my ear.

"There's one more person I have to talk to."

CHAPTER 44

THE NEXT MORNING, the sun beamed down on me. I lifted my face and inhaled the brightness. I thanked God for gently reminding me that every day was a chance for a new start.

I wrote a note for Matt and left it on the dashboard of his car.

Matt, I can't thank you enough for lending me your car and most importantly for your friendship. You told me over Thanksgiving that God is love. There are people in my life I need to show that love to. I hope to see you soon in your new job with Pastor Wayne's ministry.

Lots of love,

Kate

As I packed my suitcase, memories from my first week in the dorm raced back: crashing into Daisy, Sheila's warm welcome, and the funny stories Hannah and Alice shared about life on their farm. Then there was Bobbi, and her dramatic entrance. Now there would be three empty beds in the room. I couldn't help but wonder what the official word would be for my sudden departure.

I wheeled my suitcase to the snack bar in search of someone I knew. A classmate from my God's Golden Woman class waved to me from a corner table.

"Hi there," I said. "I'm so glad you're still here. These keys belong to Matt Carlson. Could you please give them to him when he returns from winter break?"

Ignoring her startled expression, I dropped the keys into her hand before she could answer.

Lightness filled me as I raced down The Ark's driveway to the bus stop. I'd never been so happy to get on a bus before. Hours of stops, transfers, and greasy windows seemed a minor inconvenience.

When I wasn't dozing, my mind wandered to the people I'd miss the most. What surprised me was they weren't my roommates from The Ark. I'd miss Nick and his honest and passionate ways. And, I'd miss Wanda with her easy and generous love. Now that I had their cell phone numbers, I could keep in touch. If all worked out, I'd still get to see Bobbi for New Year's Eve.

I tried not to dwell on those that made me feel pain. My heart hurt for Luke and the life he'd chosen to live because he couldn't bear to disappoint Pastor Steve. If Luke only knew the secrets his uncle hid.

Every half hour, I'd unzip the inside pocket of my purse and check for Pastor Steve's dirty list. Elizabeth would surely destroy the original as soon as she returned to campus. Could I expose what he did without incriminating Bobbi? I needed time to think this all out.

An hour of daylight remained when I stepped off the bus near Grove Cemetery. My suitcase tapped out a beat on the sidewalk as I pulled it the few blocks to the front gate. Black wrought-iron doors guarded the entrance like a portal to another time.

On any day in late December, a cemetery in New England is a desolate place. Today was especially bleak; heavy clouds had rolled in. A few green wreaths on tombstones provided the only color.

It took a few minutes, but I found my landmark, the statue of a cherub angel. Placed over the grave of an infant, the angel buried its face in its palms. Heavy wings drooped on its rounded back. It was the most heartbreaking statue I'd ever seen. Someone, maybe the mother, had wrapped a pine garland around its base. I brushed some old snow off the wings.

I walked to Ma's grave. There were no signs of recent visitors except for the zigzag footprints of some birds. Their tracks reminded me of tiny broken crosses.

On the day of Ma's funeral, a brilliant blue had colored the sky. A mound of dark earth sat piled on the deep green grass next to her grave. I didn't expect to see the hole Ma would go into or her bronze casket balanced on poles over it. Trying not to lose it, I focused on the minister.

He didn't know Ma, but he said some kind words about her life and finished with the ashes-to-ashes and dust-to-dust

Bible verse. Some workers lowered her with hidden straps. Dad approached the dirt pile, picked up a handful, and tossed it down the hole. He looked at me, Pam, and BB with watery eyes. I knew he wanted us to do the same.

I swallowed hard and prayed I wouldn't stumble. I scooped up a fistful of dirt, and without looking down, spread my fingers and let the dirt fall through them. A Beloved Mother floral wreath caught my eye. I pulled a red rose loose and returned to my spot beside my sisters. Pam and BB repeated what I did.

A siren cried in the distance, bringing me back to the present. "Ma, I still have that rose. It's in my Bible near Psalms, pressed between some sheets of wax paper."

My breath hung in the cold air.

"You know what, Ma? I never understood you. I know a lady who has five foster daughters. She gave all those girls second chances. You had us and were angry all the time. Punishing us just for being kids. Yet you were nice to Gram, even though she was a mean alcoholic and made you live with strangers. I worried that your rage might be inside me too. But I know it's not. I'm not you."

Warm tears fell down my chilled cheeks.

"We were good kids, but you decided to check out on us." I could barely speak for the sobs. "All you had to do was take care of yourself. Just take your medicine. You didn't have to die."

A blinding clarity sliced through the tangled roots of my guilt. I grasped the rough top of Ma's tombstone to steady myself. "I didn't cause your death. I'm not accepting the blame for it any longer."

Shaken, I knelt on the snow. I was going to be all right. From deep inside, the word *mercy* bubbled up. The Bible taught that mercy was showing compassion to someone who had offended you. To me it meant being mighty and humble at the same time.

"Ma, I forgive you."

Something moved in a shrub, startling me. A gray speckled dove cooed and flew away. Was it a symbol of peace from Ma? I rose with damp circles on my knees and saw my patient suitcase waiting for me to take the next step.

At the wrought-iron gates, I turned one last time. "Ma, I won't be back for a while, but I'm taking the best part of you with me. I'm taking your strength."

The sky darkened to a deeper shade of gray. Heavy snow-flakes drifted from the sky and covered my tracks with a fresh coat of white.

I was ready to go home.

ACKNOWLEDGMENTS

I'D LIKE TO THANK the wonderful people involved in my writing journey.

To Polly Letofsky and Kirsten Jensen, at My Word Publishing, who gave me expert advice and guided me through the publishing process.

To my editor, Kristen Hamilton, who amazed me with her proofreading skills. To Shira Lee Designs for creating a powerful book cover and Sari Esserman for sharing her beautiful artwork. To layout designer, Victoria Wolf, who brought the interior of my book to life.

I could not have written this book without the encouragement of my many writing teachers at UC San Diego. In particular, I'd like to thank Carolyn Wheat for keeping it real. Through my classes, I've met many wonderful writing buddies. Thanks to Penne Horn, Colleen Kendall, Julie Schwartz, and Vicki Beck for staying with me throughout the years. I'd also like to thank my earliest reader, Joan Sonner, who helped me with her editing abilities.

To my sisters and friends who have provided encouragement, please know how much I value all your advice, feedback, and support.

I could not have made it to the finish line without the support of my husband, Marc, and my daughter, Lindsey. They must be as happy as I am to see this book completed.

ABOUT THE AUTHOR

VAL AGNEW grew up in New England where she spent a year living in an evangelical school with strong cultish tendencies. When she got the courage to break free from their teachings, she packed a U-Haul and followed the warm weather to San Diego. There, she worked in the communications field and met her husband. They have one amazing nature-loving daughter.

Her travel essays have appeared in the *San Diego Union Tribune* and her poetry has been published in *Tidepools: A Journal of Ideas* at MiraCosta College.

She is active with the Big Brothers Big Sisters organization with a focus on mentoring girls in military families.

Her passion is haunting local and distant cemeteries in search of angel statues.

You can learn more at www.valagnewauthor.com.

BOOK CLUB INVITATION

Invite Val to your Book Club!
As a special gift to *Lost in The Ark* readers,
Val has offered to visit your book club
either by Zoom or in person.
Please contact Val directly to
schedule an appearance.
val@valsroad.com

CPSIA information can be obtained
at www.ICGtesting.com
Printed in the USA
LVHW101942210422
716875LV00001B/143